JESSICA SORENSEN

SHATTERED PROMISES

A SHATTERED PROMISES NOVEL

D1522299

For information:
jessicasorensen.com

Cover Design and Photography:
Mae I Design
www.maeidesign.com

Interior Design and Formatting:
Christine Borgford, Perfectly Publishable
www.perfectlypublishable.com

Shattered Promises (Shattered Promises, Book 1)
ISBN: 978–1482652222

PROLOGUE

W HY DO PEOPLE laugh? What makes them cry? Smile? What allows them to love? These are the questions I've asked myself for nearly the last twenty-one years.

What makes people feel?

I don't understand what produces emotion and I'm supposed to be writing a paper on human emotion for my Sociology class. I've been camped out on a bench in the center of the campus quad, studying the interaction of nearly the entire student body that goes to the University of Wyoming, and I still don't understand.

What is it? Why do they hold hands? Kiss? Laugh? What the hell is making them look like there are rainbows and sunshine everywhere?

It is a warm fall day and leaves are fluttering across the dry grass. The branches are bare and the air is laced with rain. My jacket is balled up on the bench beside me and ear buds are stuffed into my ears. "Wonderwall" by *Oasis* plays through the speakers, the lyrics trying to surface an emotion buried deep inside me, but, like usual, it's just a spark that quickly fades.

I jot some notes about a couple making out on the steps in the front entrance of the main office, which is a large brick building that has a historical look to it. Their hands are all over each other, feeling every inch of one another's skin, like they want each other more than anything. I don't get it. I never have. For as long as I can remember, I've never been able to feel any emotion. Sadness, happiness, love; they are all just words to me. They have no more meaning or importance than the shoes on my feet.

When I was younger, I never thought much about it. I moved through my life like a robot, and I was fine, but lately, at least for the last few days, questions are surfacing. Maybe it is the fact that Professor Fremont, my Sociology professor, has been on a human emotion kick lately. Most of his lectures relate to the drive behind emotion. Perhaps his words have finally stuck the pin into my thoughts.

Why have I never felt anything? Am I broken? Crazy? Or are there just some people who go through life like me—peacefully disconnected?

I scribble the thought down, shut my notebook, and get to my feet, deciding to call it quits for the day. I gather my things into my bag and head across the campus toward my parked car. I used to live in the dorm, but it's the start of my Senior year and I made the decision to move out on my own. I'm sure it was a huge favor to the person in line to share a dorm with me. I tend to frighten people with my internal impassiveness. I was the same way in high school. Most of my life, I was the outcast weirdo with no friends. It made sense. I mean, how can I make friends when I can't smile, laugh, or even relate to people?

As I pull my car keys out from my pocket, a nagging feeling overcomes me, like I forgot something on the bench. I glance over my shoulder, squinting against the faint stream of sunlight flowing through the air. The bench is empty. My eyes sweep through the crowd and I get the impression that someone is watching me, but everyone seems to be engulfed in their own business.

Burying the impression, I turn back around and step off the curb. That's when the heat hits me, like a kick to the stomach. I hunch over and my keys fall to the ground. It hurts, like fire's melting my skin and scorching my hands, however my skin looks as pale and smooth as it always has. I try to straighten back up, forcing my shoulders upward, but something stabs into the back of my neck. I reach around and feel the warmth of my skin scorching against my trembling fingers. There is something else there, though—something invisible, possessing my body, as if hot liquid spills through my veins and pools inside my heart.

I can't breathe—can't stand. My knees buckle and I collapse to the ground, the rocks dig through my jeans, into my skin, and my palms split open as I press them into the ground to hold my weight up. Every bone in my body feels like it is cracking open from the emotional pressure. Every hurtful word, every sad moment, every lonely second I've ever experienced pours through me like a rampant river and submerges my body, drowning me in my own tears. My fingers shake as I touch my wet cheeks.

I'm stunned. Shocked. Terrified. Because, for the first time in my life, I'm crying.

CHAPTER
ONE

Three months later . . .

I FEEL ALIVE as I follow him down the slender hallway, bordered by maroon walls and lit up by antique lanterns. The way he moves with slow, confident strides is hypnotic. My heart knocks inside my chest, excited and nervous. My pulse speeds up when he glances over his shoulder at me. He is gorgeous; dark-brown tousled hair, broad shoulders, bright green eyes. I'm helpless as my legs carry me toward him. Even though I don't know who he is, it feels like I do. I just can't place from where.

Music plays from within the building and vibrates against the walls. There is heat in the air and it makes my skin damp beneath the short leather dress I'm wearing. It's strange because I never wear dresses, but I never walk down empty hallways chasing strangers, either.

He turns to face me, walking backwards, and his tongue slips out of his mouth to wet his full lips. I swear to God, I almost die as the urge to lean forward and bite *his lip rushes through my body. I've never felt this way before. I've never felt much of anything, until now.*

"Are you sure you want to do this?" he asks, pausing at the door at the end of the hallway.

I nod eagerly, even though I have no idea what he wants me to do. "Yes."

An unhurried smile curves across his lips and the muscles of his arms flex as he shoves open the door. Inside is a small room, with blood-red walls and floors the color of ash. There's a dresser in the corner, a room divider against the back wall, along with a metal-framed bed.

I press my lips together and cross my arms over my chest, wondering if I'm getting in over my head.

He motions for me to step in as he holds the door open. "Ladies first."

I enter, fiddling with the bottom of my dress and struggling to keep my balance in my high-heeled boots. "Are you sure they won't find us here?" I ask, turning in a circle to examine the room.

He closes the door and turns around to face me with his hands behind his back. He studies me intensely and it makes me squirm. "You know, you're not like I thought you'd be," he says, taking a step forward. "Yet, at the same time you are."

"That makes no sense." I take a step back, trying to blink away from his gaze, but I am trapped by feelings I can't control.

"It makes perfect sense." He takes another step and then another. I match his moves until my back brushes the wall. He places a hand on each side of my head, pinning me between his arms and leans forward until there is hardly any space between our lips, our bodies are aligned. "You just don't know it yet."

I can smell the faint scent of his cologne and feel the heat emitting from his body. "Are you sure we shouldn't be running? They won't stop until they find me."

He shakes his head with his eyes focused on me. Up close, I can see little specks of blue inside the green and the largeness of his pupils. "We'll be fine. I promise I won't let anything happen to you."

Conflicted with whether or not I believe him, I swallow hard. "Are you sure, because . . ."

He places a finger across my lips. "Shh . . . When I promise something, I mean it."

I nod my head and my eyelids flutter from the feel of his skin on my mouth.

"I won't let anything happen to you." His finger trails down the front of my neck to my chest and I shiver as he inches closer, closing his eyes.

The first touch of his lips brings an uproar of heat to my skin that surges down my neck and my chest before hitting me straight in the stomach and coiling downward, causing me to let out an embarrassing moan. I start to recoil, but he only seems more eager to kiss me as his tongue slips deep inside my mouth.

The taste of him is familiar and comforting, yet full of danger, want, and need. I feel the back of my neck grow hot with a fire that rips through my body as a hunger possesses me. My head races a million miles a minute with thoughts of getting closer to him. I clutch onto his arms, digging my nails into his skin, drawing a line of blood as I press my body against his. What the hell is happening to me? I've never felt this way before. I need to breathe—I need to run . . . God, but I want to stay.

His hands wander down my body; across my breast to the bottom of my dress. As his fingers graze my bare thigh, he sucks on my tongue and pulls me closer. Gripping my legs, he scoops me up and urges them around his waist. The feel of him pressed up against me makes the fire burn hotter. I'm burning up. I swear I'm literally on fire.

He groans against my mouth, biting at my bottom lip as his hands roam upward beneath my dress and cup my ass. My legs constrict in response and tighten around his hips. His muscles tighten, but his tongue continues to explore my mouth, entangling with my tongue, tasting me, turning me on in ways I don't understand. God, I want to understand, though. So badly.

"Gemma," he breathes as his lips kiss a path down my jawline to my neck, where he sucks on my skin, nearly driving me crazy.

"How do you know my name?" I ask as my fingers tangle through his soft hair and my head falls back.

He shakes his head, pulling away for just a second, and his eyes are glazed over. "I don't."

I don't understand what he means, but as his fingers move between my legs, I forget about everything. The spark of his touch causes me to suck in a sharp breath. My chest heaves as I shut my eyes and dig my fingernails into his shoulder blades as more intense emotions emerge. I slide my hands underneath his shirt, feeling the lines of his muscles and the smoothness of his skin.

He laughs against my lips and then his tongue slips back inside my mouth, but it feels different. His lips . . . they don't feel the same and there is something on them that feels like cold metal.

I open my eyes and my breath catches in my throat. He's changed into someone else. His brown hair is now blond with blue tips and a silver ring is looped through his bottom lip. His eyes are bright blue, like the sky, and his skin is as pale as snow.

"Who are you . . ." I breathe, but I think I know.

The stranger stays silent and leans forward to kiss me. I wonder if there is something wrong with me as his tongue encourages my lips apart and I only clutch onto his lean arms, instead of pulling away. His skin is like ice and he tastes different and exciting. My body feels like it's going to explode from the torridness. His hands grip my waist, his nails digging into my skin as he draws me closer, crushing my body against his, and my skin beads with sweat. He mutters my name, threading his fingers through my hair and tugging at the roots until my head is tipped back. Then, his mouth moves for my neck. His teeth gently nick at my skin and it stings a little, but feels amazingly good at the same time; like some kind of euphoric venom dancing threw my veins.

As his hands search my body, the warmth of his touch gradually decreases. Instead of heat, I feel cold. His hands wander up the front of my dress, his palms gliding against the leather until he is cupping my breasts. I let out a moan, but numbness consumes me. And the cold. Why am I so cold?

My eyes snap open. Towering behind him is a figure wearing a black cloak with the hood pulled over its head. The eyes are yellow and flash fiercely as it steps forward with its bony hand stretched outward.

I jerk away from the guy's arms and lower my feet to the ground. "Oh my God," I stutter with my eyes locked on the monster.

His brows knit. "What's wrong?"

Before I can respond, the monster unhitches its jaw and opens its mouth. My scream echoes through the room as its ice-cold breath suffocates both of us and we fall to the floor—

The lyrics of "Closer" by *Nine Inch Nails* fill my head. I rub my eyes and blink the tiredness away as I hit the off button on the alarm. The cold and the heat still linger in my body, just like they do every damn morning because I can't shake that dream. I wrap my blanket around myself with the prickle gnawing at the back of my neck, pumping fear through my body that I can't shake. My emotions are still so new and I have a hard time controlling them; especially, when my dreams get me so riled up. I have no idea how to cope.

Ever since the crying incident a few of months ago, my life has altered in more ways than one. Everyday there's a new experience, whether it's as simple as finding something amusing or crying for hours over the loss of my childhood and adolescence—the regret of endless lonely days.

It is early in the morning and the pink afterglow of the sunrise paints the mountains. I climb out of bed, get dressed in a pair of black jeans and a red tee, and fasten my long brown hair into a ponytail. I take a good look in the mirror at my violet eyes, pale skin, and long legs. Whenever I look at my reflection, I can spot something hidden in my eyes; like a secret, but it could just be the alarming shade of violet just throwing me off.

After I lace up my black boots, I grab my keys and head for the front door. I have to pick up a few things from my grandparent's house. I moved in with them when I was one, after my parents died in a car accident. After I graduated, I moved out without saying a word. I'm not even sure why I did it, only that at the time it seemed like it was something I was supposed to do.

I've barely spoke to them over the last few years, but yesterday they called me up threatening to throw some of my things away, so I figure I'll head over and get them before my classes start. Besides, the sooner I get it done, the sooner I'll never have to talk to my grandparents again, which will make us *all* happy.

IT'S RIDICULOUSLY COLD in Laramie. The roads are frozen with salt sprinkled across them and icicles hang from the trees. There are snowmen decorating the yards, ice glazing the rain gutters and branches, and the roofs of the houses are piled with snow.

When I arrive at my grandparents' two-story, red-brick house my insides wind into knots as every memory attached to the place surfaces. My grandparents are the coldest people I know and have always been dead-set on ignoring me as much as possible. It didn't really bother me when I was younger, since I couldn't experience things like pain and anguish, but now, I fucking despise them. It's an overpowering feeling, which is why I hate coming here. The feeling owns me, makes me say things I normally wouldn't, and turns me into a different person—a bitter person.

I climb out of the car, zipping my coat up as I walk toward the side door. Right as I reach the bottom of the porch, the door swings open and a guy steps out. He is tall, solidly built and has his hood pulled over his head with the front of his jacket zipped up to his chin. He also wears sunglasses, so he's nearly covered up. At first, I think *robber,* but he seems too serene and confident. He stares at me for a moment with his feet planted on the top step. He seems stunned that I'm here—at my own house—when it should be the other way around.

"Hi," I say with a small wave as I step up onto the bottom stair. "Can I help you?"

He shakes his head, and with one swift spring of his toes, he grabs onto the railing and launches himself over it. He lands gracefully on the ice and then hikes down the driveway, kicking up snow from the ground.

I scratch at the back of my neck as the prickle starts to manifest, but it wilts before an emotion can develop. I glance at my hands as a tingling sensation fizzles across my skin and then my gaze lifts back to the guy who is rounding the fence line. As he nears the end of the yard he turns his head and looks at me. A magnetic current courses through me and I almost run to him. As soon as the feeling hits me, he looks away and vanishes around the corner. The sensation dissolves and I'm left both confused and kind of empty.

Shaking my head, I tug open the door and step into the kitchen. Sophia, my grandmother, is standing over the stove tending to the hissing pans as the smell of bacon fills the air. My grandfather, Marco, is reading a newspaper at the table. They both seem uncomfortable, fidgety, but that's nothing new. They've been that way for as long as I can remember.

Marco peers over the newspaper at me and his black, oval glasses slide down the brim of his slightly crooked nose. He is a reserved man who likes to avoid confrontation at all cost. "Good morning, Gemma," he mumbles with a subtle nod.

It's the same conversation we've had since I was eight: a polite hello and an eager good-bye; as if we were nothing more than acquaintances. It takes a lot, but I manage to strain a smile. "Good morning, Marco." I point over my shoulder. "Who was that person that just walked out of here?"

"No one," Sophia replies and at the same time Marco responds, "The paper boy."

I skim back and forth between them as I question their honesty. "The paper boy? Wasn't he about my age?"

"Your stuff's boxed up in the room upstairs," Sophia says, ignoring me. The bacon sizzles as she taps her high heels on the tile floor. She is wearing a floral dress with a white apron tied over it and her auburn hair is twisted in a bun. She is a very proper person; always neatly dressed and the house is always clean.

"Okay." Shaking my head, I walk across the kitchen toward the doorway. "I guess I'll go get it and be out of your hair then."

"Sounds good to me," she says curtly and resumes cooking.

Rolling my eyes, I disappear into the foyer and hurry up the stairs to my old room. This has always been the extent of our relationship: she says how much she dislikes me being around and I try my best to ignore her. It was easier to deal with when I couldn't get pissed off, but now it takes a lot of control not to scream at her.

The once tan walls of my room have been painted a bright red, the shelf in the corner is stripped of my music collection, and the dresser drawers are open and empty. I walk over to the stack of boxes near the foot of the bed and I run my finger along the label. Memories stab at my brain like sharp nails.

Empty.
Lonely.
Hopeless.

I'm broken inside.

"Gemma's junk," I read the label out loud. "I guess it's probably true . . . none of this stuff ever really meant anything to me." I wish it did, though. I wish I had a connection to something—anything.

Sighing, I backtrack to the door and peer out into the hallway, making sure no one is there, before shutting the door. Kneeling down beside my bed, I reach underneath it and run my fingers along the bottom of the mattress until I find the papers. Fumbling with the tape, I peel off the photo. It's ripped in half, faded, and frayed, but from what I can tell, it's a picture of a woman with flowing, long, brown hair, blue irises, and a snow-white complexion. I once found it while cleaning under the stairway and kept it because I believe it's my mother. I've hidden it under my bed because if Sophia found it, she would have taken it away. She hates it when I bring up my parents. The only thing I know about them is that my mother's name was Jocelyn and I only know that because it's on my birth certificate, which doesn't list my father's name and Sophia refuses to give me an explanation as to why.

I haven't looked at the photo since I've been able to feel. It's strange, the idea that it could be her. It makes my chest compress and I forget how to breathe. As tears threaten to spill out, I quickly get to my feet and tuck the picture into my back pocket. Sucking in a deep breath and forcing back the tears, I pick up a box and carry it down the stairs.

Marco is no longer in the kitchen and Sophia is taking off her apron. "Are you all right carrying those out by yourself? Marco's back has been bothering him again."

I nod as I observe a silver-framed photo of Marco and Sophia hanging on the wall next to the kitchen table. They are standing on the shore of a lake. Marco has his hand in front of his face, shielding his eyes from the sunlight and Sophia is to the side of him, smiling. On her collarbone I can see a hint of tattoo. The picture always confuses me because Sophia doesn't seem like someone who would have a tattoo. She also doesn't seem like someone who would have children of her own, either. Yet, she my mother's mother.

"I was wondering if we could talk about that thing I mentioned last week," I ask, shifting the box onto my hip, hoping she doesn't notice that I'm lying. "It's for a history paper I'm working on. I kind of need to know a thing or two about my parents."

Sophia turns away from the stove. "I thought I told you not to bring them up—that I didn't want to talk about them."

"Well, I kind of need you to." I set the box down on the table. Actually, I don't. I just want to know for myself. "Otherwise, I might fail and I'm so close to being finished, the last thing I want to do is fall behind schedule for graduation."

She turns off the stove and narrows her eyes at me. "It doesn't matter. We are not going to talk about your parents. Ever."

"Why not?" I ask, battling my anger. "What scares you so much about the idea?"

With her hands on her hips, Sophia storms toward me, her high heels clicking forcefully against the tile. "Do you think it's easy for me to talk about my daughter's death? Do you like to make me hurt?"

I hold my chin high, refusing to cower back. "No, but it feels like I should know something about her. About both my parents. In fact, you should have told me about them a long time ago."

Her skin turns a ghostly white and lines form around her eyes as she gives me a harsh look. "We will not talk about this ever again. Do you understand?" She hurries out of the kitchen and, seconds later, I hear her bedroom door shut.

Tears sting at my eyes, but I force them back. I won't let the sadness win. I'm tougher than that. I've lived without the knowledge of my parents for twenty-one years for hell sakes.

Opening the back door, I step outside. Even though a blizzard has blown in, it feels warmer than in the house.

BY THE TIME I pull up to the campus, I'm late for Calculus and there's a test today. My grade is already nearing the seventy percent mark, so I can't miss it. Swinging the car door open, I hop out into the snowfall. Deciding to leave the boxes in the trunk, I rush across the campus yard, the snow crunching under my sneakers. I keep my eyes on my watch, watching the minutes tick down. I speed up to a run, but then pause when I approach the salted sidewalk as the prickling sensation stabs at my neck.

Dammit.

I wait for an emotion to rise and take me over, wondering how complex it will be, but a few seconds go by and I feel nothing, so I force my feet to move and step up onto the curb. As my shoe touches the ground, my skin heats and my gaze zeroes in on a guy walking toward me from across the parking lot.

I'm almost certain I've seen him before, but can't place from where. My neck tingles again, little pin prickles, like the day my tears were unleashed for the very first time. I'm flooded with a desire to chase him down, rip off his clothes, bite on his neck, and do all the dirty things I've been dreaming about. I might have acted on the impulse, too, but a snowball smacks me in the face and diverts my gaze from him.

I wipe the snow from my cheek and glare at the thrower. "Didn't you see me standing here?"

A heavyset guy with a beanie on surrenders his hands in front of him as he backs toward the entrance of the campus. "Sorry, I was aiming for him." He nods his head to my right at a lanky guy with a hoodie pulled over his head.

I pluck chunks of snow out of my hair as I rush toward the entrance doors and catch up with the guy I've been having dirty thoughts about right as he swings the door open. He steps to the side and holds it open for me, like a true gentleman. I bite my bottom lip to keep my irrational, lust-filled emotions contained, and walk in; my heart hitting the inside of my chest. *Keep moving forward. Don't stop.* My thoughts are weaker than my feet and I halt, peering up at him.

My heart stops as recognition takes over. I know him. Well, too. A faint spark is flickering deep inside my memories, but I don't understand how. All I know is that I can't breathe. Or maybe, I am breathing for the very first time. Maybe this is what it is like to feel alive.

Then it hits me. He's the guy from my dream. He's even more gorgeous in person; tousled, dark brown hair and the greenest eyes I've ever seen. His long limbs are carved with muscles, and confidence radiates off him from the way he stands to the look in his eyes. He wears a black hoodie and dark jeans that hang low on his hips. I can't seem to take my eyes of the patch of skin that shows when he raises his hand to run his fingers through his hair, making his shirt ride up a little.

When our gazes collide, I'm shocked by a zap of electricity that fires through my body. The size of my eyes amplify as the feeling expands, coiling into my stomach and burning between my thighs. A gasp escapes my lips as my body quivers from the rush. I've felt this before, many times in my dreams, but, God dammit, it feels so much better in real-life.

A look of intrigue and fascination masks his face as he watches me, like he's waiting for something momentous to happen.

Does he know me? Does he dream about me, like I dream about him? How can any of this be possible?

I extend my hand toward his chest and slide my palm up the front of his shirt; needing to touch him, be close to him. His heart thuds underneath my palm, matching the erratic beat of mine and his eyes widen, his gaze flicking to my lips and for a brief, but earth-shattering moment, he looks like he might kiss me.

"Do I know you?" I ask as my fingers brush the top of his collar and electricity rips from my fingertips to my toes.

Suddenly his expression slips into a scowl. "I'm sorry, but did I give you permission to put your hands on me?" He sidesteps around me and lets the heavy metal door slam into my elbow.

"Ow." I rub at the pain on my arm as every ounce of my elation cracks, shatters, and falls to the floor. "What the hell was that for?"

He shoots me a harsh look and my mouth drops open. "Next time, hold the damn door open for yourself."

Fucking asshole. It's amazing how one second I feel like I'm in an eternal state of ecstasy and the next I'm boiling in a pot full of rage, all because this sexy stranger opened that delicious-looking mouth of his.

He turns his back on me and strolls down the hall without a glance back; leaving me angry, irritated, and totally turned on.

Yep, there is definitely something wrong with my head.

CHAPTER TWO

F OR THE REST of the day, I try to make sense of what happened in the entryway with Mr. Sexy Douche Bag. I shouldn't have just reached out and groped him that way, but his reaction was still surprising. Maybe he's just naturally a jerk, but why have I dreamt about him? Plus, there is that strange electric connection. None of it makes sense.

The next morning, after a very rough night of nightmares, I head off to Astronomy, relieved I can finally relax. I love learning about the stars. Even back in high school, during my emotionally detached days, I would stare up at the night sky and appreciate the beauty of each one; how they seem to be separate but whole. The first time I ever experienced happiness was when I had been lying in bed one night, staring out my window at the stars shining harmoniously. The prickle showed up and I smiled as the warmth of happiness swelled inside me. Ever since then, I've felt this strange bond with the night sky, like somehow I'm connected to it.

The classroom is empty when I enter. Taking a seat at the back corner desk on the upper row, I set my book on the table and take a pen out from my bag. Although I don't have any future plans for my life, I hope that one day I can do something with the stars. I'm working on a General Studies degree because nothing seems to fit right. Whenever I look forward and try to envision my future, all I see is light.

The winter semester has barely started; there are a few extra students who show up and some who drop out over the first few weeks. I notice a girl I've never seen before around campus walk into the classroom. Her golden-brown hair is twisted up in a clip that matches the shade of her pink sweater. Her eyes are a fierce green, traced with brown liner and there's something familiar about her.

She smiles at me as she takes the seat in front of me and sets her purse onto the desk. "Hi, I'm Aislin Avery."

"I'm Gemma Lucas." I feel strange because people rarely talk to me. Around sophomore year, I started to believe that perhaps I was invisible and that people couldn't see me. "Is it your first day in this class?"

She nods and tucks a strand of hair behind her ear as she begins rummaging around in her purse. "I just transferred to UW."

"Are you a senior?"

She nods. "What year are you?"

"I'm a senior too."

"Oh, that's nice," she says, retrieving some lip-gloss from her bag. "It's nice to meet a fellow soon-to-be graduate." She turns around and directs her attention to her phone.

I stare out the window and watch the snowflakes drift down from the sky as people begin to wander into the classroom. There is a little yellow light flickering near a cluster of leafless bushes, like a lightning bug spazzing out. The longer I stare at it, the more it blends into the snow and fades away.

Strange.

I click the cap of the pen off as my thoughts drift to the guy I ran into yesterday. For most of my life, I've never thought of guys as anything more than people, figures that filled up the school hallways and ran over me like I was nonexistent. And in my past that was fine. I never felt sad, lonely, or depressed. It was as if I was an object that filled up space, moved without cause, and served no purpose. Things changed when I started to feel emotions. It isn't like I want every single guy I come across, but I do have a very vivid imagination that is fed by my loneliness. If I had actual friends, then maybe my dreams and thoughts would tone down a little.

As I put the cap back on the pen, my hand begins to tremble and my gaze automatically dashes toward the doorway. My jaw drops. The guy from yesterday is walking inside. He moves like a cat with measured stretches of his long limbs and every muscle in his body flexes underneath his grey Henley and jeans. His hooded eyes are fastened on me as he climbs up the steps toward me and my fingers nearly strangle the life out of the pen in anticipation.

Is the strange, electric heat going to appear again?

He veers down the aisle in front of me, then flings his gaze off me and drops down into the seat beside Aislin. "Did you get your schedule all worked out?" he asks, reclining back in the chair and biting at a pen.

"Kind of." Aislin grabs a small paper from her purse, places it on the desk in front of her and runs her hands along it to smooth out the wrinkles. "The office people were kind of jerks."

He looks over his shoulder as he tips back the chair and the two front legs disconnect from the floor. He arches his eyebrows at me, probably because I'm staring at him with my mouth hanging agape. There's probably even some drool on my chin.

I discretely wipe my chin with the sleeve of my jacket, relaxing when it feels dry.

Aislin revolves around in her seat and beams a grin at me. "Gemma, this is my brother Alex."

I extend my hand out to him, wondering what it's going to feel like to touch him and if it will strike up the spark again. "It's nice to meet you."

His eyebrows furrow as his gaze cuts to my hand and then back to my face. He lowers the chair legs back to the ground and shrugs me off as he faces his sister. "So how much unpacking do you have left?"

My fingers grip around the pen until my knuckles turn white and it takes every ounce of energy not to stab him in the back of the neck. Thankfully, Professor Sterling enters the classroom and begins his lecture on sky charting. The interruption calms me down.

I jot down a few notes, but my concentration keeps straying to Alex. He is leaning back in his chair with his arms tucked behind his head and his eyes are half open. His shirt is riding up and his rock hard abs are peeking out. I rest my chin in my hand and focus on the lines of his muscles, his luscious lips, his firm jawline. Every now and again, he bites down on his bottom lip and I picture myself sucking it into my mouth, biting down on it and then sucking it into my mouth again. I imagine my hands touching every inch of his body, feeling how hard he is.

I'm thoroughly enjoying how hot the mental picture

makes my body feel when he unexpectedly tilts his head toward me. Our gazes collide and a fire crackles inside me, flaming passionately; full of a need I can't quite grasp. Then he glares and the fire goes *poof,* fizzles, and I feel put out; extinguished to nothing more than a thin trail of smoke. He quickly looks away and everything goes back to normal.

As class continues, the silence of the electricity is maddening. In a twisted way, I want to feel it because it feels good, but does it really exist? Just as the thought crosses my mind that maybe I have imagined it, a sharp spark nips at my lips. It is gentle at first, barely a tingle, but it grows stronger as it streams down my neck and my skin, causing a vibration deep inside me. I flex my hands and cross my legs trying to suffocate the tingling between my thighs.

Alex's jaw is taut as he stares ahead at the front of the classroom where Professor Sterling is yammering about something that is probably important, but all I can concentrate on is the untamed desire I feel. I want to do things to him, like jump over the desk and peel his clothes off.

Alex jerks his fingers through his hair and cocks his head to the side to capture my eye. His expression is a mixture of emotions: fear, anger, longing; they mirror my own perfectly. It's becoming harder than hell to keep my hands to myself. I finally have to tuck them between my legs before I end up reaching out and touching him.

Seconds later, Alex breaks our gaze and redirects his attention to the front of the classroom, clicking his pen over and over again through the rest of the lecture.

At the end of class, Professor Sterling assigns every-one to a group to work on a project and my group gets assigned to create a presentation about Gamma-ray bursts. I hate when he does this. I thought after high school that it'd be over, but there are always a few Professors who think it's beneficial to aid each other in projects. Worst of all, he pairs me with Alex and Aislin, which has to be fate slapping me across the face. Hopefully, I can keep my Goddamn hands to myself, but at the moment the idea doesn't seem plausible.

I gather my stuff and put my books into my bag before swinging it over my shoulder. Trying not to look at Alex, I start down the stairs, but his shoulder rams into me as he exits the aisle. I trip sideways, slamming my hip into one of the corners of a desk. Something inside my skull pops and images deluge my brain like little pieces of glass.

Alex and I are in front of a glistening lake, crisp with blue ice and encircled by frosted trees. Death is in the air and the sky is opaque and ominous. Snowflakes twirl around us and the temperature is well below freezing.

"It will be alright," Alex whispers to me, his breath clouding out in front of him. His lips are purple from the cold and there are dark circles under his green eyes. Shavings of ice have formed on his eyelashes and drops of snow stick to his hair. "I won't let anything happen to you. I promise I'll save you no matter what."

Tipping my chin up, I grip onto his strong arms, like it's the last time I'll see him. "But what about you? Who will save you?"

He sweeps my hair out of my face and kisses me with so much passion it nearly melts the snow. He sucks on my tongue, his hands straying around to my backside as he pulls my body against his. They linger there momentarily before he draws back. "As long as you're okay, I'll be fine."

"But Alex," I start to protest, but a large group of hooded figures charge from the forest and my words are sucked away by the wind.

The beat of their march shakes the world as they head for us. Ice topples from the trees and hits the ground. Alex pulls me against him as flames blaze through my body and then all I see is light.

I blink back to the Astronomy classroom right as my legs give out and I fall toward the floor, but Alex's arm encircles my waist and he catches me before I hit. I freeze, stunned, feeling the heat and the intensity caressing my skin, causing more confusion.

Well, what the hell was that? A dream? In the middle of the day? Awake?

"I do know you," I say as I stare up at him and this time it isn't a question.

His hands tighten around the small of my back and for a moment he holds me, frozen, as people pass by, heading down the stairs and looking at us like we're crazy. He's breathing fiercely, his chest rising and falling, as he stares at me with confliction in his eyes; his pupils round and large, and his lips are parted.

Foggy images fill my head. "I think I . . ."

"Alex," Aislin's voice rises over the moment. "We need to get to our next class."

He blinks and then wrenches his hands away from my back, giving me very little time to get my footing. He glares at me, his eyes pooled with hatred, but I'm not sure it's directed at me. Then he trots down the stairs with his sister at his side.

I watch him leave, very aware that he never denied that I know him.

CHAPTER
THREE

I 'M PRETTY SURE I'm suffering from delusions; that my stability has snapped like a broken rubber band, and my ability to grasp reality is gone. I've been really into psychology lately, doing a lot of research about it for class and for personal interest. It's an interesting thing, the human mind. There are so many different mental illnesses that can control a person, make them think a certain way, do specific things, see things that aren't real. Schizophrenia, bipolar disorder, and delirium are just a few and, in some cases, there is very little the person can do about it. I wonder if any of those apply to me.

I'm sitting on a bench out in the cold with a scarf wrapped around my neck, fingerless gloves on and a hot cup of coffee in my hands. I've called Sophia six times in the last two days and left her three voicemails. In each one I beg her to tell me about my parents. Please. Pretty please. I deserve it. However, each call is unanswered and the silence is more infuriating than the cold-hearted refusal she usually gives me.

The campus is busy for how early it is, lots of people going to and from class. As I try to analyze what is going on in each passerby's head, I notice a person lurking near the alleyway between the main office and the building next to it. He . . . she . . . it seems to be watching me. There are shadows obscuring its identity, but it looks unnaturally disproportioned and misshapen. There's also some kind of greyish smoke lacing out of its mouth and a hood blocks its eyes, but I swear there is a faint glimmer of yellow radiating from them. As the realization of what it could be strikes me across the face, I feel a spark flare inside me.

"Do you always sit outside in the cold and freeze your ass off?" The sound and feeling of Alex's presence encases my body.

I peer up at him. "Umm . . ." My gaze darts back to the alley, but the figure is gone. Again, I question my sanity. I tip my chin up, angling my neck to look up at Alex. "What did you say?"

He stares down at me with an annoyed look on his face, but there is also a trace of discomfort in the way he stands; like he's trying to relax, but can't quite get there. His hair is tucked under the hood of a heavy coat, black boots cover his feet and there is a tiny tear on the knee of his jeans.

He glances over his shoulder where I thought I'd seen the figure, and then levels his gaze back on me. "Isn't it a little bit cold to be sitting out here?"

"It's not that cold," I lie and take a sip of my coffee, basking in the heat of the hot liquid as it spills down my throat.

He cocks an eyebrow at me and there is doubt in his eyes. "It's not that cold, huh? Then, why are your lips purple?"

I touch my numb finger to my even number lips. "I

was actually working on an assignment for sociology." Another lie.

He looks around at the snowy campus yard and heavy traffic by the stairs. His forehead creases as he looks back at me and tucks his bottom lip up between his teeth, biting on it. "I have a question."

I fold my hands on my lap. "Okay. . . ."

He peeks over his shoulder again and then vigilantly lowers himself beside me on the bench. "You said you thought you knew me? Why?"

I scroll over his green eyes, his full lips, and his knee that is only inches away from mine. It's unnerving, yet, comforting, which makes absolutely no sense. Half of me is attracted to him, like metal to a magnet, while the other half is repelled by him, like oil and water. "There's just something about how you look that seems familiar." My third lie in the last minute. I'm on a roll.

"Familiar how?" he questions with intrigue. "Because I don't remember you at all and you don't look familiar. I'm pretty sure I'd remember you with that weird eye color of yours."

Irritated beyond belief, I shrug. "I'm not sure. There's just something about your face . . . like I saw it in a dream."

His eyes flicker to my lips and then a condescending look masks his face. "In your dreams?"

"Yeah, you know, things that you see when you shut your eyes at night," I say cynically, still infuriated that he's taken a jab at my eye color.

He rolls his eyes. "I know what dreams are, but what you're saying sounds an awful lot like a pick up line a guy would use on a girl."

I reach for my coffee cup balanced on the bench beside me. "I'm not coming on to you."

31

"Sure you're not," he says smugly. "Just like you weren't when you felt me up in the doorway."

"I'm not now and I wasn't then. I was just . . ." My temper shoots heat through my body that is almost as intense as the electric feeling. If he keeps it up, I'm probably going to explode and do God knows what. I haven't yet reached that level of emotion, the kind where you lose control to the point that you do and say things that you regret. "You just look familiar to me. That's all."

"And you look like a love sick girl. Sorry to break it to you, but you're not my type so you might as well get it out of your head that anything will ever happen between us."

"You don't know who I am or how I feel, so don't make assumptions."

Discounting me, he gets to his feet and dusts the snow off the back of his jeans as my jaw practically hits the snow on the ground. "See you in class Jenna." He struts off across the campus yard with arrogance exuding from him.

"It's Gemma!" I shout, like it actually matters to him.

He glances back with a smug smile on his lips and I wonder if he's intentionally been trying to burrow his way underneath my skin. If so, it's working. I jump to my feet and trample through the snow back to the car, my skin simmering against the wind. I'm not sure what I'm more furious about. That he called me a lovesick girl. Or, that he said he isn't interested.

The only thing I do know is that I've never been this livid in my entire life.

ON FRIDAY, I have a study date with Alex and Aislin in

the library so we can put the project together. I've seen a lot of them over the last few days. In fact, they seem to pop up everywhere. Aislin is polite and Alex is . . . well, I'm not sure if there's a word for what he is. One minute he's fine—quiet, in his own little world—and the next he's making a smartass remark about me; from the color of my eyes, to my lustful fascination with him (his words, not mine). He is one of the most contradictory people I've ever met and that is saying a lot since I can barely contain my own, newly present, emotions.

When I show up to the library, they're sitting at a table in the far back corner. Alex is messing with a compass and has a contemplative look on his face as he twists the knob on the top. Aislin sits next to him and is engulfed with whatever is on the screen of her phone.

"Hi, Mrs. Bakerly." I wave at the elderly librarian behind the counter. I work part-time at the library, which is a nice job, since I love books, especially science-fiction novels. Give me a story with a witch, vampire, faerie, or anything that isn't human and I am good to go.

She pushes her finger against the brim of her nose and nudges her overly large glasses up. Then she raises her hand to reciprocate my wave and looks back to the computer screen.

I drop down in the seat across from Alex and Aislin and let my bag fall to the floor. The wind has been blowing outside and my cheeks are anesthetized from the cold. I unwind my scarf from my neck and slip off my gloves, aware that Alex is watching me attentively.

"Am I particularly fascinating today?" I glance up at him with my lips pressed together.

He's wearing another long sleeve grey Henley that shows the outline of his muscular arms and his hair is disheveled like it always is. I've learned over the last few days that it's his trademark look and it is a nice one, but I always have the compulsion to run my fingers through it. He sets the gold-plated compass down on the table and for the briefest second it looks like it's orbed by a golden light, but by the time I blink, it's gone.

He folds his arms and leans over with a displeased expression, but amusement dances in his eyes. "Not really. Only that you have a candy wrapper stuck in your hair. How about you? Anything particularly fascinating about me today?"

"Nope." I comb my fingers through my hair until I find the plastic wrapper. Balling it up, I stuff it into my pocket, and then drape my coat over the back of my chair.

"Yeah, right." He smirks. "In fact, you look a little flushed by my presence."

Just keep calm. Keep calm. "That's from the cold outside." I cup my hands onto my iced cheeks to defrost them.

"Sure it is." He enjoys this—getting under my skin.

"Oh my God." Aislin gasps. "Gemma, you're frozen."

"I got about halfway here and then had to go back to the car because I forgot my phone," I explain, rubbing my hands together to thaw them. "I think it's only like two degrees outside."

Alex measures me up with his head cocked to the side. "You were supposed to be here fifteen minutes ago."

"I drive slow when it's snowing." I reach inside my pocket to silence an incoming call as my phone begins to ring. "I don't have four-wheel drive."

He glances over his shoulder at the window where snowflakes flutter down from the clouded sky. "It's not that bad out there."

"It's completely bad," I retort, irritated that he's

wiggling his way under my skin again. It's as if I have no power over my emotions when it comes to him and I've only known him for a week. How will things progress the longer I know him? "I could barely see."

He scrutinizes me. "Then maybe, you should have stayed home."

"I would love to have stayed home," I quip. "In the warmth, reading a good book, but you guys insisted we had to do this here."

His gaze bores into me as he nibbles on his lip. Last night, in my dreams, I'd bitten on that lip several times, along with the blonde stranger's. "Actually, that was Aislin who insisted. I was perfectly content at the idea of everyone working on this on their own and that way we wouldn't have to see each other."

My lungs are twitching to release the scream building up inside them. "Are you always this much of an asshole or do you just save it for me?"

He leans over the table more and our lips are so close they almost touch. His breath is hot against my skin and there is a challenge in his green eyes, as if he's daring me to argue with him. "I save all of it just for you."

Aislin snaps her cell phone shut. "Okay, I hate to break up your little moment, but I have to go." She collects her coat and purse off the back of her chair as she stands up. "There's an emergency at the . . . restaurant where I work and I need to go in."

"What kind of emergency?" Alex questions as he slumps back in his chair.

"I don't know." She shrugs and slips her arms through the sleeves of a fur-trimmed coat. She flips her hair out from beneath the collar and hitches the handle of her purse over her shoulder. "I just got a text saying that they need me to come in as soon as possible."

Alex looks unconvinced. "Bullshit. You're bailing so you can go out with that dude you met last week."

Aislin points her finger at him. "Be nice while I'm gone. I mean it. And get some stuff done. You've been slacking and letting Gemma and I pick up your workload." She waves at me. "See you later, Gemma."

I give her a small wave as she walks toward the exit, pressing buttons on her phone. Alex and I watch her until she disappears out the doors.

When he looks at me again, he seems nervous. His posture's stiff and he keeps fidgeting with his sleeves; pushing them up and then tugging them back down. "So, I guess it's just you and me."

"I guess so," I mutter as electricity caresses my skin.

Silence stacks around us and I begin to fidget. Each tick of the clock, thump of a book being put on the shelf and each whisper only add to the awkwardness.

Alex begins tapping his pen on the table as if he thinks he's a drummer. He's eyeballing the corner of the library where a tall, blond girl, wearing a short skirt is browsing through a row of books. As she bends over to search the bottom shelf, Alex slants his head to the side to get a better view of her ass.

So that's his type.

The longer I contemplate her being Alex's type, the more infuriated I grow. The cause behind the manifestation of these feelings is unknown, which makes the situation that much more frustrating. Every time he taps that damn pen, the potency of the sparks surges. They no longer feel like soft kisses, but like little bites from a thousand gnats.

"Can you cut the tapping out?" I ask him, releasing

my death grip from the chair. I put my elbows on the desk and press my fingertips to my temples. "It's hurting my head."

He tears his gaze away from the blond and the corners of his lips quirk. "Probably not. In fact, it's very important that I don't."

I slouch back in my chair and blow out a frustrated breath. "Why are you such an asshole to me? Did I do something to you that I don't know about, besides touching you without permission?"

"Kind of."

"Can you tell me what, then? So I won't do it again."

"Nah, I'd rather not."

I pierce my fingernails into my palms as the prickle jabs at my neck and blots my vision with red. "Why not?"

He shrugs as he drags his teeth along the top of the pen and his tongue slips out from his mouth. "It's complicated."

"The story of my life," I mumble, breathing through the last of my rage. The feeling has passed. Thank God.

"What's so complicated in your life?" He tosses the pen on the table and crosses his arms over his chest. "You seem like you have it easy, if you ask me."

"You barely know me," I say. "So don't make assumptions about me. For all you know, I could be a recovering crack addict, struggling to keep my sobriety."

"Are you?" He doubts.

I scowl at him. "No, but the point is that I could be."

"But, you're not." He pauses. "You know, you could always try to explain the complexity of your life to me, so I don't have to make assumptions. Maybe it'll turn out that I'm a really great listener."

I'm flabbergasted. "You seriously want to hear about

my problems? You want me to pour my heart and soul out to you? Be my best friend?"

He winces at something I've said. "I wouldn't go that far."

"Then, why are we even talking about this?" My fingers seek my jacket on the back of the chair and I prepare to make a dramatic exit. "I think that day on the bench you made it pretty clear that you didn't like me and that you don't want to get to know me."

He meticulously watches me for a moment, then his eyes sweep around the room like he's about to do something wrong. "Okay, here's the deal. I promise I won't be a jerk anymore." He checks over his shoulder again and then reduces the volume of his voice until it's low and husky. "In fact, I'll be really nice to you. And I mean — really, really nice."

I remain calm on the outside, but on the inside, I'm a violent storm of emotions. Some are fueled by rage and others by the sexiness of his Goddamn voice. "Why?"

"Why what?"

"Why are you suddenly going to be nice to me? When all you've done is be rude and insult me. What's the catch?"

"When did I ever insult you?"

"Yesterday, in class, you said that my eyes were," I make air quotes, "'Weird' and that they throw your concentration off whenever you have to look at them. That was the second time you've taken a jab at them, too."

"I didn't mean that as a bad thing," he says with a nonchalant shrug. "They're just distracting because they're . . ."

"Violet," I finish with my eyes fastened on him.

"Actually, I was going to go with different." There's a tiny indication of a smile on his lips. "But, violet works.

It's not a bad thing, though. Different is good. It's normal that's overrated."

"The first time we met, you let the door slam me in the elbow," I remind him, lowering my voice as Mrs. Bakerly glares at me from behind the counter. *Shit.* The last thing I need is to lose my job. I fold my arms on top of the table, lean my weight on them, and incline my body forward. "And, you got mad at me because I . . ."

The smile that breaks through his face is so radiant that his eyes sparkle under the lights. "Because you touched me."

I roll my tongue in my mouth trying to contain my aggravation. "It still didn't mean you had to be rude to me."

"I know." He appears genuinely sincere. "And, I'm sorry about that. I was having a rough morning."

I evaluate him. Can he feel the electricity, too? Because I sure as hell can. He seems content, calm, and perfectly in control with his shoulders relaxed and his eyes soft. "It hurt when the door hit my elbow."

"And again, I'm sorry." He looks around the room again, paying extra attention to the door where a few people are wandering in.

"Are you expecting someone?" I ask, craning my neck to look around at the door and the shelves. "Or are you looking for an escape route."

"That depends on if you're planning to try and attack me again," he quips, his lips teasing upward. "Like when we first met."

"I didn't try to attack you," I protest, narrowing my eyes at him. "I just put my hands on you."

"Without permission," he points out with that damn cocky smirk on his face. "Tell me, do you always do that with people you don't know?"

"Do you always let doors slam on people that you don't know?" It's like we're running around in circles, bantering and bickering like an old couple. I need to leave and put a stop to it, but it's the most interaction I've had with another human being and, despite the negativity, I'm kind of enjoying myself.

"Again, you touched me without permission," he says. "What did you expect to happen?"

"You know what, you're so right." I hold up my hand, showing him my palm. "You see this scar right here." I trace my finger along a faint white scar and let sarcasm drip through my voice. "I put my hand on this guy once and he cut my hand open, but I guess it was okay because I put my hands on him without permission." A total bullshit lie, but I'm trying to make a point.

He leans back in his chair, positioning his fist in front of his mouth to conceal a smile. "Sounds like the perfect punishment." He reads through my bullshit lie like an open book.

I roll my eyes and let my hand fall onto the table. "Look, I'm sorry for touching you. I just . . . I don't know why I did it."

"Because you're attracted to me," he states with over-confidence. "But, don't worry, you aren't the first."

I shake my head and melodramatically move my hand toward my bag as if what he said is the most absurd thing ever. I decide then that I will leave and prove a point; that despite the fact that he is telling the truth, I don't have to listen to him.

Quickly rising from the chair, he reaches over the table and seizes my wrist. Bringing my hand to the table, he traps it there beneath his. "Listen, I'm not much of a people person, so sometimes I say things that come off as . . ."

"As you being an asshole." I'm angry, irritated, as well as extremely hot and bothered by his touch.

"That's one way to put it." He smiles, but then it fades into a frown. "But, if you'll let me, I swear to God, I'll be nice. In fact, I promise I will."

I stare at his hand on my arm and his fingers cup around my wrist. "People make empty promises all the time."

"I never promise anything unless I mean it." He loosens his grip and shifts the position of his hand so it's extended over the table. "So, I'm promising you that I'll be nice."

I mull it over and then put my hand in his, feeling as though I'm betraying my self-worth, but it's worth it just to get some peace for the rest of my time here. As soon as our skin comes into contact, it's like my mind has been sucked into a pressurized bottle and my brain torrents with vivid images.

Alex presses his hand to mine and there is a river of blood streaming down his forearm. "I promise I'll never let anything happen to you."

"Forever?" I ask, my hand trembling against his as warm blood spills down my arm.

He smiles. "I promise." He leans over the small box situated between us and the candles burn luminously from inside the dirt cave. "And I never promise anything unless I mean it."

As I look into his eyes, I only see truth and when he kisses me, pressing his lips to mine, devouring me, tasting me and feeling me with his free hand; I know that he's all I want.

I gasp, jerking my hand away as my heart squeezes inside my chest. "*Shit.*"

He calmly draws his hand away and rests it on the table. "Are you okay?"

"Yeah . . ." I take a deep breath, my pulse frantically pounding against the outpouring of adrenaline in my body. I search his eyes, looking for a sign that he experienced the same thing. "Are you okay?"

"I'm fine." He reaches toward a stack of books on the table. "Maybe we should get to work."

What is happening to me? These things . . . these images . . . what are they? I press down everything I'm feeling, the perplexity, fear, the longing, and I nod.

"Can I ask you one more question?" he asks as I flick the cap off my pen.

I nod, distracted by my thoughts. "Sure."

"Where did you really get the scar?"

I stare down at the thin line running across my palm. "I have no idea . . . I can't remember."

He doesn't seem alarmed by my answer, instead, he appears satisfied. He begins highlighting notes with a bright yellow marker and I do the same. Finally, after searching through an entire stack of books and finding nothing, I decide to go look for more in the Astronomy Section and see if I can find anything on Gamma-ray burst. Alex doesn't ask where I'm going because he's caught up in flirting with Blondie.

I'm squatting down searching the slim selection of books on the bottom row, when someone walks up behind me. Electricity gyrates through me and I know its Alex.

"Finding anything useful?" Alex asks, flopping down on the floor next to me with his back up against the shelf. "Because the stack on the table Aislin dug up is practically useless."

I slide a book out from the shelf and shake my head.

"The selection here's crap. We might have to go to the library across town." I turn around and sit down on the floor. "They have a better selection."

"Or we could just bail on the project all together."

"Why are you even in the class?" I open the book, turn around, and sit down on the floor. "If you don't like the subject. It's not even required."

His grins. "An easy A."

"It's not that easy," I assure him as I skim through the chapter titles. "Take this project, which is turning out to be a pain in the ass."

"Then why are you taking the class?"

"I just love the stars, I guess."

"Are you sure that's it?" he questions with assumption in his tone.

I try to stay calm, but the fact that he's assuming stuff about me makes me uneasy. What if he knows about my weird connection with the stars—how would he know? "No, that's it. Just a love for them."

His lips part and there's a strange look on his face as he leans in. "I think I need to . . ." The blond-haired girl comes strutting up the aisle, swinging her hips, and he trails.

"Well, looks like you have a stalker," I mutter.

A smile takes over his face. "Jealous?"

My fingers drift to the back of my neck, which is free from the prickle and any new emotions. "I can one-hundred percent assure you that I'm not jealous."

He finds me perplexing as he studies me, but then the blond girl stops in front of us, and all his attention goes to her and her cleavage bursting from her top.

"I forgot to give you my number," she says and holds out a torn piece of notebook paper with a number scribbled on it.

Alex reads it over and the girl waits with her bottom lip in her teeth and her arms crossed. When he doesn't say anything, she asks, "So you're going to call me, right?"

Alex's eyes scale up her body to her face. "Absolutely."

She smiles and then shoots me a dirty look before walking away. When she disappears around the corner of the aisle, Alex balls up the paper and chucks it into the shelves across from us. I give him a funny look and he simply shrugs.

"What?" he asks. "I'm not interested."

"But you just told her you would call."

He shrugs again and then absorbs himself in a book. "Don't pretend you're not glad I just threw that away," he says without looking up.

I run my finger down the page, trying to act uninterested, but there's no use trying to deny it. He laughs softly under his breath and then silence settles between us as we read through pages and pages of book after book. Somehow Alex begins to shift toward me and I don't notice until there's only a whisper of air between our bodies. I should ask him to scoot over, but I don't really want to.

He scoots over more until his shoulder magnetizes to mine. I freeze as my skin ignites and combusts like a flare, sending my body into a shuddering fit. Alex stiffens, but doesn't move. I slant my head toward him our eyes locked.

"Once upon a time there was a princess," a small boy smiles as he walks through the grass with a little girl. "And she was the most beautiful princess in the world."

"Was she smart?" the girl asks, spinning in circles with her hands out to the side.

"She was the smartest girl in the world," the boy says

and grabs her hand to stop her from spinning. "And the strongest, but she didn't think so."

I blink the image of the children away, move back from Alex, and inhale sharply. What is that? And why has it only ever happened with Alex?

"Are you okay?" Alex's eyes examine me over like he's hunting for broken pieces hidden inside me. "You look pale."

I allow my hair to create a veil between us as my head tips forward. "I'm fine. I just have a headache."

"Are you sure?"

I nod, turn the page, and lean to the side to get away from the sweltering heat.

Alex releases out a slow breath, then tosses the book on the shelf and gets to his feet. "I think I'm going to bail out early."

I don't look at him. "Okay." *Yes, gorgeous, beautiful guy, bail out. Bail out now. Run away from me before you find out just how crazy I am.*

He starts to walk away, but dithers at the end of the aisle. "You're absolutely sure you're okay?"

I nod. "I'm fine."

He leaves me alone with a stack of books. I sit there reading through them, trying to pretend like I'm fine. That nothing is wrong. That I'm completely normal. But I'm only lying to myself. Things are far from normal—they aren't even close.

CHAPTER
FOUR

LOFTY TREES ENCLOSE *around me. It's dark. The moon is an orb that makes the mountains look like rolling shadows and the snow is a sheet of crystal. A light radiates brightly in the distance as I hike through the forest, heading deeper into the trees, moving for it, my mind begging me to get closer.*

As I step through the last of the bushes and out into the open, the light glows resolutely, like the stars above my head. I want to touch it—need to touch it.

"Don't touch it," a deep voice that I know very well rises over my shoulder.

I turn around to face it. "Why not?"

He's resting against a tree with his arms folded and he's dressed in dark jeans and a long-sleeve, black shirt. The radiance of the moon illuminates his face, making his eyes sparkle. "Because you don't want to. Trust me."

"You're standing out in the middle of the woods at night," I reply. "That doesn't scream trustworthy."

An amused smile tugs at his lips as he stands up straight. "I followed you out here." He walks toward me, narrowing the gap between us. "I thought I told you to wait inside the house."

I glance behind me at the light in the center of the snow, which has faded into a weak glimmer. *"What is that?"* Right as I say it, the light suffocates out.

Alex stops inches away from me and the warmth of his breath brushes my chilled cheeks. *"Gemma, you shouldn't be wandering around out in the woods by yourself. It's dangerous."* He leans in a little as he says it and our lips almost touch.

"It's just a forest," I say, breathless, and then joke, *"I'm pretty sure all the bears are in hibernation."*

He lets out a soft laugh. *"That's not what I'm talking about."* He places a hand on my upper arm and lets out a sigh. *"We should go back to the house."*

I move forward and graze my lips across his. *"What if I don't want to?"*

The connection of our mouths causes a zap of static to erupt and I let out a soft moan. His body tenses, but his warm tongue willingly enters my mouth. He tastes like mint and it melts me on the inside as his hands slip up the sides of my neck to my cheeks and then up to my hair. He pulls at the roots, tipping my head back so he can search my mouth more thoroughly.

"You feel so good," he murmurs against my lips as his hands slide around to my back and he pulls me closer. *"So fucking good."*

His words make me want to rip his clothes off. I feel around until I find the bottom of his shirt and then I sneak my hand underneath it, feeling his cold, but soft, skin, and his sculpted muscles.

"Fuck! Your hands are cold." He inhales a sharp breath, his muscles tensing, and then he lets out a low laugh that sounds very close to a growl. Suddenly he

jerks back and his eyes dart over my shoulder. "Run."

"What?' I say, but he's shoving me forward, back toward the house that's on the other side of the trees.

I stumble backwards as groups and groups of soaring figures ascend from the trees. They're everywhere, their eyes reflecting against the snow and the ice like fireflies.

Alex's arm snakes around me and he guides me behind him. "No matter what happens, make sure you run." Reaching into his pocket, he pulls out a knife and poises it out in front of him.

"What are you going to do—"

Before I can finish, he runs at them with the knife out. One steps forward, while the others open their mouths. The pale glow of the moon lights up the swirls and lines of their breaths as it fogs and laces around us like smoke. I duck to the ground as a cloud of it heads toward my face and envelops my body. An arctic chill sucks the breath from my lungs as I sink into the snow, no longer in control of my body.

I'm so cold and I can't breathe.

The last thing I see is Alex's body sinking lifelessly into the snow, then screeches envelop around me as a blanket of ice encircles my body, crushing my skin into my bones.

I'm dying, being smothered by the cold, and Alex is already dead.

I open my mouth and with every ounce of pain I'm feeling, I force out a scream that cuts through the night like a jagged blade.

I bolt upright in my bed, screaming at the top of my lungs and clutching at my blanket. Sweat drips from my forehead and trickles down my neck as my heart threatens to leap out of my chest. My gaze zips forward at a barrage of blinking eyes surrounding my room. They're everywhere, so blinding I can't tell where they're coming from. The air is cold and I can feel a breeze engulfing my body.

I jump up, flailing my arms as I trip toward the door, but by the time I reach it, the yellow eyes are gone. All that's there is the emptiness of my room and the darkness outside. I hurry over to the window, daring a peek at the parking lot outside. Most of the parking spots are filled and the lights on the carports are on. I can't see anything; no yellow eyes . . . no monsters . . .

I flip the lights on and press my hand to my heart as I slide to the floor. I feel defeated and alone as I take in my limited surroundings; the single nightstand with a simple lamp and my empty bed where no one else has ever been.

Empty. It's the one word that sums up my life.

Gripping on to the last of my will, I push myself to my feet. I need to try and get some answers; maybe then things will be a little easier. Heading out to the kitchen, I turn on the coffeemaker and then drop down at the computer desk in the corner of the dining room and open my laptop. I type in 'realistic, reoccurring dreams.' Links about physics pop up.

Even though it seems crazy, I click on a link and begin to read the article. "*Reoccurring and very vivid dreams may be the window into future events that are going to happen. Or, some people believe that it may be a surfacing memory that a person has repressed as a coping mechanism.*"

Are my dreams either of these things? Have they happened and I just can't remember? Or are they going to happen? Sighing, I shut down the computer and get dressed in jeans and a black t-shirt. I pull on a coat, slip on my boots and then pour coffee into a stainless steel mug before heading out the door; feeling exhausted and emotionally drained.

I've been dreaming about the monsters for two months and I'm worn out. I just want a break from the images, and the feelings they manifest. It would be nice to maybe get an explanation, too.

I FEEL HUNG over and it's my busy day, too; three classes *and* work. I'm sitting in Astronomy, half-alive with my eyes shut, an elbow propped against the table with my head resting against my palm. I'm just about to fall asleep when someone drops down in the chair beside me. The zap of electricity hits me at almost the same time the person sits and I jump in my seat as my eyes fly open.

"Sorry, I didn't mean to scare you." Alex sets his book on top of the desk and smiles. "I thought I'd sit by you today, if that's okay?"

I check over my shoulder, making sure there is no one behind me that he might be talking to. "Are you being serious?"

His eyebrows dip together as he shoves up the sleeves of his black shirt. "Yeah, why wouldn't I be?"

I sigh, sitting up straighter. "Because I thought your nice-guy act would be an exclusive, one-time event."

He seals his lips together, stifling a laugh. "Well, it's not. Besides, Aislin isn't here today and usually I cheat off her, so I thought I'd cheat off you instead."

I shake my head as a smile slips through. "Whatever. You know the quizzes in this class aren't multiple choice. There are questions that you have to answer in your own words."

"I'll just change a few words. No biggie." He raises his hips to take out his phone from his pocket as it begins ringing with "Save me" by *Unwritten Law* as the ring tone. He checks the screen and then presses the side button until it shuts off before returning it to his pocket. "So how's your day going?"

"Fine, I guess." He's being normal and it's weird. Maybe he suffers from a mental illness too, because he is about as bi-polar as I am.

"You seem unsure." He slants his head toward me, grinning. "I thought that was a pretty simple question?"

"It was," I say, unzipping my jacket as the heat amid us intensifies. "I'm just a little out of it."

"Tired?"

"Yeah, kind of."

It becomes quiet and I find myself wishing we'd go back to arguing, just so I don't have to endure the silence.

"Wasn't class supposed to start like five minutes ago?" Twisting his wrist, he glances at his watch.

Kinking my neck, I confirm the time on the wall clock behind me. "Yeah, but Professor Sterling is generally fashionably late."

Alex stares at the doorway as he deliberates something. "I say, if he's not here in five minutes, we skip out and go do something else. I need a break anyway. We could go on a short-lived road trip."

I start opening my notebook, but pause. "You want to skip out on class? With me?"

He shrugs, his gaze situating on me. "Yeah, why not?"

I shrug coolly, but, on the inside, I'm a nervous wreck. "Because you'd be with me."

He looks a little bit guilty. "That doesn't sound so bad.

Think about it. You, me, coffee and an endless amount of road."

I attempt to read him, but he's a book full of blank pages. "Where would we go?"

He holds my gaze forcefully. "Where do you want to go?"

The possibilities are infinite and my mind begins to conjure up all kinds of ideas. "How about the beach? I've always wondered what the ocean looks like and how the sand would feel between my toes."

He rubs his lips together, thoughtfully. "It feels nice." A dark smile breaks through. "Especially, when you're at a nudist beach and you can be completely naked."

Something heats from inside, like I'm beginning to get embarrassed, so I say the only thing I can think of. "Yeah, but what happens when sand gets lodged in uncomfortable places."

He snorts a laugh and smiles. It's a real smile, too. One that doesn't convey heaviness beneath it. "Good point." He pauses. "So you've really never been to the ocean?"

I shake my head. "I've never left Wyoming. At least, I don't think I have. I might have when I was a baby and still lived with my parents, before they died, but I . . ." I realize I'm rambling.

The guilt in his eyes magnifies. "What happened to your parents?"

My shoulders stiffen as the heaviness of the topic falls against my chest and crushes the oxygen out of me. I can barely breathe—barely think. "They died in a car accident."

Frowning, he looks down at his watch again. "Who did you live with while you were growing up?"

I reply with as minimal disdain as possible. "My

grandparents."

There's a hint of compassion on his face. "You don't like them?"

I focus on the front of the classroom, wishing he'd stop talking about the subject because it feels like a knife being plunged into my heart. "No, they're fine."

He examines my face with disbelief. "I'm sorry I brought it up."

I open my book and fan through the pages to distract myself from the pain. "It's fine."

His eyes explore my face, my eyes, my hands; like he's trying to unravel my thoughts. Eventually, he relaxes and his mouth curves upward into a playful smile. "Should we go?"

Outside the window is a layer of white snow, covering the grass and parking lot. It looks like a winter-wonderland out of some fairy tale; a kingdom made of ice and snowflakes. "You seriously want to go on a road trip with me?"

He verifies it with a nod. "I seriously want to go on a road trip with you."

My heart pounds inside my chest, enthusiastic and willing. There's a pause. We turn heads, lock eyes, then start to rise to our feet, but Professor Sterling chooses that moment to come whisking in with a handful of tests.

Alex's mouth curves into a lopsided grin. "Guess I'll have to take a rain check."

"I guess so." Sighing, I lower back into the chair.

Professor Sterling has a briefcase in his hand, as well as the tests, and he sets everything on the podium in front of the classroom. He looks a little off today; his suit is wrinkled, his face is unshaved and his hair is a little shaggy. He appears grungy as if he's travelled back through time to the 90's. He stares at the whiteboard for the longest time, with his arms crossed and his chin propped on his fist. When he turns around, his eyes scan the classroom. It doesn't seem like he's even looking at us; more like he's looking through us, as if we are nothing more than transparent statues.

"Today, I'm going to tell you a little story." He walks up to the board and picks up a marker. The tip squeaks as he draws several lines across the board and then puts the cap on, before returning the marker to its place on the tray. "About a fallen star."

I exchange a glance with Alex and he smiles, elevating his eyebrows. "I think someone's had a little bit too much to drink today."

"I don't think he drinks," I say, staring at the picture on the board. It's drawn in blue with lines that shoot out from the end of a very sloppily drawn star.

Alex leans over the desk toward me. "Trust me; he does. I smelt it on his breath one day."

I nod, but pick up my pen and take notes anyway.

Professor Sterling paces the front of the classroom with his hands behind his back. "There's a legend that a very long time ago a meteorite fell from the sky and landed up in the mountains that surround this valley."

People in the classroom glance around at one another and an eerie calm sets in, as if we all agree that he's snapped. I'm going to give him the benefit of the doubt, however, since I know what it is like to potentially be crazy. Plus, there is something about what he's saying that strikes a nerve and a vibration of a memory whispers a story I can't remember the words to.

He strolls behind the podium and I swear his gaze loiters on me as he takes in everyone. He picks up a marker and climbs up in the stool behind the podium. "Although, some believe that it wasn't a meteorite, but an actual fallen star."

A hand shoots up in the air and Professor Sterling points the marker at the culprit; a straggly built guy that has very bad acne. "Yes, Philman."

"It's Philip," the guy corrects and slouches forward as he flips the page of his notebook. "And if a star actually hit earth, we'd all be dead,"

Professor Sterling shakes his head as he hops off the stool. "Not if it was a piece of a star. Sometimes, when stars get spinning beyond their normal acceleration speed, pieces break off. Some may be large while others are as tiny as my finger." He strolls up to the board and scribbles jagged lines across the star, making it look like it's broken.

"But, if it hit, wouldn't we all know about it?" a girl from the front row calls out as she fans through the pages of her textbook.

He readdresses his attention back to the class, facing us as he throws the marker onto his desk. "Not if someone hid it before it was discovered."

"But who would do that?" the girl responds and picks up her pen to take notes.

The grin on Professor Sterling's face is haunting and sends a chill up my spine. "Someone who wanted a lot of power."

I'm engrossed in the irrationality of the story. Fallen stars. Power hungry people. It's the making of an interesting novel.

"Maybe, he's high, too." The feel of Alex's breath steals my focus.

I look away from Professor Sterling to Alex and am

stunned by how close he is. "I think he's just telling a legend."

"Maybe." He smiles as he reaches over and tucks a strand of my hair behind my ear. He slides his finger down my cheekbone and jawline before moving it away. There's a slight tremble to his hand, but he plays it off with a cocky smile. "Or maybe, he's just high or drunk."

Touch me again. Please touch me again. I've never been touched like that before, except in my own imagination. I'm hypnotized. Petrified. Controlled. I can't look away from him, even when he reclines back in his chair and concentrates on the front of the classroom while chewing on the end of his pen. I forget about paying attention. I forget about everything for a moment.

We don't talk for the rest of class, but halfway through Professor Sterling's lecture, Alex moves his leg toward me, inching it closer until his knee is resting against mine. The contact is mind-blowing, amazing, and mystifying. I'm not sure if he's done it on purpose or if he is just getting comfortable. Either way, I'm glad.

I'm glad about a lot of things at that moment.

ALEX LEAVES IN a hurry when class is over, barely uttering two words to me. I try not to take it personally since the guy is more up and down than I am, but it does bother me. How he'd been acting during class was great and fun and I've wanted both of those things in my life for a while. He takes those things with him the moment he exits the door, though.

I head around the back of the school where my car is parked. I usually park out front, but it was overly crowded today. The snow is coming down hard and I can barely make out the outline of the cars. With my chin tucked down and my hood pulled over my head, I fight my way to where I guess my car is parked.

As I near the back row of the parking lot, I'm overtaken with the strangest feeling that someone is following me. I shift my bag up my arm, telling myself I'm overreacting, but then I hear a whisper. It's feeble at first; however, it grows noisier and more coherent.

"Gemma." A hand grabs my arm and I'm basked in the warmest rays of sunshine that have ever touched the earth. It's magical and makes me feel powerful.

As a warm sensation sails across my skin, my legs give out and I crumple to the ground, hitting the ice hard. As I shoot upright, I don't feel pain, but I'm off-balance. With my hands out to the side of me, I squint through the flurry of snow. In the distance, there's a figure; lofty, with wide-ranging shoulders. It looks an awful lot like the figure I've seen in the alleyway near the front entrance; the one with the glowing yellow eyes. *Shit.*

I move to run, but a thick fog swims out from behind a car and heads toward me. It's tinged black, like ashy smoke, and it gyrates around me, starting at my feet and working its way to my head. It mixes with the snow that floats up from the ground. I can't see a damn thing, except for the eyes moving toward me.

It can't be real. Things like this only exist in dreams, but, as the temperature plummets, and my skin turns a gruesome shade of blue, I make a decision.

It's time to run like hell.

I drop my bag and whirl around, preparing to run, but I slam into something rock solid. I swiftly back up with my hands out in front of me and panting for air. Through the fog, Alex surfaces, and relief washes over me. He puts his fingers up to his lips, urging me to be quiet as he takes my hand. There's no spark of electricity from the contact this time, and I feel hollow. It feels strange and unnatural, but as he pulls me to the left, I run with him, trusting him completely.

As we near the cars, I glance over my shoulder and search for the monster. The fog has divided and I have a clear view of it. It's more terrifying to look at in real-life. It is excessively tall with rotting skin and purple and black veins. There are bits and pieces of flesh missing, revealing bones and muscles. A black cloak drapes down its body to the icy ground. The fog that conceals the parking lot is streaming from out of its mouth and it makes a hollow noise with each breath. It's terrifying and the fear sears the image of it into my mind like a tattoo I'll never be able to get rid of.

Alex jerks me around a car and we hunker down behind its side. Fog dances around us and the wintry air is like needles to my skin. I begin to shiver and chatter uncontrollably.

"It's going to find us," I say through chattering teeth as I turn to face him.

He doesn't respond and he looks a little out of it.

"Alex," I whisper, waving my hand in front of his face. "We should run. Those things . . . They . . . they'll kill us both."

He seems unaffected, stoic and immobile. I wave my hand in front of his face again, but he doesn't blink. What the hell is wrong with him?

I'm about to pinch him to snap him out of his trance when a deafening shriek cripples the air. I jump to my feet as the monster steps out from in front of the car. I spin toward Alex to shout at him to run, but he isn't there. I reel back around, but the monster has vanished, too. It's all gone; the fear, the need to get away. Everything transfers back into place; the fog lifts and my body warms up.

There's a swishing sound and then I'm being pulled back. I'm no longer standing, but lying alone in the middle of the parking lot; my face pressed against the ice, and my cheekbone feels swollen and bruised. I sit up and cup my cheek. There isn't a single speck of fog in sight, no monsters, no Alex. Everything is just as it should be.

Except for my head.

It's like I zoned off in the middle of the day while I was walking and fell down. I'm pretty certain that I'm going to have a bruise. Letting out a massive breath of air, I search between the cars in the parking lot and behind a nearby tree, just to make sure. All seems right in the world. My skin has turned to its normal shade of pale and the memories of what just happened are already drifting away.

How many damn times is this going to happen to me? Maybe it's time to see someone and get my head checked out.

I scoop up my bag, dust off the snow and watch the cars back out of their parking spaces. I'm losing it. I'm really going crazy. Either that, or someone is seriously messing with my head

CHAPTER
FIVE

F OR THE NEXT couple of days, Alex doesn't show
up to class and I don't see him in the halls. I try not
to think about it too much, but it's all my mind goes
to. While I wait it out, my nightmares become cleverer.
The scenery starts altering to darker places, like cemeteries and gothic clubs. One even takes place in a yard full
of bones. The sequence of events never changes, though.
I'll be with Alex, or sometimes with the blond stranger,
and *BAM*, the monsters will show up, we'll suffer and ultimately die.

For a faltering instant, I consider telling Marco and
Sophia about what is going on—trying to seek help—but
then, I realize that will only add to my insanity. So I keep
my mouth shut, letting my nightmares haunt me, own
me, consume my nights and leave me wishing for a friend
or someone I can talk to about them.

I'm working in the library this morning. It's a quiet
day and I find myself missing the busy work of putting
books away and checking books in and out to distract me
from my thoughts of monsters, heavy make out sessions
and the realization that I might be lonely for the rest of my

life. As I place a worn book onto the top row of a shelf with my feet propped on the bottom and my arm stretched as far as it will go, I hear someone move up beside me.

"Need some help?" Alex is leaning against the shelf with his hands in his pockets. He has on a black-fitted t-shirt again, a pair of faded jeans, black boots and there are flakes of snow in his brown hair. He looks like he's trying to be relaxed, but can't quite get there; his posture's a little stiff. "You look like you do."

Every emotion I've ever felt crashes through me and throws off my equilibrium, like I've been tossed onto a tilt-a-whirl driven by crack. "I'm good, but thanks." My shoe clips the corner of a cart as I retreat back and I almost fall on my ass.

Alex's fingers press roughly into my hips as he grabs ahold of me and stops me from falling. "You know, I'm starting to notice that you have a knack for falling, especially when you're around me."

I back away from him, my entire body searing from his touch. "That's a clever observation, but I'm always this way."

He presses his hand to his heart, feigning offense. "So, it's not just me?"

A soft laugh escapes my mouth that sounds a lot like a dying goat. "Nope, sorry."

I pause, analyzing how I should approach my much needed question. "Hey, this is going to sound weird, but you didn't happen to . . . um . . . by chance were you out back a few days ago?"

"Out back? Of the campus?" he asks and I nod. "Nah, I've never been out there. Why?"

I feel my already crumbling world break into even more pieces. "Oh, it's nothing. I just thought I saw you while I was walking to my car, but I guess not."

He stares at me silently like he's trying to read my mind. "Do you want to talk about something?"

I'm stunned. "With *you?*"

His lips bow upward and his eyes glimmer mischievously. "You say that like I just asked you to have sex with me."

I'm pretty sure my heart stops, dies in my chest and ceases to exist. I'm in shock, embarrassed and completely enthralled by the sound of the words coming out of his mouth. I need to say something, to break the unnerving silence that has overtaken us, but all I can do is stand there and gawk at him. He starts to squirm more and more the longer the silence goes on and his smile dissipates. Finally, I bail and start up the aisle, pushing the cart along with me, concentrating on the squeaking of the wheels to deflect my concentration from him and to give him an out to run like hell from weirdo girl.

I catch a flash of yellow from my peripheral vision, but this has been happening intermittently since my delusion with the monster in the parking lot and the light always fades when I turn my head. So I ignore it.

"I'm actually glad I ran into you." Alex comes up behind me again, scaring me half to death and making me drop the book I'm holding. He quickly scoops it up and gives it back to me. "I was supposed to be coming by to see if you could meet up at my house later tonight."

I take the book from his hand. My voice comes out sharp as I ask, "What? Why?"

He snorts a laugh. "Relax, I don't bite or anything. I just wanted to know if you can because Aislin wants to finish up the project tonight. In fact, I think her head is going to explode if we don't."

"Oh." I slide the book on the shelf, frowning. "You've been gone for a few days."

A lazy grin creeps up on his face. "You noticed."

I scale up his rock-solid body and I detect a squirm on his part, which secretly pleases me. "It's hard not to notice when you're gone."

His smile expands. "Are you coming on to me?" He moves his arm so it's on the shelf beside my head and his voice drops to a deep whisper as he leans toward me. "Because if you are, I'm going to have to warn you that you shouldn't. It's dangerous—I'm dangerous."

I arch my eyebrows as I put a book on the shelf without taking my eyes off him. "Now, that sounds like a come-on line."

He bites at his lip as his smile practically takes over his face and he widens the space between us by stepping back. "What do you say? Can you come over later to work on the project?"

I stretch my arm behind my back, feeling around for a book on the cart. "Yeah, that works for me, I guess."

"You sound disappointed," he muses with a grin. "Is it because of the project or because you'd be around me?"

I pick up a book and read the number on the binding, pretending to be indifferent even though I have a rabble of butterflies in my stomach. "It's neither. I'm just tired today. I haven't been sleeping very well." I put the book on the shelf and turn around, only to notice that he's diminished the space between us again.

"Why?" He slants forward and places a hand on the shelf, so the crook of his arm is beside my head.

"Bad dreams," I say and sigh when he frowns. "I sound like a little kid, don't I?"

He shakes his head. "No, but what are the dreams

about?"

Monsters. Death. You and your sexiness. "Just stuff . . . things . . . You know what, it's not important. They're just dreams."

"Maybe it would help to talk about it. Holding stuff in only makes things harder."

"What are you, like a psych major or something?" I joke.

He shrugs. "No, I'm undecided."

"What year are you?"

"A senior."

"That's a little late to be undecided," I say, wondering if he's lying. I retrieve another book off the cart, astonished that he can detour me from my worries. He's made me feel better and normal; my thoughts less heavy. That is all I want from life; a clear head and direction. "Don't people generally declare majors around their sophomore year?"

He edges to the side as a guy ambles up the aisle, whistling an off-key tune. "What are *you* majoring in?"

I scoot the book into its correct place on the shelf. "General Studies."

"Isn't that about the same as undecided?" he accuses and captures my gaze. "It's like saying I can't make up my mind, so I'll just have a vague major to get by."

"Yeah, maybe," I mumble, deflated. He's struck a touchy subject. My future. My indecision. The fact that I never can envision myself doing anything.

His gaze flicks to my lips and he inhales slowly. "If you ever need to talk, you can come to me."

I eye him over. "Are you being serious?"

"As serious as I was when I said we should skip out on Astronomy and go for a road trip." A leisurely smile unfolds across his face and he sticks out his hand. "Here, give me your phone."

Confused beyond belief, I take my phone out of my pocket and give it to him. He swipes his finger across the screen to unlock it, pushes some buttons and then hands it back to me, brushing his finger along the inside of my wrist. Even though it's probably accidental, my heart and mind connect in a lively dance that nearly sends my knees buckling.

"I'll see you later, Gemma." He winks at me before he reels on his heels and vanishes around the corner. I feel a tug inside my chest and for a second it feels like he's ripped my heart out and taken it with him. I feel disconnected as I read the notes section of my phone:

24432 Monarch Road Apt 34

Meet Aislin and me there at 9:00 pm tonight so we can finish the project.

I put my phone back into my pocket and begin putting books on the shelf, letting the puzzlement, anticipation, and sheer loathing entwine inside me, like a tethered knot, until they form one single coherent emotion.

Numbness.

I REMAIN NUMB the rest of the day; oblivious to anything except my work task. If someone approaches me with a question, I answer with as few words as possible. It's like I've died or traveled back in time to when I was unemotional and withdrawn; my body still moving, but my soul and spirit disconnected from each other.

The feeling lingers during the entire drive to Alex's place, which is in a nice area where all the buildings have a similar, newly-built look to them. His apartment is located at the farthest corner building, on the upper floor. It's snowing hard and by the time he opens the door, my hands and lips are numb, like my heart.

Except suddenly, it isn't.

The sight of him launches my body into a fit and a massive volume of emotions surge through me, toward my heart, like they are racing. I'm just not sure which one will get there first: anger, passion, sadness . . .

Lust.

Alex has a serious case of bed-head, but it looks so sexy and touchable. He also doesn't have a shirt on and his jeans hang low on his hips. His flawless skin is stretched over his solid, tight muscles and a black circle, trimmed by a golden ring of flames, is tattooed on his ribcage. As he raises his arms to brace his hands on the doorway, my gaze skims lower, my breath clouding out in front of my face.

"Are you going to come in?" he asks, pleased that I'm ogling him. "Or, just stand there and enjoy the view."

Oh dear God, oh hell almighty. I've never experienced mortification, but I'm verging toward it at this moment; not quite there, but close. "I wasn't enjoying the view," I lie and not very well.

He rolls his eyes, then moves back and I walk inside, stomping snow off my boots before I step onto the carpet. He shuts the door behind me, picks up a plaid shirt off the back of the sofa, slips his arms through the sleeves and does up the buttons; covering up those wonderful abs of his. "Aislin's not here yet."

I nod, glancing around at the bare white walls, the empty counters in the kitchen and the two chairs that surround the small, square table in the corner. There are boxes near the back of the room, a coffee table in the center, and a hallway leading to somewhere. That's it. His house is about as vacant as my old bedroom, which is sad.

"How long has it been since you moved in?" I ask, feeling the awkwardness filtering the air.

He shrugs as he heads for the refrigerator in the kitchen. "A few weeks ago or so."

I unzip my jacket and wander around gawking at the labels on the boxes: *dishes, bedroom stuff.* "Weapons?"

"It's a hobby."

A hobby for what? "That's an interesting hobby . . . why haven't you unpacked yet?"

He takes two cans of soda out of the fridge and kicks the door shut. "I'm used to living out of boxes."

Returning to the living room, he offers me a soda as I aim a questioning look at him. "How come?"

He sits down on the couch as he flicks the tab of the can. "When I was younger, my dad moved us around a lot, so it became easier to keep things packed. It's part of life now, I guess. Honestly, I'd have no idea what to do with stuff all over the house."

I nod as I tap my finger at the tab, internally cringing at the silence that settles in. "When's Aislin going to be here?"

He kicks his bare feet up on the table. "Her boss made her work late. She called me about thirty minutes ago and said she was going to be like an hour late."

"Oh." I take a sip of my soda, unable to think of a single word to say to him, but I've never been much of a conversational wizard, only on rare occasions.

"You can sit down." He pats the spot next to him on the couch. "I don't bite."

What if I want him to bite me? I blink the thought

away, set my leather jacket on the back of the kitchen chair and join him on the sofa. The electricity scorches my skin, dispersing through my body and blood roars in my ears. I press the ice-cold soda can to my forehead, feeling like I'm on the verge of passing out.

"Do you have a headache?" Alex tips his head back and takes a sip of his drink with his eyes on me the entire time. He moves the can away from his lips and observes me with curiosity. "I have some Tylenol in the cupboard."

I shake my head. "I'm fine. I'm just a little tired."

"Is it your nightmares? Are they keeping you up at night?" There's laughter in his tone.

"You know I really wish I wouldn't have told you that." I grimace and swallow a large mouthful of soda.

He sets his can down on the table. "Why not? I'm just trying to get you to smile. You don't do that a lot."

I shrug, flipping the tab until it snaps off. "Don't you think that at twenty-one years old, people shouldn't have nightmares? It seems like I should be passed that?"

He shakes his head, takes the broken tab from my hand and discards it on the table. "Nah, nightmares and dreams last forever. It's part of life."

"Yeah, I guess." I hesitate. "Do you have them?"

"Have nightmares?" he asks with a quirk of his lips. "Not really, but I'm completely dead inside so nothing scares me."

I analyze his expression. It's one of passivity and gives no detection on whether or not he is joking.

"I'm being serious," he says with a one-shouldered shrug. "It's how I've been forever, hence the reason why I'm a douche bag and rarely feel bad."

He's the most perplexing person I've ever met, besides myself. "You're not being a douche right now. In

69

fact, you haven't been much of one the last few times I've been around you."

"Yeah, give me some time. It takes me a while to warm up." He is unreadable; there's an indifferent expression on his face, his mouth sits in a straight line, his eyes give nothing away. "I have this theory." He changes the subject as he scoots to the side, relocating closer to me on the couch. "About you."

I force down the massive lump in my throat. "What kind of theory? Or do I not want to know?"

The cocky gleam revisits his eyes and he stretches his arm along the back of the chair so it lies beside my head. "The kind where I think you're extremely innocent."

That is the last thing I expected to come out of his mouth. "Excuse me?"

"I can tell these things," he says as his fingers tangle through my hair. "It's a gift."

And Mr. Sexy Douche Bag returns. I withdraw my head away from his hand as the jolt of electricity webs my thoughts. "Just because you think something doesn't mean you have to say it out loud."

He grins haughtily and reaches for my hair again. "The simple fact that you can't even deny it, tells me I'm right."

"Don't touch me." I start to get to my feet, but his fingers spread over my thigh and he forces me down, kind of roughly.

He rotates to the side on his hip and his body conforms over me. "I'm not trying to make you mad." He kneads my thigh with his fingertips, causing an effervescent feeling to coil up between my thighs. I cross my legs to suppress a shudder as my head hits the armrest of the sofa. "Only to get to know you a little better."

I'm conflicted between slapping his hand away and letting his fingers sneak up my leg further. "You said you warm up." I can't take my eyes off his hand on my leg.

His eyebrows knit and his hand stops traveling upward. "What?"

"To being a douche." I smack his hand off my leg, even though it nearly kills me. Then I place my hands on his chest, noting the racing of his heart, and push him away from me so I can sit up. "But there was no warming up. You went from hot to cold in about two seconds."

He looks down at his hand as he flexes his fingers, appearing befuddled. "You know, you're nothing like what I expected." He elevates his chin and meets my eyes. "The first time I saw you, I expected you to be quiet and less . . . feisty."

Was that a compliment? My lips part to question, but his phone starts playing "Mad World" by *Evergreen Terrace* and my words drift off as he answers it, gets to his feet and heads down the hallway. I grab my coat, slip my arms through the sleeves, and zip it up. It's definitely time to go. Assignment or not, it's not a good thing to be here. He drives me crazy, in both really bad and really good ways, and it is emotionally unhealthy.

As I open the door, a below-zero breeze carries into the house, blustering snowflakes across the floor and against my cheeks. There's a snowstorm blowing in as usual. Tucking my lips underneath the collar of my coat, I start to step out.

"Gemma, wait," Alex calls out. I pause with one foot over the threshold, waiting for . . . something. "I want you to go somewhere with me."

I turn my head toward him and lower the collar away from my face. "Are you being serious?"

He's slipped a pair of boots on, but the laces are still undone. "I'll knock it off. You just get me all riled up for some reason." He lowers himself onto the edge of the coffee table and kicks his boot up on his knee to tie up the laces. "But I promise I'll be Mr. Nice Guy the entire time." He pauses, setting his foot back down on the ground and amusement sparkles in his eyes. "I cross my heart and hope to die."

An image presses up at the back of my mind and pops in my head like a burnt out light bulb.

"Cross my heart and hope to die," someone whispers.

A little girl with long brown hair spins circles in a field with her arms out. "Stick a needle in your eye?"

"Stick a needle in both eyes," the voice answers with laughter.

I flinch and then for no reason whatsoever say, "Stick a needle in your eye?"

I half expect him to return my question with the same response as in the memory, but all he does is stand up and nod. He grabs his coat off a hook in the wall and then moves past me, steps outside and gestures at me to follow.

"What about Aislin?" I ask as he locks up the door.

"She's actually going to meet us at the place." He puts the house key in his pocket, turns for the stairway, and zips up his jacket as snowflakes stick to his brown hair. "Although, I don't think we'll be getting any of our project done."

I trot down the stairs after him, holding onto the railing. "Why not?"

He reaches the bottom of the stairway, dusts the snow out of his hair, and glances over his shoulder at me. "Because we're going to a party."

I slam to a stop, slip on a patch of ice, and smack my

elbow on the railing as I try to catch myself. Alex's hands snap out and his fingers enfold around my waist, saving me from a very painful fall. The sparks attempt to fire up against my skin, but the air is freezing and the sensation is muffled.

"You're very accident prone." He releases me and tugs his hood over his head. "You need to relax. It's just a party and we're not even going there to join in. We just need to pick something up."

I follow him down the sidewalk, hiding my hands in my sleeves to keep them warm. "Then, why are you bringing me with you?"

He shrugs as he swerves to the left and heads toward the carport. "I find you entertaining to be around. You say things normal people wouldn't say." I frown and he shakes his head, smiling, as he adds, "It's a good thing so stop pouting."

It almost sounds like a compliment. Stunned, I shove all my reservations aside and follow him, drawn by an impulse that I have no control over, as if I'm a puppet. Or a lovesick girl. Either one isn't that flattering.

CHAPTER SIX

A LEX DRIVES A 1969 cherry-red Camaro with black leather on the inside. It's the sexiest car I've ever laid eyes on and I'm not even a car person. It's embarrassing to admit, but it kind of turns me on a little or maybe it's him driving the car that is getting my insides throbbing. That way sounds a lot better.

He drives fast, which is extremely dangerous for how icy the roads are, but, for some unknown reason, I trust him; somehow I know that he'll never let anything hurt me. I keep my seatbelt buckled, though, listening to the engine purr as I watch the curves of the road.

It's getting late, the sky is black, the snow is thick, and the headlights light up the way. The inside of the car smells like cologne and there is a hint of a lilac sent. I realize there are pressed flowers hanging from the rearview mirror. I reach up and spin them around, glancing over the browned edges and the crisp stems.

"I didn't picture you as a flower person," I tease, releasing the flowers and rotating in the seat to face him, drawing my knee up with me.

He has one hand resting comfortably on top of the

steering wheel and the other is on the shifter. "You're funny." He flashes me a grin as he slows down for a very sharp corner. "Someone gave them to me."

"A girl someone?" I request casually as I shuffle through his playlist on the iPod.

He nods and I feel my heart sink in my chest, ram against the inside of my stomach, and rile up the motion of my blood. "Yeah, she gave them to me quite a while ago."

I feel like an idiot. This whole time I've been drooling over him and I never bothered to ask if he has a girlfriend. "Oh, sorry. It doesn't seem so bad then. To have them, I mean; especially if she means something to you."

He twists the string, securing the flowers to the mirror, his eyes glazing over as if he's floating back into a memory. "I should probably take them down."

"Why? Did you break up with the girl?" Could I be any more obvious?

He releases a breath trapped in his chest and wraps his fingers around the shifter. "No, she died; quite a while ago."

Me and my excessive questions. Dammit. The sorrow in his eyes makes me feel like an asshole. "I'm sorry, I wouldn't have brought it up if I—"

As his fingers brush just above my kneecap, the sound of my voice withers. "It's okay. It was a long time ago and I've moved on."

He doesn't sound like it. In fact, this is the first time I've ever seen any real, raw emotion from him. He looks lost, ripped apart from the inside, broken, beaten and guilty. I wonder what happened to this girl, but I don't dare press any more than I already have. His hand leaves my leg and I decide to end the conversation, before I say anything else stupid.

THE PARTY IS in a cabin that's located in the middle of the mountains. The car gets stuck in the snow three times during the drive up as the road becomes packed with more snow, narrowing the roads. It's pitch black by the time we park in front of the cabin; the sky is so gloomy there isn't a single speckle of starlight.

The red interior lights of the cabin highlight the shoveled pathway that leads to the front porch and the red glow makes the snow look like it's soaked with blood. There is music blasting from the inside that has an entrancing, sexy beat and the deep bass rattles the windows. There are people making out on the steps, the mixing of their breath swirling in the cold air as their hands wander and grope at each other. *What am I about to walk into? An orgy?*

Alex turns the headlights off, removes the keys from the ignition, then opens the car door and steps outside. He tucks the keys into his pocket and lowers his head to peer in at me. "You comin'?"

I glance warily at the porch and then at the trees beside it, recollecting my dream. "What kind of party is this?"

"The kind where you have to take off your clothes just to get in," he says and my expression falls. He shakes his head, grinning. "Relax, Gemma. It's just a party. I promise you'll be okay."

Another promise. I climb out of the car and meet him around the front. Walking side-by-side, we head up the pathway to the house. None of the people kissing and feeling each other up notice us as we pass by them and step into the warmth of the house. I begin to take a breath, when the smell of smoke, alcohol and sweat consumes my nostrils.

The place is crammed with people taking shots and sipping beers. There's a cloud of smoke from a very packed smoking section near the sliding glass door and the sexual tension from the dance floor is like poison in the air. Some of the things they're doing are making my cheeks heat with excessive blood flow.

My body tenses as Alex's breath touches my ear and his hand grazes the small of my back. "Relax, I promised you'd be okay and I never break a promise. Remember?"

My shoulder jolts upward from the nearness of him as I nod. "I'd be a little bit more comfortable if I knew why we're here."

He leans over my shoulder and I tilt my head to the side to meet his eyes. My depth perception is off and I almost end up kissing him. "I just have to pick something up." He threads his fingers through mine and pulls me toward the crowd.

I can't stop staring at our interlocked fingers, even as stray elbows and shoulders slam into my ribs and sides. No one's ever held my hand. Ever. In fact, I've never even been hugged, that I know of.

"Don't drink anything offered to you," Alex calls out over the music as a woman dressed in a short black dress whisks by us with a tray of green Jell-O shots.

Nodding, I coordinate with his steps, staying as close to him as possible. As we approach a hallway my gaze falls on a woman dancing by herself in the corner. She has a margarita glass in her hand and is spilling her drink everywhere as she shimmies her hips to the music. As her head tips back, her hair moves and each strand forms a head. It looks like she has snakes in her hair; like she's Medusa. My eyes widen as one of the snakes hisses in my direction and I gasp. *Holy shit.*

"Gemma," Alex's voice rises over my thoughts as he squeezes my hand.

I blink and her hair doesn't look like snakes anymore, but long, black locks of hair. I divert my concentration to Alex.

He's watching me inquisitively. "Are you okay?"

I nod, suddenly aware that nothing can help me escape the hallucinations, nightmares and daydreams. They're going to haunt me for the rest of my life. Or until I finally go off the deep end and get locked up.

Alex's eyes are locked on me as he backs the rest of the way to the hallway, leading me along with him and, again, I feel safe. I walk with him, step-by-step, maneuvering through the people effortlessly, and I'm temporarily put into a state of euphoria. He doesn't look away until we reach the end and he opens a door, pulling me inside after him before shutting the door. It's quiet. And mellow. And normal.

"What exactly are they smoking out there?" I inquire as I examine the small room. There is a queen-size bed, covered with a black comforter, and the walls are red just like the lighting flowing from the ceiling and everywhere else in the house.

Alex starts opening the drawers of one of the dressers and digging through them. "Who knows? Maybe Peyote."

I'm not sure if he's being serious or not. "I thought I saw something weird."

His chin tips up and there's an inquisitive look on his face. "Like what?"

I shrug and my hands fall to my side and I sit down on the bed. The springs creak below my weight. "A woman with snakes for hair."

He lets out a soft laugh as he shuts the drawer. "Don't worry. As long as you don't see anyone with fangs, we're fine. Or a guy with a snake tattoo on his neck. If you see someone with that, then we'd need to run."

Did he inhale some of the peyote? "Um . . . what?"

He winks at me and dimples appear as he smiles. "Relax, he's not supposed to be here, even though it's his house." He shucks off his coat before he places his hand on the wall.

"What would happen if he was here?" I wonder as he runs his fingers along the wall.

Drawing his elbow back, he raises his fist beside his head. "Then, he'd probably try to kill me." With one swift swing, he hammers his hand through the wall. Sheetrock crumbles, breaking off and falling to the floor as I jump to my feet.

"What are you doing?" I hiss. "You just punched a hole into someone's wall!"

He shakes his hand and dusts bits of debris off his knuckles. "Obviously."

I kick a large chunk of wall out of the way and step up beside him. "But, what about snake tattoo guy?"

Standing on his toes, he snakes his arm into the hole. "I already told you he isn't supposed to be here. Besides, he may try to kill me, but it doesn't mean he can." He draws his arm back and there's something silver clutched in his hands.

I move forward and lean over to get a better look. "What's that?"

He quickly stuffs it into his pocket. "It's nothing you

need to worry about."

I cross my arms and step back. "You drag me up to a party where people are smoking peyote and there's a guy that may want to kill you. You punch a hole in the wall and take out something, but I shouldn't worry about it?"

He stares at me musingly. "I didn't drag you out here. You came of your own freewill."

I open my mouth to argue, but he's right. "Fine, you're right. Can we go now?"

His gaze never wavers from me. "Do you want to go? Or do you want to stay here a little longer . . . with me?"

"I . . ." Why can't I answer that question?

His eyes flicker to the bed and then settle back on me. The starvation in his eyes both pulls me and pushes me away. I'm afraid, yet curious of what will happen and where the night will take me if I dare to do something out of the norm. "We could hang out here for a while."

"What about snake tattoo guy?" My voice squeaks and I clear my throat. "What if he shows up and tries to kick your ass?"

"Again, he can try," he says with a grin and reduces the already limited space between us. "But it doesn't mean he can."

The defensive wall I've built around myself slowly crumbles. "Okay."

His eyebrows arch in surprise. "Okay? You want to stay?"

I nod. "Yeah, I want to stay."

Again, he glances at that damn bed. What is he thinking? I sure as hell know what I'm thinking and it requires a lot of time on that bed. "I'm going to go get us something to drink." He speaks slowly as he steps back. "Wait here."

"I thought you said not to drink anything offered to

me?"

His lips quirk as he opens the door. "That excludes me." Before I can respond, he walks out and shuts the door.

I collapse on the bed, letting out a breath I hadn't realized I've been holding. What am I doing here with a guy I barely know? I have a feeling the night is only going to result in trouble, yet, I don't seem to give a shit.

I roll on my back and stare up at the cracks in the ceiling. I start counting each one as my nerves begin to short-circuit through my blood, taking each limb over and ultimately my heart. The prickle stabs at the back of my neck and I feel out of control and helpless, then I feel nothing. A numbing sensation takes me over and my body starts to sink into the mattress. Immobility consumes each nerve. I'm paralyzed and as the images form in front of my face, all I can do is watch as my spirit detaches from my body. I float away into the ceiling and, seconds later, darkness immerses me.

WHEN MY FEET touch the ground again, I'm standing in the middle of a field. The night sky is covered with stars and there are crickets chirping from the grass. The air smells like lilacs and the warm breeze caresses my cheeks. A feeling of peace has overtaken me and I stroll through the grass with no direct destination.

If I had one wish in my life, I'd wish that I could stay and feel this way forever. Content and weightless with no worry or sorrow of the past. No confusion about life or how I feel. It's right then that I realize just how lonely and discontent I am. How empty I feel even though I'm a bundle of emotions. I've never lived, never loved, never done anything.

Moments later the feeling is stolen away with a gust of wind. I turn around and the tall grass hisses at my legs. In the distance of the land, two figures surface. One is tall and the other is very short. They are holding hands and step slowly as if they are savoring the moments of their journey.

"We're almost there," the tall figure says. It's one of the loveliest voices I've ever heard from a woman; not too high or too low. She wears a dress and her long hair dances in the wind. I wonder what she looks like, but as she gets closer, I realize her face is obscured and distorted with a haze.

The shorter figure's face is also distorted, but I see that she has a skip to her walk, like she is happy to be here. "I'm so excited!"

"I know you are, honey," replies the woman, swaying her arms and giving the little girl a swing. "And you should be. There is a lot to be excited about right now."

I watch them with fascination. Who are they? Deep down it feels like I know the answer, but my mind can't quite connect it together, like it's missing a piece of the puzzle.

I remain motionless in the field as they near me. I start to lift my hand to wave at them when they get close enough, but they walk by me as if I'm nonexistent, as if I'm a ghost. Maybe I've died back on the bed in the cabin and this is the afterlife?

"Hello," I call out, trailing after them.

Neither of them flinches nor makes any move that tells me they heard me as they continue on with their conversation. I speed up and chase after them. They stop beside a large oak tree that stretches to the dark sky. The moonlight glimmers across their faces and the only details I can make out about them are that they have long hair and fair complexions.

"Here we go. This spot is perfect." The woman raises her hand to the sky and points at the stars. "See that one right there?"

The little girl's head tilts up. "Yeah, I see it, Mama."

"That one's yours," the mother tells her. "That spot right there."

"It belongs to you," the mother continues, sadness filling her voice. I wonder if my own mother ever talked to me like this when I was a baby. Did she love me? Did she want to make me happy? I only had a year with her and I can't remember a single aspect or detail, nothing.

"For forever?" the girl asks, spinning in a circle with her arms out and her head tipped back as she basks in the moment.

"I hope not," she replies sadly and picks up the girl.

The girl throws her arms around her mother and they hug each other as if nothing else in the world matters. It's a feeling I will never understand. I shut my eyes, no longer able to bear something I wish I had, but know I never will. I may be able to feel now, but that doesn't mean I can travel through the past and have moments like these with my mother. I know this. Somehow I know that my life will be short, that I'll be very lonely, and that when it all ends, I'll only have myself.

CHAPTER SEVEN

WHEN I OPEN my eyes, I'm lying on my back on the bed at the cabin, no longer staring at the ceiling, but at Alex's worried face above me. My arms rest lifelessly out to my side and, for a moment, I can't move. When Alex places his hand on my cheek, the connection launches a zap to my heart and brings my body back to life.

I gasp for air as my lungs expand and I urgently reach for my eyes to wipe away the tears that are streaming down my cheeks. Alex leans back, giving me room. My body aches in objection as I sit up, blinking my burning eyes.

I don't look at him, but I can feel him watching me. "I think I should go home," I say, smearing away the last of my tears onto the sleeve of my shirt.

"You're crying." He leans forward and tips his head, moving into my line of vision. His eyes scan my face. "You're really crying."

I swing my legs off the bed, attempting to stand, but my muscles are taut and I fall right back down. "People cry all the time. It's part of life."

"Yeah, but usually people cry when they're upset or when something horrible happens to them." His eyes roam to the window and he stares at the silhouettes of the trees. "Did something horrible or sad happen to you?"

I shake my head, but it feels like I'm lying as vague memories press at my mind. Even though I've never been able to feel it until now, my life hasn't been a walk in the park. I basically raised myself since I could walk, cooking dinner for myself by the age of six when I could read the instructions to the microwave dinners. I walked myself to the bus stop in the below zero weather. I sat in my room countless times, staring at the wall and wondering what I was supposed to do with myself because everything felt pointless. There isn't a single picture of me because no one has ever wanted one enough to take it. I'm told all the time that I'm not wanted. Is all this considered horrible?

He smoothes my hair out of my eyes, tensing as our skin comes into contact. "You blacked out. It took me forever to wake you up."

"I'm fine," I lie and try to get to my feet again, but my legs give out again and I collapse back onto the bed, giving up.

His tense expression alleviates and his voice is soft, begging. "Gemma, there's obviously something bothering you, so just tell me what it is."

"It's called life." I meet his eyes. "Now, would you please take me home? I feel sick."

He shakes his head. "You were fine when I left the room. What the hell happened?"

I was fine when he left, and then I wasn't. Just like when I was working at the library. Then he showed up and then left, leaving me numb. A realization clicks inside my head: what if it is him that is making me feel this way, or the absence of him anyway? "Who are you?"

His expression shifts as he looks at me like I'm crazy, making me feel small and insignificant. "I'm Alex." He speaks to me like I'm a moron.

I kneel up on the bed, trying to gain some confidence against his overbearing gaze. "I know what your name is, but what I'm wondering is, who you are as a person?"

His eyes never leave me. "Why?"

"Because I want to know."

"But, why?"

It's like a game to him. A fucking mind game. "Because ever since I met you, things in my life have gotten a little . . . weird."

He chews on his lip, unflustered. "Weird how?"

"You know what, let's just go." I start to get up, but his fingers snag my elbow and he yanks me back down on the bed.

"You're not going anywhere until you tell me why you were crying." He rolls on his hip, forces me on my back, and traps me beneath him.

Longing swells through my body and I bite my lip hard to suppress a moan. "Get off me."

He shakes his head as he transfers his weight so that my legs are confined underneath him and our bodies touch strategically, chest-to-chest, leg-to-leg. "Fight all you want, you can't do anything about it. I'm the one in control here." He pauses as I scowl and our chests brush as we breathe in sync. "Now, please, will you just calm down and tell me why you're flipping out? I thought I was doing well with the whole douche bag thing."

"You were." I swallow hard from the feel of his breath stroking against my cheeks and the way my nipples brush against his chest every time I take a breath. I've never been this physically close to anyone and my mind is racing with anxiety, anger and a craving to touch him everywhere. It's too much. I'm going into an emotional overload and it feels like I'm going to combust. I try to wiggle my arms between us, but he seizes my arms and lures them above my head.

"Get off me!" I need help, but I'm shit-out-of-luck. The music is so loud and it even muffles the noise in the room. "Please!"

He forces my arms together and holds them in one of his very large hands. "Not until you tell me why you're flipping out."

"Because physical contact freaks me out," I lie, arching my body into his in a lame attempt to force him off me.

He moves his body upward out of my reach, but still keeps a hand on my arms. "I can tell when you're lying by the way you're biting your lip." He lets his weight descend back toward me. "Just like I can tell when you're pissed off by the way your jaw tenses." His body is back on me and I lay immobile beneath him as he continues with his voice softer. "Just like I can tell when I'm embarrassing you because your cheeks turn pink." His face lowers towards mine and I notice for the first time that he has a faint scar just below his eye. His breath is hot against my ear and neck; my eyes uncontrollably shut as he whispers, "Or how I can tell when you're getting turned on by the way you get distracted and how your body shudders."

The insinuation of his words encloses around me and my body shudders, just like he's accused. Something snaps inside me. I break. Splinter apart. Pieces are now missing. I raise my head and surprise him as I touch my lips against his. I push past the forceful amount of electricity slashing through me and instead of kissing him, I suck his bottom lip into my mouth.

Then I bite down hard.

I'm not even sure what the point is. Whether I'm pissed off or so turned on that I've lost the capability to rationalize my actions. I rest my head back on the mattress and wait for him to hop off and call me a freak.

Instead, he stares at me as his tongue slips out from his mouth and wets his lips. "Fuck, you drew blood."

Before I can even begin to be embarrassed, he lets out a deep growl and seconds later his lips come down on mine. Holy fucking hell. I've never felt anything like it. It's all gone; the worry, the sadness, the emptiness. I can barely breathe as his tongue slips inside my mouth and entangles with mine. I have no idea what I'm doing, but I go with it and allow his tongue to search my mouth. My skin feels like it's melting, but in a good way. As I lift my hips up, pressing our bodies together, the heat spirals out of control. I want to be closer—need to be closer—but it doesn't seem possible, since he's lying on top of me.

His hand is still holding my arms and he tightens his grip as his other hand slides down my body to my hip. He digs his fingers into my skin as he moves his legs so that mine are free. Seconds later, I have them fastened in a vice-grip around his waist. His body tenses and his breath catches in his throat. Drawing away, he looks into my eyes and I think he's going to say something insulting, but then he lets out another low growl that sends vibrations all over my skin and he crushes his lips into mine again. The innocent kiss suddenly turns reckless as his hand slips underneath my shirt and he cups my breast. I've never felt this kind of ecstasy before. It's intoxicating. Overwhelming. Complete. I finally understand what the big deal is.

"I've wanted this for forever," he murmurs, which doesn't make much sense.

But I don't really care at the moment

I writhe my hips up against him, feeling his hardness between my legs. My head becomes foggier as he kisses and feels me all over. I want to rip his shirt off, feel his skin and feel the passion, the spark, the connection. As every ounce of my self-control withers, I wiggle my hands out of his. Maneuvering them between us, I begin to fumble with the buttons of his shirt. When I reach the last one, he catches my hand and stops me.

He removes his lips from mine, props up on his arm and peers down at me. His lips are swollen and his eyes are glazed over like he barely understands what is going on. "We should slow down," he pants, looking conflicted.

I instantly frown. "Why?"

Looking torn, he glances down at my hand trapped in his and then back at me. "Because we should." He loosens his grip and frees my hand. Like a magnet, my fingers move for the last button and I flick it undone.

As my fingers graze his stomach, his lips seal against mine. His tongue urges my mouth apart and when it enters mine, the warmth nearly swallows me. Pressing my hands flat onto his stomach, I feel the rhythm of his breathing, the rise and fall of his chest, the warmth of his skin.

I begin writhing my hips against his again, letting go as he moves his lips away from my mouth and start trailing kissing down my neck. Each one is soft, but full of desire. I want more—need more. I'm confused by my thoughts and what my body wants. It's like I've been starving for years, nearly dying of hunger, and his kisses are finally satisfying the ever-growing starvation.

As he approaches my collarbone and takes a nip at my skin, I delve my fingers into his shoulder blades. With one last buck of my hips, something explodes inside me and, for a second, I'm free from the world I've never felt I belonged in. There is no pain, no loneliness, no fear. Everything I'm feeling at the moment is real.

Apparently, the light bulb above our heads has the same idea. It flickers and then glass shatters everywhere. I wince as sharp, hot fragments of glass land on my skin.

I freeze. Alex freezes. Time seems to freeze. Alex shifts his weight and the next thing I know he's climbing off me, leaving me in the dark surrounded by hot glass that is sharper than the mortification I feel at the moment.

He flips a lamp on, but I don't dare look at him as I sit up, plucking the pieces of glass off me. He walks around in front of me and begins picking glass out of my hair without saying a word. The silence says more than words ever could.

"So that was . . ." He drops a piece of glass onto the floor and then runs his hand down his arm, brushing some off his sleeve. "Interesting."

I angle my neck back to look up at him. His hair is a mess, his lips puffy, and he looks perplexed. And lost. And, well, a little horrified. I feel suddenly ashamed. I've never felt like this before and I don't quite understand it.

"We should probably go." His eyes travel above my head to the ceiling.

I tip my head back, tracking his gaze to the broken light fixture that is making a low buzzing noise. "How do you think it happened?"

He shrugs, flicking a piece of glass off his sleeve. "Faulty wiring."

"Does that stuff cause light bulbs to explode?"

He avoids looking at me and his tone is clipped. "I don't know. I'm not an electrician."

I suck in a breath as I stand up. Running my hand down the front of my jeans, I clear the remaining glass off and then depart for the door. "Alright, let's go then."

I'm overwhelmed. Baffled. There are thoughts in my head that need resolution, but I don't know how to seek it. Tears pool in the corners of my eyes as I hurry for the door and out into the crowded hall. There are even more people littering the room than when we arrived and even more smoke filtering the air. I hold my breath and tuck in my elbows as I begin to squeeze through the sweaty bodies that smell like salt and alcohol.

Fingers wrap around my upper arm and I'm jerked back as a current of heat charges through my body. Alex guides me back toward the mellower end of the hall.

"I'm sorry," he says it so softly that I'm not sure I heard it correctly.

I look at him. "Sorry for what?" The list of reasons is endless.

Releasing my arm, he rakes his hand through his messy hair, making it stick up more than it usually does. "I just . . . I don't know. Panicking, I guess. But I shouldn't have snapped at you." It's physically paining him to say it. His hand falls to his side and he hesitates. "But, that can't happen again. We have to . . . we have to be friends. Just friends."

It sounds like a copout line. I cross my arms, trying to protect myself from the feelings of humiliation eating away at me. "I didn't even know we were that."

He huffs out a breath as his head falls back. "You're going to make this difficult, aren't you?"

I expand my hands out to the side of me, nearly hitting a woman as she whisks by. "I'm not doing anything, except being honest. I don't know you. You don't know me, at least, not very well."

He lifts his head back up and there is a frown puckering at his brow. "But, I do."

I shake my head, fighting to stay composed. "How come—" The music switches to an upbeat rhythm that pounds through the speakers and asphyxiates my tone. People start going wild, banging their heads and gyrating their bodies against each other. I inch closer to Alex, even though the heat and the disgusted look on his face is ripping my heart into a thousand pieces of nothingness. "How come you're fine one second and then suddenly, completely offish? I don't get you. At all. And it's like you do it on purpose. Like you . . ." I trail off as he stares at me, biting at his lip, seeming amused. "Why are you looking at me like that?"

He shakes his head as he grins. "It's nothing." There's a pause and he stares at my mouth. "I just realized that I'm going to have my hands full."

I'm not sure what it is; the stifling heat or the wounding of my pride, but I suddenly lift my hand to hit him. He starts to smile, but then all humor leaves his face as his gaze dashes over my shoulder. He quickly grabs my arm and tugs me down the hall toward the bedroom door. Pressing his hands to my back, he shoves me forward. I trip over my feet and land on the bed.

"What the hell are you doing?!" I sit up as he slams the door and spins around.

He puts his finger to his lips, shushing me, then he races over to the window. Peering outside, he reaches into his pocket and draws out a small pocketknife. He flips the blade open and turns to me with the sharp end aimed at my heart.

"Is that what you stole out of the wall?" I inch away from him with my hands out in front of me.

He glances at the knife, then lowers it to his side and shakes his head. "No." His boots thud against the floor as he paces with his fists clenched. "Remember that snake-tattoo guy I was telling you about? Well, he's here."

I keep my eyes on the knife in his hand. "What are you going to do?"

"I don't . . ." He spins toward the window and flings it open. A nippy breeze howls at my ears and snowflakes encircle around me. "We're going to climb out the window."

There's no way I'm going to jump out the window and into the snowy forest. I've hated the forest ever since my dream. I'm already too close now. Shaking my head, I kneel up and back away across the bed. "Why can't I just walk out the door and meet you at the car? He's not after me?"

He turns to me and there's a cautious look in his eyes. "Well actually he kind of is."

I climb off the bed and stand up on the other side to maintain some distance between us. "How am I a part of this?"

He sticks out his hand. "It doesn't matter right now. You need to come with me—we need to get out of here."

I arch my eyebrows at his hand. "Not until you tell me what's going on."

Letting out a frustrated sigh, he rounds the bed in quick, determined strides, so I have little time to react. Before I know it, he's right in front of me. "That's a really long story that I don't have time to explain at the moment." He laces his fingers through mine and hauls me toward the open window. "I just need to get you out of here. I should never have brought you here."

I remove my hand from his and glance out the window at the forest that stretches aimlessly into the night. "Then why did you?"

His gaze interlocks with mine. "Because I can't seem to stay away from you for some Goddamn, annoying reason."

Uncertain how to react, I seal my lips and climb up onto the windowsill. Swinging my leg out, I glance back at him. "You're coming, too, right?"

He nods, but his gaze darts to the door as it swings open. I catch a glimpse of yellow that flickers as a cape flaps and then I'm being shoved out the window. Luckily, we are on the first floor, and the fall is short. I land in the snow bank and sink into it. Falling onto my hands and knees, I dig my nails into the snow and claw my way forward, dragging my legs out of the snow bank. Rolling onto my back, I stare up at the window I've just fallen out of. It is freezing and dark, and there are shadows moving all over inside the house. I can see two figures in the room, fighting against each other, swinging their fists and there's a lot of loud banging. I push to my feet and back away, undecided. Should I run? Or wait? As I turn toward the car, I hear a soft thud and I spin around. Alex has jumped out the window and is running for me. Within a beat, he's grabbing my hand and then we are running like hell around the house. His skin is cold and his body blurs against the darkness. I struggle to keep up, my legs stretching to their maximum length. I'm moving so quickly that I run into him as he stops and it's like colliding with a wall made of ice.

"What is it?" I stagger to the right as he begins to move

again, detouring around a fence and then heading toward the trees. My legs fight to keep up with him as he picks up the pace. I can barely see anything; the sharp features of his face and the solid outline of his body blends with the dark. "We're seriously not going in there, are we?"

As we reach a small opening where the trees break apart from one another, he stops and glances from left to right. Then he releases my hand and turns in a circle, looking lost as he takes in the trees. His hair is crisped with frost and the way he moves his legs, without quite bending his knees is strange.

"What are you doing?" I breathe and the cold stings my lungs. "Did you get injured? You look like you're walking funny."

He remains silent as he hikes toward the trees, crossing his legs with each step. He no longer has the knife in his hand and there's something off about him—he is too quiet.

"Alex," I hiss and chase after him, keeping my head low to the ground because the branches of the trees clip my head. "What are we running from?"

He looks at me from over his shoulder and the moonlight reflects in his eyes. His pupils look hollow as if every last speck of emotion has been emptied. He smiles and it's like looking at a ghost. Something's wrong.

I shuffle backwards with my hands poised out to the side. The ground is slippery and snow keeps falling from the branches of the trees and down the collar of my coat. Alex doesn't utter a word to me, he only observes me. The recollection of a memory runs over me like a truck and my knees almost give out. I've dreamt about this place before. I was in the trees, it was dark, and the moon was bright. I brace a hand against a tree and squint through

the dark. Through the darkness, a dim flicker of light surfaces. I want to run, but my legs are bound to the ground
by my fear.

"Why did you bring me here?" I demand. "And who
are you really?"

He folds his arms across his chest and stares at me,
unresponsive. His stare is weighted and overpowering.
My body longs to be near him, but the rage inside my
head keeps me put.

"Answer me!" I shout and the sound echoes for miles
and snow shivers from the bare branches of the trees. My
body shakes from the wrath inside me. "Do you know
what's going to happen? Is that why you brought me out
here? Because you want it to happen?!"

Again he's silent, like a mummy with their lips stitched
shut. The shadows of the branches cast across his face and
the wind howls around us. I pry my hand away from the
tree and force my feet to move. I know what is going to
happen and I need to get out of here, with or without him.
In a slow, lethargic movement, I rotate around and drag
my feet through the deep snow. The sky is a sheet of black
and my bearings are mixed up from the cold that possesses my limbs. I'm lost. I glance over my shoulder and Alex
is gone. He has bailed on me; left me out here in the dark.
I'm not sure if that is a good thing or a frightening one.

"Shit," I curse as I circle around a tree, hunching over
as I try to track my footsteps back to the cabin. The light
glimmers in the distance, beckoning me to come closer
and I keep winding around the trees, trying to get back to
the cabin, but all that seems to happen is I grow nearer to
the light. It is getting colder and the moonlight is fading
behind the clouds.

I halt at the sight of lofty shadows emerging from the

trees. They're just a hallucination, like in the parking lot. It has to be. However, as the figures surfaces move closer, the fear that races through my body and rams into my gut and chest is very real.

"Gemma, what are you doing out here?" Alex winds around the last of the trees and steps out into the open. The remaining stream of moonlight casts across his face and his eyes look normal again, not empty. There are scratches on his face, his jacket is torn, and his hair is disheveled. "Why the hell didn't you run to the car?"

My gaze drifts to the knife in his hand. There's blood on his knuckles and on the blade. "You took me out here."

He stops a distance away and his eyebrows dip together. "What are you talking about?" He's close enough now that I can see a thin river of blood streaming down his wrist.

"You're bleeding?" I dare a step closer to him.

His shoulder moves forward and he examines the blood pouring out of his arm. "It's just a scratch."

I shake my head. "No, it's bad."

"I'll live, but we have to get you out of here." He offers me his uninjured hand, but I don't take it. "Would you just come with me?"

"I don't know." I look over my shoulder, noting that the light in the distance has vanished. "I can't . . . I don't . . ." Confusion is overwhelming me. I want to run to where the light disappeared. I want to run away from Alex. I want to run away *with* Alex. I have no idea what to do. I'm pretty sure I am the most confused human being that has ever lived.

"Gemma!" Alex's angry voice cuts through the night like a knife to flesh.

Goosebumps dot my skin and my heart thrashes

against my chest. I can feel my ribs about to crack, unable to endure such a heavy emotion. I back away, the snow crunching below my shoes. "I don't know what to do."

"Follow me." The voice is softer and more soothing than Alex's, yet when I turn around it is Alex standing behind me. Only he isn't injured and he doesn't have a knife. His skin looks paler, like the snow and his eyes like coals. My eyes glide back and forth. There is an Alex on each side of me, both waiting for me to take their hand.

The inevitable has finally come. I've snapped, fallen off the cliff called reality and submerged into the darkness where imaginary things walk, talk and are real to me, but no one else. It seems like everything is moving in slow motion and I'm linked to each aspect that surrounds me; the expanding of the icicles as the temperature descends, the sounds of branches snapping, the inhale and exhale of Alex's breath.

"Gemma." The injured Alex takes a cautious step forward. "Don't listen to it. It's not real."

I whip my head back and forth between them. "Listen to *it? It's* you. I don't . . ." I tug my hands through my hair and yank out the roots as I try to sort through what's happening. "Oh my God, I'm crazy."

"You're not crazy." His feet move gradually and carry him closer to me, while the other just stands there. "That thing is . . . well, it's a mirage, kind of like a trick of the eye. It doesn't really exist. I promise." With each step, he leaves a trail of blood in the snow, which makes him seem realer than the other. He bleeds, has veins and a pumping heart. I know because I can suddenly hear it.

"Don't listen to it." The mirage-in-question purrs. "You need to come with me." His voice sounds controlled and his face flickers, fading in and out. Shock waves through me and I stumble backward away from him. He isn't real. He's a ghost, unruffled and transparent. "Don't run. If you do, you'll die."

My head snaps in the other direction and I do the exact opposite. I run like hell toward the injured Alex. Before I know it my hand is in his and we are running away from the mirage.

"What's going on!" A branch snags my cheek and splits open my skin. I cup it as warm blood pools out of my skin.

He shakes his head, the blood from his arm dripping onto me, the liquid warm against my skin. "I'll explain later . . ." His words are sucked away by the sound of the wind.

As the heaviness of the cold presses down on my body, I realize I know what's going to happen because I've dreamt about it only days ago.

The ground begins to quake as tall figures march through the trees. Their eyes glow across the snow and icicles begin to crisp the trees that surround us. Fog snakes through the trunks, coiling and spiraling, heading in our direction. Alex speeds up, moving at a pace I'm not capable of keeping.

"Alex," I choke against the cold as my feet slip out from under me. His hand glides up my arm and he helps me get my balance before I fall. "I can't . . ."

He practically lifts me up and carries me, my feet leaving the ground. Moments later, we break out from the trees and into the yard of the cabin. My feet touch the ground again and I'm moving on my own. The car isn't too far off and Aislin stands beside the driver's side, bundled up in a coat and hat, her arms crossed and her eyes narrowed.

"What the hell were you thinking?" She moves away from the car and stomps toward us, tightening the scarf around her neck. "Bringing her up here."

Alex sprints toward her with me in tow as the people on the porch of the cabin watch us. "Now's not the time for lectures." Alex doesn't slow down, nearly running over her, and she has to jump out of his way.

"What the hell is going on?" She rushes after us with worry written all over her face.

Alex slams to a halt when we reach his car. "Gemma's seeing mirages."

Aislin's head whips in my direction. "You did what?"

Before I can respond, Alex interrupts, "And they've found her." He pats his pockets and then takes out his keys.

The color drains from Aislin's face and beneath the cast of the porch light, her skin looks green. "The Death Walkers? How?"

My insides weave into knots like they are made of thorns that want to tear at my insides. "Death Walkers?"

Alex swings his car door open, dives in over the console and reaches toward the glove compartment. "Yeah, big, tall creatures that look like the walking dead." He takes something out, slams the console shut, and jumps out of the car.

My heart stills as his words echo in my head. I glance at the trees, the people on the porch, and then back at Alex. "And have glowing eyes?"

Alex and Aislin freeze and they look at me as if I'm nuts. Maybe I am. Perhaps this is another dream and I'm going to wake up at any moment. "How do you . . . never mind. You can explain later." He turns to Aislin. "You gotta transport us out of here."

"Transport?" I ask at the same time Aislin says, "Why?"

Alex's fingers close around my upper arm and his eyes stay on Aislin. "Because there's no way in hell we're going to out run them."

I lurch my shoulder forward, trying to wiggle my arm free from his grip, but his fingertips dig deeper into the fabric of my coat. "What the hell is going on? Someone better start explaining or I swear to God—"

"Or, you'll what?" Alex waits with a condescending look on his face.

Furious, I lift my knee and move my foot toward his shin. He dodges out of my way and then drags me around to the passenger side. Aislin chases after us as she retrieves a purple object from her pocket. "I only have the amethyst with me. I'm not sure it's powerful enough to take all three of us anywhere."

"Make it work." Alex's voice is piercing as he yanks open the door. "We need to . . ." His eyes widen as they zone in on the trees behind us.

I track his gaze and every last hope for my sanity evaporates. Frost webs along the fence that encloses the cabin and moves in contours and patterns across the ground toward our feet. The frozen air intoxicates my lungs and bites my skin. A screech rattles the air and hundreds of yellow eyes flash through the forest. I can hear Alex and Aislin talking . . . something about getting out of here and transporting again, but I can't focus on anything but the glowing eyes. The other Alex is standing out in the middle with them, as if he's on their side.

"Why are you out there?" I ask as Alex steers me by the shoulders toward the open door. Aislin has climbed into the backseat from the driver's side and has a crystal and a black candle on the center console. He gently pushes my head down with his hand and shoves me into the front seat. I fall in and bang my head on the roof as he slams the door shut. I sit up as he hurries around the car, climbs into the car and slams the door.

He hammers his fist against the lock on the door. "Lock your door," he commands and I obey without hesitation.

"A mirage." Aislin leans over the console and stares out the window at the Alex marching with the cloaked monsters. He looks almost the same, but not quite solid. "And if there's one, then that means—"

"It means we need to get the hell out of here," Alex cuts her off as he slips the keys into the ignition. He turns it and pumps the gas pedal. "So get your spell going."

Aislin kneels up on the back seat with the black candle in front of her and a chunk of amethyst in her hand. She flicks the lighter, lights the wick, and begins to mutter incoherently underneath her breath. What is she doing? Black Magic?

"I have to get out of here," I sputter as the engine revs up and then dies. "Now."

The monsters are getting closer. The ground is trembling against their steps; the trees and house shudder. Screams from inside flow to the outside as ice rushes across the ground and swallows the house. The people inside ram their bodies against the ice chunk that had once been their home. They're trapped.

"We have to help them," I mutter in horror as their bodies are crushed and blood splatters the ice. It's like watching a horror movie, only it's real and it chokes at my throat. My lungs . . . they don't want to work anymore. "Oh my God . . . we have to . . . we have to do something."

"Shit." Alex ignores me and punches his fist against the steering wheel when the car refuses to start. There's still blood flowing from his arm, but it has slowed to a trickle. "God dammit, Aislin, get us the hell out of here. The cold has frozen the fucking engine."

The windows frost over and I can't see the house. Fog swirls through the vents of the heater and fills up the car. The temperature bottoming below freezing. I can't feel my fingers or my lips. As the monsters near the car, I panic. I know how this will end if I don't get away. They'll kill me. I've seen it every night for the last few months.

I reach for the handle of the door, but Alex grabs my elbow. "You aren't going anywhere."

"Yes, I am. Now, move." I wrench my arm and scoot closer to the door, but his strength overpowers me and he hauls me back by the arm. "You don't understand. I have to get away from them . . . They'll—I . . ."

"No, *you* don't understand." Alex lugs me over the console and just about knocks the candle over. I kick my legs and twist my midsection, trying to get away from his grip, but his fingers delve into my hips. He picks me up as if I weigh nothing and sets me on his lap so I'm straddling him. "If you get out of this car you'll die."

"If I stay in this car, they'll kill me!" I clamp my hands down on his shoulders and push back until my back presses against the steering wheel. "I've seen it happen a thousand times. And they're going to kill you."

Shock masks his face. "You know what those things are?"

I crook to the side and try to duck under his arm, but he lowers it, barricading me in. "This is not the first time I've seen them . . . And would you please let me go. I'm not going to sit around in the Goddamn car and wait for them to come and freeze me."

"Do you have a Goddamn death wish or something?" he breathes fiercely in my ear as his arms snake around my waist. "Do yourself a favor. Shut the hell up and listen to me."

I raise my arm to slap him across the face, but he grabs my hand and clasps it in his own. "Please, let me go." I'm starting to cry and I don't understand why. Yes, I'm scared and cold, but there's also something else there I can't quite decipher; almost like I'm suddenly aware that I'm about to lose any future I have. That it will all end and the possibilities I haven't yet gotten to experience will forever remain unknown.

The temperature continues to plummet as layers of ice build over the car and the roof begins to concave under the pressure. Cloaked creatures are everywhere, their eyes flickering as aggressively as the flame of the candle. Their capes flap in the wind and create a canopy over the car. The temperature drops beyond cold. Death is in the air.

"Holy shit," I breathe, shaking my hand, which has tinted purple. "What's happening to me?"

Alex encloses his hands around mine and brings them an instant relief from the cold. "Try to relax, okay? Aislin will have us out of here in just a second." There's sincerity in his eyes which I've never seen before and the electricity connects me to him, forcing me to submit to him.

Aislin is doing some kind of voodoo witch thing with the candle and the amethyst and it's creating a cloud of violet smoke. The smoke slips into my lungs and burns like a fatal toxin.

I cough and my head falls into Alex's shoulder "What is she doing?" I whisper, clutching onto his arms.

"Just stay calm," Alex lulls as his hand runs up and down my back. Sedation takes over my mind and I slip into a state of exhaustion caused from the chill that has tugged my body close to a state of hypothermia. Or maybe I'm dying. *Death*. It seems right, like all the pieces of a puzzle have finally been connected. "I promise everything will be okay. Just trust me."

And I do, because at the moment he's all I have. So despite the fact that I've seen two of him and that he keeps talking about mirages, Death Walkers and transporting, I close my eyes and fall against him as my body is rendered motionless by the cold.

The car gives an abrupt jerk to the side as one of the creatures charges into it. Fog swarms beneath the crevasses of the doors and windows and ice glazes my skin and stings my lungs. I want to sleep. Forever. Yeah, that doesn't sound so bad.

"Stay awake." Alex's voice sounds so far away. I crack my eyes open and he hugs me against his chest and kisses my forehead. The gesture brings warmth, but is rapidly erased as the car rocks again "Aislin, hurry up."

"*Per is calx ego lux lucis via,*" Aislin whispers from the backseat. The fire lights up against her face and her amplified eyes.

The ice that has built around the car begins to fracture and chip away. I can see the mirage Alex, watching me from outside, his face becoming clearer with each fragment of ice that breaks off. There's something in his eyes that tells me I'll see him again many more times and that he'll bring me harm, perhaps even kill me one day. And looking at him feels I'm finally looking into my future and instead of life, I see him and, in him, I see my death.

A purple glow erupts through the car and the windows

implode. Glass flies everywhere and Alex's arm comes up over my head to protect me. I let out a scream as a thick darkness weaves into my body and steals every aspect of myself away and again, I'm left feeling numb.

CHAPTER
EIGHT

"WHAT IF WE were to die tomorrow?" I'm lying on my back in a grassy field staring up at the night sky with my hand out to the side of me. "Would you be happy?"

"I could die right now and I'd be happy." Alex rolls on his side and props himself up on his elbow.

"That's such a line," I say, but my insides flutter. "You seriously can't come up with anything better than that?"

He laughs gently as he eyes my lips. "Oh yeah, is that so?"

"Completely so." I wet my lips in anticipation.

Grinning, he positions his body closer to me. Pivoting onto his hip, he flips on top of me and covers his body over mine. The hardness of his chest presses against me. With each inhale and exhale, I grow more anxious at what's about to happen. Because I know that something amazing is about to happen.

"Gemma, I'm happier right now than I've ever been," he whispers. "Even if we're being hunted."

The moonlight mirrors in his eyes and a pale light rings around the pupils. I want him, more than I've ever *wanted anything. So I let myself have him. Grabbing onto the front of his shirt, I crush his lips onto mine and seal us together.*

I pull away to whisper, "Me too." Then I fasten my legs around him firmly and he presses down in response. With each breath, my nipples stroke against his chest, and trigger warmth between my legs. My fingers drift down the front of his chest and underneath his shirt. He follows my lead, his palm gliding down the front of me, and then his fingers sneak up the front of my shirt. While his one hand tangles in my hair, his other hand cups my breast and his thumb grazes across my nipple. A fire ignites through my body, but it isn't satisfying the hunger inside. I need to be closer to him. Desperately.

Moving my body back, I sit up, forcing him to give me room. Grabbing the bottom of my shirt, I yank it over my head and chuck it over into the grass. I shake my hair out and my bare chest heaves as he deliberately takes me in.

"What are you doing?" His eyes are glossed over like he's high. "You know we're not supposed to be doing this."

I kneel up in front of him, vulnerable, knowing he can shoot me down. "I don't care. I don't care about any of it anymore. Let me die, but let me die happy."

His eyes scroll up my stomach, to my chest, and conclusively reside on my eyes. He reaches behind his head and tugs his own shirt off. His chest is solid and his stomach is lined with muscles. I want to touch him, more than anything. We move for each other like magnets and, as our bare chests collide, passion crazes every single part of me. I'm happy. Blissfully, mind-numbingly happy.

And in the end, that is all that matters.

A LIGHT FLASHES and is echoed by an explosion inside my head. My vision resurfaces and my face is inches away from the floor. My nose smacks against the hard wood and my bones pop. I moan as pain erupts through my nose and jaw.

"God dammit." I roll over to my back, clutching my nose and staring up at a red ceiling. "Where am I?"

Flipping onto my stomach, I push up to my feet. The room is small, the walls are red, and there's a leather sectional sofa in the corner. Bookshelves line the room, along with windows, but curtains block the view outside. "Am I dreaming?"

"No, you're very much awake." A hand comes down on my shoulder and a surge of electricity spirals down my arm. I reel around, swinging my hand and slap the hand from my shoulder.

"Relax." Alex stands only a foot away from me. There are cuts on his face and on his arm. The front of his shirt is torn and there is glass in his hair.

"Are you okay?" Aislin is behind him, observing me from over his shoulder. Her face is streaked with lines of mascara like she's been crying and some of the ends of her hair have been singed.

"Gemma," Alex says when I don't respond. He exchanges a look with Aislin and then moves toward me. "Tell me what you're thinking?"

I'm conquered with the compulsion to throw my arms around him and I step toward him, but the feeling dissipates. The memories of what happened rematerialize—the madness, the mirage, the monsters—and I back up with my hands out in front of me. "I'm thinking you need to get the hell away from me." A sharp pain throbs to the surface of my left rib and I hunch over moaning. "Something hurts." Alex moves for me and my hand shoots up. "Stay away from me. I mean it."

"I'm not going to hurt you." He pauses, waiting for me to settle down. I take a deep breath and keep my eyes targeted on him as he makes the rest of the journey toward me. "You need to hold still. You're bleeding."

I'm suddenly aware that blood is dripping down the back of my hand. I lift up the edge of my coat and see a small piece of glass sticking out of my ribs. "That's disgusting."

He chuckles under his breath. "Yeah, but I think you're going to be okay. In fact, you seem subdued."

"I feel subdued." Like if my emotions are malfunctioning. I straighten my shoulders, even though the pain is crippling, and compel what little irritation is left inside me to show itself. "You think I'm going to be okay? Seriously. Because my mind is racing so fast, I can't even grasp what just happened." I throw one of my hands in the air. "I mean, what was all that?"

"Just relax," Alex insists and then turns to Aislin. "You better go find Laylen and see if he has a first aid kit or something . . . Although, I'm still trying to figure out why you transported us here at all. Seriously, out of all the places to go, you brought us here?"

"It was an accident." Aislin's cheeks go pink as she tucks her chin down and lets her hair veil her face. "And you should be grateful I got us out of there before . . ." She glances at me, then trails off and hurries for the door. "I'll go find Laylen."

"Who's Laylen?" I wince as the fragment of glass

shifts.

Alex motions his hand to the sofa as he tears off the corner of his shirt. "Go sit down so I can look at it."

I disregard the pain and the blood running down the back of my hand. "Not until you tell me where we are and how the hell we got here. What was all that back there? Because right now, I'm thinking that I've got to be dreaming, yet it all seems so real."

"I really don't think that's the most important thing right now," Alex interrupts with a disapproving shake of his head. "Considering you have a piece of glass sticking out of your rib."

"And you have a giant cut on your arm." I point my finger at his sliced open forearm. "Yet, all you seem to be concerned with is me."

"Yeah, and my concern for you is what caused all this," he mutters. As my eyebrows furrow, he sighs. "Look, go sit down and I'll try to explain everything."

"How do I know you're you, though? What if you're that mirage thing I saw back there?"

He wraps the torn piece of shirt around the cut on his arm. "You really think I am?"

I swallow hard and glance around the room, at the bookcases, the old books that look ancient and the window that is concealed by a curtain. *What's out there?* "I really don't know what to think. Seconds ago I was in the forest and Aislin was doing all that weird witchy stuff with that crystal and candle. Now I'm in some person's house I just—I just don't get it."

He studies me as he presses his lips together and pops his bruised knuckles. "You know, you're nothing like what I thought you'd be."

"What does that mean exactly?" I ask quizzically.

"You always say things like that. They make no sense to me, just like a lot of the stuff you say."

My response seems to entertain him. He smiles softly as his fingers drift toward my cheek. I flinch as his thumb grazes across my cheekbone and my tender skin is kissed by an eruption of sparks. He draws his hand back, which has some blood on it, and he wipes it off on the side of his jeans.

He inhales and then his sturdy chest puffs out as he lets out a slow breath. "You feel that right?"

I nod my head, knowing exactly what he means, even though he didn't say it—the sparks. "Yeah . . . I think so."

"Then that's how you know I'm real. You won't feel that with the mirage."

He's right. While I was holding the counterfeit's hand, I felt nothing but hollowness and that's why I sensed something was off.

He knows things, about me—I know he does—and I need the answers more than I need air. "You know things about me?" I ask. "Don't you?"

He rubs his tense jaw and shuts his eyes. "I do."

I force the lump in my throat down. "How?"

His eyes open and it's like staring into my own, the amount of pain is infinite. "Sit down and I'll try to explain. Even though, it's going to be nearly fucking impossible."

Desperate to understand what secrets he has locked away inside, I settle on the couch, and let my questions pour out of me. "Okay, so how did we get here? And what were those things back there? Those . . . Death Walkers? And how do you know about them . . ." I trail off.

Alex is staring at me with eyes as big as golf balls. "Are you going to give me a chance to talk? Or do you want to just keep going with the questions?"

"Sorry, but they've been piling up at a very rapid rate," I say and he stifles a smile. "But, I'll try to calm down and get them out one by one."

He stares off into empty space, lost in thought. "Take off your coat."

"Huh . . . Why?"

Desire burns in his eyes. "You have to take your coat off if you want me to get the glass out of your side.

My thoughts coast back to when I had the orgasm while we were on the bed. It was the most incredible feeling I've experienced yet and I wonder how much better it would be if we were closer, touching, bare skin to bare . . .

"Gemma." Alex's voice jerks me out of my thoughts.

I blink at him and then carefully slip my arms out of my sleeves, easing my coat off. "God, it hurts."

Alex chucks his coat off, rolls up the sleeves of his black thermal shirt, and stretches his arm toward me, his fingers moving for my side.

"What are you doing?" My muscles tense as his hand nears me.

His hand freezes as I lean away from him and then he shakes his head. "Would you relax? I have to actually get close to you in order to look at that." He points a finger at my wounded side.

"Oh, sorry, I'm just nervous, considering . . ." Where do I start with that?

He understands, nodding. "I get it, but I promise I won't hurt you."

I nod, put my hands on my lap, and kink my elbow out of the way so he can get a full view of my rib and the glass wedged in the skin like a splinter. He gradually lifts the bottom of my shirt and there's a notable shake to his fingers as he inspects the area.

I suppress the gasp wanting to flee my lips as his fingers search each bump of my ribs and every spot of my skin. After what seems like an eternity, he pulls his hand back.

His eyes are amplified and his breathing speeds up. "Shit, I don't know what to do."

"Why? How bad is it?" I crane my neck and peel my shirt away from my skin to get a look at the injury myself. It doesn't look that bad; narrow and not that long. There's some blood dripping out, but not a significant amount.

Alex stares at me with a serious expression, then his mouth curves into a grin and laughter escapes his lips. "No, it's not that bad at all. The piece of glass is small, and you're barely bleeding. I should be able to get it out and stitch it up without any problems." He glances at the door. "Just as soon as Aislin gets in here with the first-aid kit."

I tug down my shirt and swat his arm with my hand. "That wasn't funny. You had me worried I was seriously hurt."

He glances at where I touched him and then back at my face. "Actually, it was funny."

"Do you even know how to do stitches?" I ask. "Or is that something else you're making up?"

He cocks an eyebrow. "What else am I making up?"

I motion my arm at the room with flourish. "Um, the fact that we're here says how much you've made up."

He props his foot up on his knee and leans back on the couch. "Actually, I never made anything up. I just didn't tell you things."

"Omission of the truth is just as bad as making shit up."

"Says who?"

"Says me!"

We stare at each other with defiance; each of us refusing to look away and let the other win.

"Besides." I adjust back on the sofa, moving carefully and cradling my side with my arm. "How do I know you haven't been lying? I've known you for like a few weeks. For all I know your name isn't even Alex." I reach over and pinch his leg. His knee jerks and his foot falls to the floor. "And, are you even real? I saw another one of you for hell sakes." I take a deep breath, staring forward as I shake my head. "I don't even know what's true and what isn't anymore . . . what's real and what's not."

He slants forward, catches my gaze and it nearly penetrates me. "Back at the cabin, when everything was happening, you said you knew the Death Walkers were going to kill you . . . how?"

"If I told you, you'd think I was insane," I say and let my head flop onto the back of the sofa. "I even think it's insane."

I feel him move and then he's above me, one of his elbows propped on each side of my head. He edges his face close and the fervor of his breath dampens my skin.

"I can completely and utterly assure you that nothing you say is going to make me question your sanity," he says softly. "I promise you, I've seen and heard it all."

I carefully consider what he says and then surrender to my doubts, knowing it can't get much worse than it is. "I dreamt about them."

"You dreamt about them?" he questions.

I nod my head and our foreheads clip. "A lot actually. For the last few months or so."

He shifts his weight and puts a gap between our faces, but not our bodies. "And what happened in these dreams?"

Heat rushes to my cheeks as I blush. "Stuff . . . I don't know. It went a little different each time, but it always ended the same."

He scans my face with a curious expression. "Why do you look embarrassed?"

I shake my head and force my gaze to remain on his eyes and not his lips. "I'm just hot."

He presses his lips together and then adjusts back in his seat, giving me some room.

I release a breath that was imprisoned inside my lungs, tuck my hair behind my ears, and stare at my hands. "It's weird, you know, because this all seems real, but my mind's screaming at me that it's not possible. That there's no way I could be sitting here when moments ago I was in your frozen car surrounded by . . ." I peer up at him as I lower my hands to my lap. "What did you call them? Death Walkers?"

He nods and grabs hold of one of my hands. "Why did you look at your hands just now?"

I push myself to look past the surging current his touch brings. "Because, in my dreams, they always turn blue, like I have frostbite or something."

He frees my hand and I return it to my lap. "That's because it *is* frostbite. Those things you saw, the Death Walkers, control the temperature of the air and since they favor the cold, they drop it rapidly wherever they are."

My eyes sting with impending tears. "This is all so much."

He opens his mouth to say something, but a loud thump from inside the house startles us both. We jump closer to each other as if we can't help it. Before I can work up a wince from the static, he has his pocketknife out and the blade flipped open.

"Whose house are we at?" I whisper, not taking my eyes off the knife. It's miniature and caked with dry flakes of blood.

He shakes his head, breaks his attention from the door, and sets the knife on a small square table next to the couch. "Laylen's. He's a friend of Aislin's . . . and mine." He reaches behind him and pulls back the curtain. "He lives in Vegas."

Outside the window, dusk is advancing and casts a pinkish glow across the bronze sand that stretches for miles. I kneel up toward the window to get a closer look. "This can't be real. None of this can."

He lets the curtain fall closed. "Well it is. Trust me." He places a hand on top of my chest. At first, I think he is trying to feel me up which seems inappropriate, considering the circumstances. "All of it is. You. Me. *Everything*."

I inhale through my nose to maintain steady breathing. "Like monsters that freeze everything, or are you talking about other stuff?"

He moves his hand away and blows out a stressed breath. "I'm talking about a lot of things. Monsters are just the beginning of it and the rest is even more confusing."

"*More* confusing? I can't even fathom how that can be possible."

"But, it is," he mutters. "Way, way fucking confusing . . . and complicated."

"I get complicated," I say, thinking about my emotions and wondering if it has anything to do with what is going on. Although, I can't connect it, it *seems* plausible. "But, what I don't get is how we got here."

He assesses me briefly, then turns sideways and slides his leg up on the sofa so his knee is pressing against mine.

"Aislin transported us here."

"Yeah, I heard you guys say that a lot, but what I don't get is *how*. One minute we are all trapped in the car and the next I'm falling on the floor." I omit the dirty dream I had about him for various reasons; one being, I don't want my cheeks to turn red again.

He dithers. "She used a form of Wicca magic."

I snort a laugh, but stop when I notice how solemn he looks. "You're being serious? Because witches and magic aren't supposed to be real."

"They aren't, huh?" he asks with a cock of his eyebrow. "Then, why don't *you* explain how we got here?"

I shrug. "Maybe it's not real. Maybe it's a delusional world brought on by the trauma of those things—those Death Walker things that are trying to kill me. Or maybe this is just another mirage and this entire house is fake."

"So, let me get this straight," he says, frustrated. "You're saying you believe in something like the Death Walkers, who, by the way, are demons, but you don't believe in magic or witches."

"No, that's not what I'm saying," I correct him. "I said that witches weren't *supposed* to be real, but it doesn't mean that I think the idea is unrealistic."

"You're extremely confusing, you know that?" he points out. "And calm. How can you be so calm in this kind of situation?"

I'm ridiculously calm and it is very unfitting for the situation. Most people would be running like hell to get away, or balled up in a corner banging their head on the wall; trying to force the madness out of their brains. "I have . . . issues . . . with fear . . . I mean, part of my brain is telling me that this is all just one big crazy delusion I've conjured up, but the other part is noting how very real everything feels. I've had some trouble in the past determining what's real, too."

His eyes scan me from head to toe and my skin electrifies like magic. Like *witch* magic. "What are you talking about? What kind of trouble? Did something happen that I don't know about."

"How would you know about anything?" I inquire with suspicion. "I haven't told you anything."

He situates a hand on my cheek and I shiver from the sparkling it causes inside me. "I know more than you think."

I freeze as the electricity sings through my veins and crashes into my heart. My lungs swell from the pressure and the position of the glass alters. The pain causes me to moan, but the tingling sensation in my lower abdomen causes me to gasp. It's the strangest noise that has ever passed my lips.

Alex must have thought so, too, because his eyes enlarge. "Are you okay?"

I slant my head back from his hand. "I'm fine. I'm just shocked because you can feel it too."

"Of course I can feel it." He sighs back in the chair. "How can I not?" He trails off, his voice softening. "But, I'm not supposed to . . . I'm breaking so many Goddamn rules."

"What rules?" I probe. "You know, you speak in riddles sometimes."

He rakes his fingers roughly through his hair and pieces stick up in every direction. I have the urge to put them back in place, but the pained expression on his face warns me that it's best not to touch him. I tuck my hands underneath my legs to keep them restrained. "How the hell am I supposed to explain to *you* how important *you* are? It's fucking impossible." He stares at his scraped up hands, turning them over as he examines them.

"How important *I* am?" I scan the room, even though it's obvious he's talking to me, and aim an incredulous look at him. "I think you're getting me mixed up with someone else because, trust me, there's nothing important about me."

"You have no idea how wrong you are." He sucks in a slow breath and then raises his chin up to look at me. The intensity in his eyes makes me shrink back. "You're the most im—"

"I found one." Aislin races into the room with a proud look on her face. She's carrying a first-aid kit and her hair has been pulled back into a bun. She's also taken off her coat and boots.

Alex instantly springs to his feet like he's guilty of some heinous crime. "It took you long enough. Jesus, what the hell were you doing?" He joins her in the middle of the room, frowning. "You seriously cleaned up? God, Gemma's bleeding out here and you go wash up."

"I'm fine," I say, but they either don't hear me or don't care what I have to say.

"I had glass in my hair." She shoves the first-aid kit at him. "And it took me a second to find Laylen."

"Sure it did." There's insinuation in his tone. "Just like it always does."

"Whatever, Alex. It's not like that between us anymore and you know it." She flips her hair from her shoulder and then puts her hands on her hips. "And, just so you know, Laylen's going to stay away until . . ." She glances at me, then leans closer to Alex as she lowers her voice.

I can't hear what they are saying. I hunch over, leaning forward to listen, but all I gather is something about "staying away" and "blood." I give up and rest back against the couch with my arm draped over my stomach. I'm tired so I shut my eyes and let the numbness of approaching sleep consume me. It seems like I should be terrified out of my mind and I guess I am, in a sense. If Death Walkers or some other strange creature came running in, I would run, but I also feel empty. Not like how I had before I could feel. It feels like I've emptied all my worries. I'm no longer in this madness alone. Alex is here. And Aislin. And I guess this Laylen guy—whoever he is—is here, too. I'm not just roaming around the world solo, seeing bizarre things and otherworldly creatures. They can see them too. So, whether they are real or not, it's a relief to know that I'm not the only one who's crazy.

"All right, but Stephan's going to be pissed," I hear Aislin say and then footsteps head toward the door.

"Are you sleeping?" Alex's voice drifts over me and I crack open my eyelids. He stands above me with the first-aid kit tucked under his arm. There are worry lines around his eyes and across his forehead.

"Who's Stephan?"

He sets the first-aid kit on the table, flips the latches open and lifts up the lid. "My father."

"Your father." That isn't what I expected. I sit up and scoot to the edge of the sofa. "Really?"

"Really." He nods, then snatches a throw pillow from the recliner nearby and places it on the sofa beside me. "Lay down so I can get that piece of glass out of you and I'll try to explain what I know while I do."

"Like why the Death Walkers haunt my dreams? And why you think I'm so important? And also, why I saw another one of you more than once?"

He freezes. "You saw the mirage more than once?"

I nod. "But I thought I blacked out or something and it was just a dream. Now, though, I'm second guessing that thought. I'm second guessing all my original thoughts."

"That's probably a wise idea." He rummages around in the kit and takes out square pieces of gauze and some Band-Aids. "It might help you believe what I'm going to tell you." His hand stills as his eyes wander up to me. "Are you scared yet?"

I analyze my emotions; confusion, inquisitiveness and eagerness are flowing inside me, causing chaos. Fear is absent, though. "I think I'm good. Although, I'm confused."

He scratches his head like it's the weirdest response he's ever heard. "Alright then, lie down and I'll do my best to eliminate some of the confusion."

I lie down on the sofa and situate my head on the pillow with my arms resting at my sides. "Is a mirage like a doppelganger?"

He gapes at me with a needle in his hand. "How do you know what a doppelganger is?"

I shrug. "I read a lot."

His hand falls to the side and he almost stabs himself with the needle. "Again, you surprise me." He pauses with a look of contemplation. "Gemma, were you always like this? Growing up, I mean? Or were you . . . different?"

I'm not ready to answer that question yet, but the simple fact that he's asked it leads me to believe he knows things about me and my past. "You go first."

Sighing with frustration, he bends over so he's hovering over me. "Okay, try to hold as still as possible while I do this."

I fix my eyes on the ceiling, trying to think of something else besides the glass lodged in my side and the fact that he's about to tug it out. All that I can think of, though, is that the red ceiling reminds me of blood and I'm very aware of every jerking movement. I flop my arm over my face, seal my eyes shut, and inhale through the pain. It's easier than I expected, but, for some reason, I have a hunch that what lies ahead is going to be more painful.

"Are you doing okay?" he whispers. "You're not going to pass out on me, are you?"

I shake my head from side to side, but my ribs are on *fire.* "I'm good."

"Okay, it's all over." He sounds choked so I open my eyes. In his palm is a long, but thin piece of glass. "This little thing right here is what was in you."

"That's it?" I pick it up and turn it over in my hand. "It's so small."

"Yeah, I know, but it was in pretty deep." He takes the glass from me and tosses it into the first aid kit. Then he grabs a cotton ball, unscrews the lid of the rubbing alcohol bottle and douses the cotton ball with it. "Gemma, I'm really sorry."

"For what?"

"For this." He presses the cotton ball onto the open wound on my rib. It feels like someone has dumped gasoline on my skin and lit a match. My skin is blazing with a fire that's invisible to the naked eye. I squeeze my eyes shut, bite down on my lip, and try not to scream bloody murder.

"Sorry about that." He removes the cotton ball from my skin, which is soaked with my blood, and discards it into the kit. "I just thought it would be better if I caught you off-guard. That way, you wouldn't anticipate it."

"I don't . . . God that hurt." I complain and my voice cracks.

"Now, I just have to stitch it up." He pauses and I open my eyes to see what he's doing. His gaze is aimed at my side, but not the one that is split open; the opposite one that is free of gaping holes.

I start to sit up. "Is there another one?"

He flattens his palm against my stomach and settles his gaze on my face. "Don't move until I get it fixed up." He shifts his body, then jerks his hand away and flexes his fingers as if my touch has burned him. "Anyway, the cut isn't very big, so it shouldn't take me that long."

"Are you sure you're going to be okay?" I ask, lying back down. "You seem out of it."

"I'll be fine." His voice comes out sharp and he quickly clears his throat. He takes out a spool of string and begins unwinding it around his hand.

The atmosphere between us has been killed by awkwardness and discomfort, which doesn't make sense. Moments ago, I felt fine with him.

"So . . . are you going to explain to me why *you* think I'm so important?" I ask.

"Yeah, give me a second." He refuses to look at me and snips the end of the string with a pair of scissors. "But you have to promise me two things first . . . The first is that you have to promise that you'll try to keep an open mind about what I say."

"Okay, that seems easy enough," I assure him with confidence. "What's the second thing?"

He drops the scissors into the kit. "That you'll let me finish talking before you start freaking out."

A chill slithers up my spine and I shiver. "How do you know I'll freak out?"

He squints his eyes as he raises the needle and loops the piece of clear string through the end. "Because any sane person would freak out at what I'm about to tell them; even someone like you who seems to welcome the crazy."

"I don't welcome it," I state. "I just don't know how to react sometimes."

He stations the needle just above my ribcage. "I know, but this might push you over the edge, so I need you to try your hardest to keep it together. It's important."

I nod, but deep down, I know that it can end up out of my hands if the prickle makes a grand appearance. "I'll do my best." His hand dips toward my exposed stomach and I recoil because I absolutely hate needles.

"I'm not even sure where to begin." He rubs his hand across his face and his concentration sidetracks to stitching me up. "Hold still," he instructs and I hold my breath as he guides the needle through my skin.

Somebody kill me and put me out of my misery. It hurts like hell, but I know if I move, it'll only increase the pain. "Jesus, that hurts." I breathe through gritted teeth as I stab my fingernails into the leather fabric of the sofa. Tears fill my eyes and one slips down my cheek as I pant violently. "So bad."

"Sorry," he apologizes before making another stitch. He kneels back and gives me a moment to catch my breath. "You gonna make it?"

I bob my head up and down and look at him through my watery vision. "Yeah, go on. And start talking to me. It'll distract me."

He sketches his finger down my cheek and wipes away a tear. He rubs his finger and thumb together as he stares at the teardrop, then his face twists with bewilderment.

"It's just a tear," I remark, equally as bewildered.

He nods and wipes his hand on his jeans. "I know."

He applies another stitch, weaving through my skin and it shoots the pain through all of my limbs. "Do you remember that fallen star story Professor Sterling told, the day I finally decided to sit by you in class."

"The one where you teased me about going on a road trip?" I attempt to smile, but it's too much work.

He doesn't seem amused as he twines the needle through my skin again and the he positions his other hand on my stomach. All of my attentiveness channels to his fingers. On my skin. My eyelids flutter as my body bows up. The warmth. The hum. It even numbs out the pain a little. I want him to move them across my body, touch me in places I've never been touched before.

"Gemma?" His hoarse voice brings me back to reality.

I blink dazedly at him and realize I've bowed my body up against his hand. "Huh?"

He stares down at me with his forehead creased, then his neck twitches and he clears his throat. "Did you hear what I said?"

I lower my body, shake my head, and admit, "Umm . . . no."

He presses on my stomach and directs my untamed body back down. "I asked if you remembered the secret group that hid the star."

My brain is hazy and I can't form intelligible thoughts. "Yeah . . . I remember the story vaguely, but I have no idea why you're bringing up something we talked about in Astronomy class. It was just a story."

He shakes his head. "No, it wasn't. It was based on fact, although, Professor Sterling didn't know that. In fact, he didn't know a lot about what he was talking about that day."

"You make it sound like he was possessed."

"Because he was."

I can't take it anymore. I prop up on my elbows, causing us to smack heads. "By what, a ghost?" I press the heel of my hand to my throbbing head.

He rubs the spot on his forehead where mine smacked. "Not a ghost . . . a mirage."

"You mean, there's another Professor Sterling?" I gape at him unfathomably. "Like there's another you?"

"Neither one is actually us." He places his hand on my shoulder and gives me a gentle push back to lie down. "Now lie back down so I can finish the stitch. You're already going to have a wicked scar. Let's not make it worse."

I lie back on the couch, rest my head on the pillow and put my arms to the side of me. "If they aren't *you,* then what are they?"

He pauses. "Foreseers."

I fold my shirt up a little more because blood is starting to seep out of the wound again. "Like psychics?"

He frowns. "You know what Foreseers are?"

My shoulders rise and fall as I shrug. "I read about it once. They can see into the future or something."

"That definition is really vague," he says. "There's a lot more to them than seeing the future. They can create images that aren't real—make people see things that aren't real. It's kind of like a game to some of them."

I gulp, taking it all in. "You think one's been messing with me?"

He nods. "I do, ever since Professor Sterling showed up and wasn't quite himself."

I rewind through everything that's happened and remember how that day Alex had been particularly nice to me. "Is that why you did it? Why you were being nice and asked me to go on a road trip with you."

He twists the lid onto the rubbing alcohol. "No, that's not why. I'm not even supposed to be nice to you." He makes an *oh-shit* face as he says it.

I pierce him with a stern look. "Why?"

"I'm getting to that." He moves closer to me. "You remember how he mentioned there was a power hungry group that might have hid the star."

"He didn't say group," I clarify. "He said person."

"Well he should have said group." He quickly makes another stitch. It happens so fast, my body barely registers the pain. "The secret group is called *Custodis de Vita*."

"The *Custodis* what?" I begin to sit up again out of instinct and he puts his hand on my waist to restrain me.

"The *Custodis de Vita,*" he repeats as his fingers enfold around my skin. I want him to move them lower and see how it feels. I seriously have a screwed up head. "It's a secret group that's not necessarily power hungry, but doesn't want power to fall into the wrong hands."

It's too hard to focus on what he's saying while he touches me. I lift his hand off my stomach and breathe freely. "So much better."

He glances at his hand inquisitively and returns his line of gaze back to me. "Care to share what that was about?"

"What is that word? Like Latin or something?" I evade the question.

He stares at me intensely with his head slanted down. It blocks out the light and his pupils are massive, taking over his eyes. "Yeah, it means Keepers of Life, but for short, we call ourselves The Keepers."

"Keepers of Life." The words feel foul leaving my lips. "It sounds like a cult."

A chuckle flees his mouth. "It's not, though. We

actually protect the world from dangerous things."

"*We?*" I study his expression; unyielding and full of truth. "So you belong to this *Keepers* group?"

"And Aislin. And . . ." He covers his mouth with his hand and coughs into it. "Marco and Sophia."

I lay inert, letting his words sink into my body, like a disease. The dots are starting to connect and images of things I've never remembered before stab unruly at the back of my mind; Sophia sharpening a sword, Marco talking on the phone about a battle.

"So, what you're telling me is that Marco and Sophia, the people who've raised me since I was one, belong to some secret group that protects the world from evil?" It sounds unbelievable, just like every other damn aspect of my life. Saving the world from evil and demons and vampires . . . God, what if there really are vampires? "And that you know them?"

He doesn't answer, but through his silence, I have my answer. It's like a piece of the puzzle has been jammed into place. "Holy shit, you were there that day, weren't you? That day I went to get my boxes." I start to sit up, but I feel pain from the stitches and I immediately fall back. "You were that guy in those sunglasses, the one who wouldn't talk to me."

The quietness stretches on forever. I can't believe this—I shouldn't believe it. Yet, I do, which only makes the situation more of a maze.

"What are you thinking about?" He applies another stitch through the cut and cocks his head to the side, measuring me up with a powerful gaze that melts at my thoughts.

"That you're lying," I say quietly. "That you're full of shit and messing with my head."

"That's completely understandable," he admits. "I get it. I really do. But, it's the truth, despite the fact that it sounds absurd." The needle snags my skin and my hand instinctively flies toward the pain. Alex grabs my hand before I get ahold of the stitches. "Whatever you do, don't touch it," he cautions and I can feel his pulse hammering through his fingertips. He's nervous. Or scared. And I'm . . . I don't know, because there isn't anything there yet. Confused, yes, but, other than that, I haven't linked to an emotion yet.

I pull my hand away from his as distrust claims my body. "Why hasn't anyone mentioned this to me before? All those years I lived with Marco and Sophia—those weeks I knew you—why not just say something?"

"You think we could just come up to you and say 'Hey, I work for this secret group that fights evil?' Yeah, that goes over really well with people."

"You could have said something . . . less intense, but something like 'Hey, I have a secret life you might not want to know about.'"

His eyes are heated. "Would you have wanted to know about it though? If I'd said something like that to you."

"Yes," I say without contemplation, which more or less means it's the truth. "I don't like being in the dark about stuff."

"Easier said than done," he mumbles and then lets out a discouraged sigh as the needle snakes through my skin. "But back to the story because it really will explain a lot more for you." He pauses and I wait, pondering where the hell he's going with this. He takes a deep breath and concentrates on his hand as he makes yet another stitch. "That star I was telling you about had a lot of power. That's why we . . . the Keepers, went and got it in the first place.

If it fell into the wrong hands, then . . ." He trails off.

"Then what?" I press. I feel it coming, the calm before the storm. Whatever he is going to say will break me apart and I'll be left stitching myself back together.

He shakes his head. "Nothing. Let me try this again. Those Foreseers I was talking about, well one of them made a prediction that a fallen star was going to prevent the end of the world from happening." He picks up the scissors and trims the end of the string off.

The stab at the back of my neck is dull, but detectable. *"The end of the world."*

He chucks the scissors back into the kit, takes out a roll of tape and some gauze. "When I say 'end of the world,' what I mean is there's this portal that's supposed to open sometime . . . although, no one knows exactly when."

I stare expressionlessly at him. "A portal? Like a deep hole will open up and swallow up the world? Or, all hell will rain down? Or, zombies will walk out and take over the world?"

"You don't believe me." He arranges the gauze over the stitches and secures it with tape. Then he puts everything back in the kit and shuts the lid. "I'm all done with the stitches, so you can sit up if you want. Just be careful, though. If you move too fast, you might rip them open."

I tug my shirt down and gradually sit up. My side feels strangely tight and my head is full of thoughtless nonsense.

Alex sits down on the sofa next to me, drapes an arm behind my head and relaxes his knee against mine. A spasm of heat coils up my inner thigh and my knee jerks upward.

"What is that?" I ask as I stared down at our knees. "That electricity I feel whenever I'm around you? What is it? Does it have anything to do with this?"

He plays with my hair, twisting a strand around his finger. "I have no idea what causes it. I really don't."

I shoot him a look. "You have no idea what it is? At all. Or, are you just omitting the truth, as you so nicely put it."

He rolls his tongue to keep from smiling at me as he releases my hair. "Nope. I've never felt anything like it until you came along."

"Yeah, me neither," I mutter, combing my fingers through my hair to smooth it back into place. "Until the first time I met you at the school . . . that day you let the door slam in my face . . . but even when I ran into you at Marco and Sophia's house, I felt something."

He pulls a guilty face, but then he seems surprised. "Really? That was the first time you felt it? *Ever?*"

"Yes, why do you look so surprised?" I ask. "You just said the same thing."

"Because you're different," he says and I frown. He kicks his boots up on the table and crosses his legs. "I'll get to why, but give me a minute. I have to finish explaining the portal story, because it's kind of like background information."

"To what?"

"To you . . . but back to the portal because you need to kind of understand that part before I go anywhere else with it." He pauses and I'm pretty sure he's holding his breath. "If it opens up, it'll let millions of Death Walkers out and you've seen what they can do, so I'm sure you can guess how that would end the world."

I place my hand on the arm of the sofa and bring my knee up onto the couch as colorful images flash through my mind, little pieces of memories clipping together, forming a story.

The ground is an ice-rink, the buildings are tall statues, and the sky ripples with clouds that shower down a heavy snowstorm. In the distance, there is light—fire— and when it mixes with the snow, there is nothing but chaos.

"By ice," I whisper as the images shatter into pieces and dissolve.

His phone beeps and he glances at the screen. "Exactly." He scrolls through his screen and hammers his fingers against a few buttons, seeming preoccupied, yet he continues on with his story. "There's this guy named Demetrius, who's the leader of all the Death Walkers, and he wants this portal to open. Basically, the fallen star is the only thing that has enough power to keep the portal from opening."

"Do you still have the star?" I wonder and then raise my hands in front of me. "And, I'm only asking that question out of curiosity. I'm still not sure if I one-hundred percent believe what you're telling me."

His gaze rises from his phone and there is a look in his eyes that I don't like. "Yeah, we still have it. We kept it hidden so Demetrius couldn't find it. For the first few years after the Keepers found it, we had a Shifter transfer the star's energy into different objects to keep its location a constant secret." He stops. "Do I need to slow down? You look lost."

I shake my head. "Kind of lost. Kind of overwhelmed. But you can go on."

"Okay, but a warning, the next part is going to be very hard for you to hear." He glances down at his hands, and then turns them over, so his palms are facing the floor, and he looks vexed. "Just try to stay calm, okay?"

It feels like thorns have veined their way through my stomach and are poking at my insides. "I'll try."

He sucks in a deep breath and takes my hand in his. He traces his finger along the scar on my palm gently and it makes me feel a little bit better at the moment. "An accident happened a few years after we found the star. Theron, the Shifter I told you about, was attacked by Demetrius while in possession of the object that was holding the star's energy and, during a moment of panic, he accidently placed the power into a . . . woman."

My heart thumps inside my chest, like a drum, beating louder and louder. "What happened to her?"

"Nothing. The energy didn't end up in her." His hand tightens around mine. "She was pregnant when it happened and it ended up going into her unborn child."

My heart thumps and thumps and I can barely hear the stale calmness in my voice. "Then, what happened to the baby?"

"She lived, but the star's energy is still trapped inside her. For some reason—and no one knows for sure, because no one has ever come across anything like it before—no Shifter could transfer it out of her." He presses his lips together as my heart roars inside my chest. "A few years after it happened, the mother died, but not because of the star." He watches me attentively. "She was a Keeper and her name was Jocelyn."

My heart stops, but I still can't hear a sound.

Jocelyn was my mother.

And suddenly I understand what has been wrong with me for the last twenty-one years. I'm not crazy.

I am the star.

I'm not sure what to do with this information. My brain is in overdrive, racing with different solutions trying to make it so it can't be possible, but it all comes down to a list of things.

The dreams.

The monsters.

The mirages.

The weird images always popping up in my brain.

The detachment from the world.

My lack of emotions.

They all seem unreal and so does a star's energy being inside me. Put them together and they make sense. I come to the conclusion that he's telling the truth and I do what anyone would have done.

I run away from the painful truth because it's just too much to take.

CHAPTER
NINE

MY LEGS CARRY me across the room, my lungs fight against the ache from the stitches. I make it to the door before his long arms wrap around my waist. He's careful not to touch my stitches as he strengthens his hold and drags me backwards.

"Let go of me!" I shout as I throw all my weight forward, but he's stronger than the average person. He puts no effort into his movements as he picks me up until my feet are off the floor and then carries me back to the couch. He sets me down and when I try to get right back up, he thrusts his hand out and shoves me back down.

"Calm down," he orders. "You're going to tear those stitches open."

My chest heaves as I breathe furiously. "I don't care. It wouldn't hurt any more than what's happening on the inside."

He looks at me with sympathy. "I understand you're probably upset, but I—"

"I'm not upset," I cut him off. "I'm content, which is frightening, because I know what you said is the truth and I don't want it to be. I wanted it to be something else;

something that can be cured with a pill or something."

He looks helpless, eyes wide and his lips still. The clock ticks back and forth, back and forth. I don't know what to say or what to do with myself. My entire life, I've had a star's energy inside me. A fucking piece of a star. I'm probably not even human.

"What am I?" I ask. My voice sounds detached.

"What are you?" Alex asks, looking at me bewilderedly as he sinks down on the couch beside me. He places a hand on the back of the couch, rotates sideways and traps me in place. "I'm not sure what you mean."

"Well, I can't be human," I say, my eyebrows knitting. "I mean, nothing about me has really been human, has it? And having a star inside me . . . That can't be human."

"You're human," he assures me and takes my hand in his. He grazes his finger across the inside of my wrist. A few months ago I would have felt nothing, but now it brings me a little comfort in the sea of absurdity I've been thrown into. "You're just a human with a lot of power."

I can feel that power through his touch and it's making me nauseous. I ease my hand away from his, but he grabs ahold of it again and guides me closer until I'm pretty much sitting on his lap.

"Look, I know this all sounds crazy," he begins with a look of determination as he puts his hands domineeringly on my hips. He lifts me up and sets me down on his lap, so my legs are on either side of him. "And I understand that you're probably scared shitless, but there's more stuff I have to tell you."

My eyes roll to the ceiling as I fight back the tears. "How can there be more . . . I don't think I can take anymore."

"Yes, you can. You're a lot tougher than you know," he

says and I lower my head to see if he's being serious. His gaze never wavers as I study him. "But here's the thing. If you don't want to hear it—if you want to be left in the dark for the rest of your life—then you need to tell me. If you want me to stop, then I will."

"I've been left in the dark for most of my life." It isn't really a question, but he nods anyway. I take a deep breath and whisper, "Tell me then."

He nods, gripping onto my hips like he thinks I'm going to try and flee again. "The Keepers lucked out because Demetrius never discovered the location of the star's power, but when you were born, a Foreseer told Stephan that if your emotions weren't controlled, then the power of the star would weaken and eventually die, along with the world. So, to stop that from happening, Stephan made the decision for you to go live with Marco and Sophia in the real world."

"How old was I when I went to live with them?" I utter softly. "Because I was told one, but I'm starting to wonder if maybe I was a little older."

"No, you were one," he replies in a flat tone. "And they were under strict orders to make sure you stayed unemotional."

I hit an eerie calm—an 'unemotional' calm. I was made to be this way—to be dead inside. To live a life of solitude. All those mind-numbing years alone, without a friend, never speaking unless a question was directed to me. It was all done on purpose? A lump builds in my throat, blocking my airway. I can't breathe.

"Gemma," he says with concern. "Tell me what you're thinking."

I suck in a sharp breath and force the lump down. "How did they do it? How did Marco and Sophia make me unemotional?"

His eyes wander over my shoulder. "I was always told that it was because they gave you as little physical contact as possible. Isolation. If someone doesn't ever know happiness, sadness, or love, then how can they ever feel it? Right?"

"Are you lying to me?" I lean to the side and he stares down at the floor behind me. "You can't even look at me."

"I'm not lying, Gemma." He looks at me guardedly. "I'm just telling you what I know, which isn't everything."

"Yes, you are," I assert, fighting down my anger; fearing if I release it, the consequences will be irreversible, especially if I end up punching him. I start to get up, but his arms wind tighter as he wrestles me down onto his lap and crushes my chest against his.

"You can't go wandering off," he says sternly. "Not until we figure out what's going on . . . why the Death Walkers are on to you."

"Let me go." I'm enraged. Furious. Pissed off beyond comprehension. I dig my fingers into his shoulders, hard.

He doesn't seem to give a shit as he picks me up and flips us to the side so he is lying on top of me. He gathers my arms together in one of his hands and pins them up above my head. I'm trapped beneath him and the scorching heat is unbearable.

"You're thinking too irrationally right now," he says. "You need to calm down, take a few deep breaths and think before you do anything."

I bend my back up and press my chest against his. "I'm thinking as rationally as anyone would in this situation. And there's all this . . . stuff in my body and head and I don't know what to do with it."

He lowers himself and I feel the hardness of his body

bear down on me. "Calm down. You're going to tear open your stitches . . . Just calm down."

I lie there, panting, and so does he. With each rise and fall of our lungs, our chests collide. I become calmer, which doesn't seem possible. Yet, it is; my erratic breathing is slowing down, my heart steadying.

He loosens up too, and isn't so tense anymore. "Now, if I let you go, will you promise to stay here and talk? No running off?"

I take a deep breath and nod, but deep down I know *I* have no control over what I do at the moment. My emotions do.

He lets go of me and pushes himself up. Then he grabs my hand and aides me as I sit up next to him. It grows quiet as he turns his head and looks over his shoulder at his back. "You know, you're fucking ruthless. You clawed through my shirt and cut the skin." He turns so I can see his back. Sure enough, I've managed to tear his shirt and his exposed skin is split open and bleeding.

"Sorry," I apologize, but there is very little sincerity in my tone.

He turns around and there's fire in his eyes. "Don't be." He clears his throat and then I clear mine.

"So, why did I start to feel, then?" I pull my legs up on the couch and tuck them under me. "That's what I really want to know. What happened?"

"No one can really figure that out. I guess Marco and Sophia noticed some changes in you over the last few months or so."

"They barely talk to me. How did they notice changes?"

"I guess you started asking questions about your parents and stuff. You even seemed sad at times."

So that's why Sophia has been upset. That's why she

won't tell me anything, but it didn't make it better. It made it worse. I feel a flicker of hatred in that moment; it's small, but there, and eager to flame bright. "And how do you play a part in this? I mean, you were at Marco and Sophia's house that morning, and then, suddenly you were at my school. I'm guessing you weren't there just to learn."

He lets out a breath. "Aislin and I enrolled in school to try and figure out what was going on with you. We were supposed to keep our distance and just observe, but that didn't work out very well."

"Are those the rules you broke?"

He shrugs. "That's just one among a very long list."

"So you're not supposed to be near me?"

He shakes his head and his gaze sweeps all over me, like he's memorizing me before he bails. "No, not really."

I think about us on the bed and just how close we've gotten. I pluck at a stray string on the throw pillow. "You broke that rule more than once."

"I know," he mutters and then lets out a sigh. "Look, I know you probably have a ton more questions, but I really need to get ahold of Stephan and figure out what's going on. The Death Walkers—I don't know how they discovered you—and we need to find that out before they track us down again."

I want to believe that when he says 'us,' he actually means *us*, but, for some reason, I feel like I'm the exclusion. Deep down, I know I'm alone in this, just like I've been my entire life. In the end, I'm the only person I can count on for anything.

CHAPTER
TEN

THE HOUSE IS enormous; an overly large living room, a large dining area and a very long hallway that has a lot of shut doors. I wonder what is behind those doors; if they are normal rooms or torture chambers or something.

"There's something else I need to tell you," he says as he comes to a stop in front of one of the shut doors. He turns to me and there's uneasiness in his demeanor.

I sigh. "Let me guess, unless you kill me right now, the world will explode." What can I say? I'm tired.

He confines a smile. "Well, I'm glad your sense of humor hasn't left you," he says and I pull an intolerant face. "Relax; it's not about you this time. It's about Laylen, the guy who lives here." He points up and down the hallway. Then, he crosses his arms. "He's not human."

"If he's not human, then what is he?"

He scratches the back of his neck as he mutters, "A vampire."

I stare blankly at him. He has to be joking. There is no way vampires can really exist. Can they?

He steps toward me cautiously with his hands at his

sides. "I know what you're thinking . . . I can see it written across your face. That there's no way vampires are real, but they're about as real as Death Walkers and you've seen those with your own eyes."

My eyes drift to the end of the hall. Light spills through the glass just above the door and creates misshapen reflections across the floor and walls. I could run away and pretend that this madness never existed. That the last few hours are a dream, which they easily could be, but I've seen too much; know too much. There is no way I can go back into the dark again and live my life just as it was. I've changed. Everything has changed.

"You're not thinking about running again, are you?" Alex asks.

"No, I was just thinking about stuff." I glance back at him. "Does he bite?"

Alex's jaw clamps down. It takes him a moment to answer. "No, since he was a Keeper before he changed, things work a little differently . . . He's more in control of his blood lust."

"Blood lust?" I've read about vampires, seen them portrayed on television shows. Some of them are depicted as sexy and their blood lust even sexier. I wonder if this Laylen guy's blood lust—should it ever emerge—will be sexy and feel good? I'm probably wondering too many things about the subject. I cover my mouth and cough to clear my throat. "And what about vampires that aren't Keepers to begin with? What are they like?"

"Let's just hope you don't ever have to find out," Alex says, then turns the doorknob and shoves the door open.

The room is bigger than the one we just left, but there's a lack of windows. The dark red walls are bordered by bookshelves and there is a long, mahogany table in the middle of the room with eight antique spindle-back chairs around it.

Aislin is in one of the end chairs, texting on her cell phone. When she sees us, she jumps to her feet and meets us in the center of the room. "Oh, good. I was just about to come get you. Did you get everything taken care of?"

Alex looks at me and then back at Aislin; I can sense something is up. "Yeah, I guess. Well, as much as I could."

Aislin sighs, patting her phone against the palm of her hand. "I can't get ahold of Stephan. It goes straight to his voicemail."

"That's odd," Alex mumbles, staring at the spot on the floor in front of his feet with his eyebrows dipped. "Did you try Marco and Sophia?"

"Yeah, they didn't answer, either." Aislin checks her cell phone screen. "Something's not right."

"Why do you need to get ahold of Marco and Sophia?" I intervene.

"Because they might know where Stephan is," Alex replies uncomfortably. "They're pretty close—Sophia, Marco and my father."

"And yet I've never met you before," I say. "Which seems a little bizarre."

"Isolation," Alex counters placidly. "They wanted as little familiarity as possible around you."

I just stare at him. There are no words. No coherent sentences that can explain how he can talk so casually about something so significant, at least to me.

"What?" he wonders. "Why are you looking at me like that?"

"Because you're so . . ." I rack my brain for the right word. "Nonchalant about stuff. It's weird."

"And you're emotional about a lot of things, which is

weird since a few months ago you couldn't even smile," he retorts, inching toward me. "You want to share any insight to that?"

I stand tall, posture straight, and my feet firmly planted to the floor. "Care to share why you're so calm? Why you can talk about my painful past as if it's a piece of dirt on your shoe."

"I don't share anything with just anyone," he says, again calm, and my hand itches to slap him.

"And vice versa." I clench my hands into fists and hide them behind my back, attempting to keep my own cool.

"But yours is important to share." He takes another step, diminishing more space between us.

I match his move and get right in his face. A floodgate opens, releasing a waterfall of emotions that severely want to wipe away the last hour or so. "In order for me to want to tell you anything, I have to trust you and, right now, I don't. It's that simple."

His eyes blacken and his voice lowers as he leans in. "You trusted me pretty damn well back at the cabin."

My hand starts to rise, to either hit him or shove him—I'm not exactly sure. I never find out, though because Aislin steps up and mediates.

"Maybe we should try calling them again?" she suggests. "It doesn't hurt to try."

Without taking his eyes off me, Alex nods. "Yeah, go ahead and try." He pauses and Aislin begins pressing buttons on her phone. "Do you know if Marco and Sophia were going somewhere? Like on a vacation or something."

I'm so stunned, I can't blink. "You do realize that I barely talked to them when I lived with them. After I moved out, we've talked on the phone maybe, like, three times."

"You were over there that day I ran into you." His hand digs around in the pocket of his jeans for his phone. "Did they say anything then?"

"Yeah, they said to get my shit out of my room," I state with bitterness seeping thickly from my throat as I gather loose strands of my hair and put them back into place. "And to never ask questions about my parents again. I'm guessing that neither of those things screamed that they were planning a vacation anytime soon."

"Gemma, this isn't a joke." Alex huffs an aggravated breath and puts the receiver up to his ear. "It's important. Your life, the world's life, depends on it."

"Oh, I know it's not." Carefully lifting my arms up, I take the elastic out of my hair and refasten it so my hair is in a secure ponytail. "I was being serious, Alex. The extent of our relationship makes sense to me now since I know," I gesture my hand in front of me and heave a breath, "everything."

He clicks the end button and stares wordlessly at me. I hold his gaze, unwavering, until the fiery connection becomes too much, then I look away and focus on a small piece of artwork on the wall. It's splattered with blues and reds and there is a grey, stone castle in the background that has a familiar look to it. "I'm sorry, okay? I'm just pissed off about . . . all the bullshit."

I hear Aislin's breath catch and Alex shakes his head, looking at her. "What? You knew she was like this when we enrolled in college, it was the reason why we enrolled."

"Yeah, but . . ." she glances at me with wide eyes. "She's so bad."

"You know I can hear you, right?" I shake my head and turn for the door. "I need some fresh air."

As my hand wraps around the doorknob, Alex's

fingers encircle my elbow. He hauls me backwards until my back is against his chest. "No wandering off alone." His arm snakes around my waist, while the other pins my arms against my chest.

My breathing comes out in silent gasps. "Is that another rule?"

"Of mine? Yes. It's called the rule of not getting yourself killed."

I slant my head back to look him in the eyes. "I just need some fresh air. This is a lot to take in."

"No wandering off by yourself," he repeats, his gaze skimming to my lips.

"I'm not a child," I remind him. "Now, if I want to step outside for two Goddamn minutes, I will." I take a deep breath and then force my arms forward, hoping he'll yield because there is no way I'm getting away by myself; he is just too strong.

His arms unstiffen and I move out of his hold; his hands sliding down my arms and along the back of my shirt as I step away.

"Stay close," he says softly as he releases the hem of my shirt.

Without looking back, I hurry to the door before he changes his mind and decides to make it difficult. Once I'm out in the hall, I free a tension-filled breath that I've been suppressing for the last few hours as I head for the front door. I'm not sure what my initial plans are other than to get away from Alex and Aislin's bluntness. They have a way of making me feel like I'm not real, like I'm a magical sword, instead of a human. It's not my fault that I'm harboring a star inside me.

WHEN I'M OUTSIDE, I know I'm not going to run away. Besides the obvious fact that I'm surrounded my limitless desert, and I have no idea which direction will take me home, I'm also scared. I don't want to die like I have in my dreams countless times. Alex and Aislin seem to know stuff that may help me stay alive and I want more answers about my past, my future and who I am. I want to know more.

I sit on the front porch as I take in the events of the last few hours. I have a cut on my side, blood on my shirt and a star inside my body. I glance over my hands and arms, then up each leg. I don't look different or anything, but I *feel* different. That's a given. Each day I feel different because each day I change inside—I grow emotionally. Sighing, I try to relax and clear my head. The desert air is intoxicatingly warm and the grey sky is ornamented with a few stars. I probably could stay here forever; and pretend nothing exists, besides me and the night sky.

"It's peaceful out here, right?" a deep, sultry voice drifts over my shoulder.

My muscles tense at the unacquainted person's arrival. I rotate my body and scan up his very long legs, his firm chest, all the way to his eyes, which are ocean blue and entrancing to look at. I've seen those eyes before; I've seen and felt all of him before. He's the blond stranger that makes a frequent appearance in my dreams.

His features are more striking in person and he reminds me of a singer in a punk rock band. The tips of his blond hair are dyed blue and sweep across his forehead and down across his ears. A silver ring threads his deep red bottom lip. He has on a black t-shirt, black jeans and black combat boots. Greek-like symbols are tattooed on his forearm, inked in black with thick lines.

He smiles softly as his gaze lands on my eyes. "You know, the last time I saw you, you were maybe four-years-old." He glances down at my chest making all the feelings from my dreams surface and steam across my skin. "You've grown up *a lot.*"

I rise to my feet with my eyes on him. He's taller in person because I'm not very short myself and he makes me feel downright diminutive. "Who are you?"

He laughs. "I take it you don't remember me." He sticks out his hand. "I'm Laylen."

My expression falls and my eyes expand as I step down a couple of stairs, undecided if I should stay or flee. Am I afraid of him? Or curious? "Laylen, as in the owner of this house?"

He lets his hand fall to his side. "Awe, I take it, you do remember me, at least, through what Alex has told you." He says Alex's name with such disdain that there has to be some bad history between them.

I feel bad because he clearly knows me and I can't recall a single detail about him besides my dirty dreams, which never happened. Or have they? I'm beginning to wonder about my dreams and their insightfulness.

I decide I'm not afraid of him and step back up onto the stair above. "I'm sorry, but I don't remember you. I just recognized the name because Alex and Aislin told me the owner of this house was named Laylen."

He moves down so he's on the step right in front of me and I have to kink my neck just to see his eyes. Up close, I note the sadness in them, deep pathways that show the scars conjoined with his heart. I want to hug him, which is strange because I'm not a hugger, but he looks so sad. "And they told you I'm a vampire."

I nod. "They did."

He waits. "And?"

"And . . ." I'm uncertain what he's waiting for me to say so I stick out my hand cordially. "It's nice to meet you."

He snorts a laugh and it makes me laugh, too. It's the most bizarre moment in a long sequence of bizarre moments because it's normal. I don't even know him, besides the fact that he has a very warm tongue and slightly cold skin, but those facts are solely based on my dreams.

Smiling, he shakes my hand and his skin is like frost on a window. "Well, it's nice to meet you, Gemma, or should I say, meet you again?"

"How do you know me?" I wonder. "Is it because of the Keeper connection?"

His shoulders lift as he shrugs. "Yes and no. We also knew each other when we were young, but it might have been too long ago for you to remember."

I search my brain for a memory of a blond hair, blue-eyed boy, but there's nothing except darkness. But that's a common occurrence whenever I try to remember something from my early past. "I'm sorry, I don't. I wish I did."

He seems doubtful. And miserable. It breaks my heart to see. There's no way an evil vampire could carry so much misery in them. "And I mean that."

We smile again and then he squeezes my hand. Why are we still holding hands? It's odd, yet, I don't pull away. I just continue to stand there and grasp onto his long fingers that feel like popsicles. It's mind-boggling, but it makes sense to my body because I want to cling onto him in any way I can. I'm attracted to him. Obviously. I understand that much, but there is also something else;

something stronger and compelling.

"You want to sit down and talk?" he asks, looking me in the eyes and I nod.

We release hands and take a seat on the steps next to each other. He leans against the railing and I recline back on my elbows, feeling a sense of comfort. The porch light radiates into the night and casts shadows across the stairs. We gaze at the desert, listening to the crickets chirp. I can make out the constellation of Cassiopeia up in the sky and a revelation hits me. Is that where my fascination with stars comes from? Maybe I subconsciously knew about the star inside me? Perhaps, I knew that a piece of me belongs up in the sky?

"So," Laylen finally breaks the silence and there's acrimony in his tone. "How's life been with Marco and Sophia?"

"It's been okay, I guess," I mutter and fix my gaze on him. "By your tone, I'm guessing, you're not a fan of them."

He laughs as he stares up at the stars. "I'm not a fan of Keepers in general."

I take in his profile; the slight crook in his nose and the firmness of his jawline. "How come?" I crack a smile. "Well, besides the obvious fact that they're liars."

"That they are," he agrees, encountering my gaze. "I'm guessing Alex hasn't told you my story."

"Story?" A bug lands on my arm and I swat at it and then wipe my hand on my jeans.

"The one where I was kicked out of the Keepers circle because I was turned."

"They kicked you out because you're a vampire?" I'm astounded. "Why? You don't seem evil?"

"Don't I?" he questions with a penetrating look.

"Because a lot of people sure think the opposite."

"I don't think so," I disagree. "Alex even told me that you have your blood lust under control." The word lust sounds funny leaving my mouth. He seems to think so too, because he can't seem to take his eyes off my lips.

"Alex is just telling you that to impress you," he says, sucking his lip ring into his mouth. "He doesn't really believe it."

"I doubt that," I say, but it sounds like a lie. "You don't like Alex because he's a Keeper?"

"It's the other way around," he answers. "Alex doesn't like me because of what I am and I choose to return the feeling."

I bite my lip and drum my fingers on my knee. "Yeah, Alex seems like he can be . . ."

"An asshole," Laylen says and grins when I look at him, but it's a plastic smile. A façade to cover up his real feelings.

"I was going to use the term douche bag," I clarify. "But yeah, asshole works too . . . Why is he like that? He told me it was because he was moody."

Laylen shakes his head disagreeing. "It's because of his father."

"Stephan?"

"Yeah, he's put it in Alex's head since we were kids that you have to be unattached and unemotional in order to be a good Keeper," he says and then mutters, "Like he would even know himself."

"You don't like Stephan?" I ask. "Isn't he a Keeper?"

He shrugs. "Being a Keeper doesn't mean anything, Gemma, regardless of what Alex tells you. You'll be able to determine for yourself what you think of Stephan when you meet him, but I'm guessing you won't like him. Most people don't." He leans back on his elbow. "And just because Keepers claim to protect the world, doesn't mean that they're good people."

Silence encircles us along with the warm air as I try to sort through the colossal volume of information I've received. While I dither in my thoughts, Laylen keeps tracing his tongue along his teeth and biting on his lip ring.

Finally, curiosity gets the best of me. "What makes you a vampire exactly?"

He bites at his lip ring again, making these sucking sounds that drive my body into a fitful frenzy and I have to sit on my hands to stop myself from touching him. "What do you mean?"

What is the correct way to ask someone how they are considered a creature of the night? The living undead? A bloodthirsty monster? Albeit, a sexy, undead monster. "I've read a lot of books about vampires," I start. "But nothing factual. So I don't know what to believe about vampires and the things they do."

He rubs his hand along his jaw thoughtfully. "You want to know what makes me a monster? Whether I bite? If I'm a killer, or if I drink blood? If I can run at an inhuman speed or if I have super-human strength?"

"It sounds like such a stupid question when you put it that way." My lips quirk. "But, I guess that's what I'm trying to ask, minus the whole killer thing. Because I don't think that."

He elevates an eyebrow. "You don't think that I'm a killer?"

I shake my head. "You're not putting out the whole 'I'm-a-demon-and-I'm-going-to-kill-you' vibe, so I'm guessing no."

"Well, you're the first to not pass that judgment on

me." He crosses his lean arms and observes me, and it only makes me feel more in tune with him. He isn't going to hurt me. I can feel it in every bone of my body and through the way the sensation of heat unites rhythmically with my pulse. "You're right," he says definitively. "I'm not a killer. I've never killed anyone; at least, that I know of."

A strange answer, but one I decide to tiptoe around, for now. "But other vampires are?"

He nods with his eyes secured on me as if I'm the most fascinating creature in the world. "Other vampires are a lot like what you've read and I'm not talking about the ones who drink blood by killing animals. These ones like to kill people; they get a thrill from it."

A chill crawls down my spine as the image of splattered blood paints the inside of my brain. "I don't get it. If people are dying because their blood was drained, wouldn't the news mention it? Wouldn't everyone in the whole world know vampires exist?"

He uncrosses his arms, swings them over the railing, and pulls himself up so he's sitting up straight. "Haven't you ever noticed that a lot of people turn their heads away from the things they don't want to see? Besides, people are excellent at keeping secrets from one another. If the right people don't want the world to know that vampires exist, then they won't know."

"Right people, as in the Keepers?"

He nods. "You're catching on quick."

I cup my hand on the side of my head. "I'm surprised I can think at all. It's been an overwhelming day."

"I bet it has." His gaze roams to the front door and the light reflects in his eyes. "Do you want to go inside and lie down? You could take a nap or something."

I'm still stuck on the fact that he's a vampire. "Do you sleep?"

He looks at me with an amused glimmer in his eyes. "You're still on that, huh?"

I lean forward and relax my arms on my knees. "I've always been into the supernatural and now I have a real vampire right in front of me. I'm not sure I'll ever be *off* it."

He smiles, I smile back and there's that link, bonding us together again. "I'm immortal." He traces his long finger along the tattoo on his forearm.

I scoot closer. "So you can't die?"

He lowers his arms from the railing. "Nope, not unless I'm staked through the heart or decapitated." I scrunch my nose and he laughs. "Am I freaking you out yet?"

I shake my head. "Nope. You'll probably figure out really soon that I can take in the crazy quite well."

He brings his knee up and places his foot on the step between us and overlaps his fingers around his knee. "I'm also stronger than the average person and I have fangs."

His teeth are flat, white, and smooth. "You have *fangs?* Where?"

"They're retractable," he says and slides his tongue along his lips. "And I only bring them out when I want to."

I think about my dream and how he bit me. Curiosity sparks inside me. "And when do you want to?"

His body goes rigid. "Let's hope you don't have to find out."

I want to find out, though. In fact, I crave it, like a dying plant craves water. Not because I want him to drink my blood and kill me, but because I want to see if it feels the same as it did in my dream; intoxicating and potent. "What else can you do?"

He bites back a smile and shakes his head. "You're a curious thing, aren't you?" He analyzes me with a tilt of his head and then his eyes shade to a dark blue. "You really want to know?"

I nod because curiosity is spilling through my veins like a drug. "I do."

His gaze lingers on me for a brief second longer and then he glances at the door before scooting closer to me. He tucks a strand of my hair out of my face and then traces a line below my eye. "Shut your eyes."

I'm thrown off a little by his touch. "What?"

He draws back his hand, sucks his bottom lip into his mouth and his lip ring slips between his teeth. "Shut your eyes and I'll show you what I can do."

I glance at the desert and then at the house. Do I trust him? Even though I hardly know him, I do trust him, but I don't understand why. Leaning back against the step, I inhale a breath of the warm air and then let my eyelids slip shut.

There is no movement, no softness of his voice, and no sounds of a dying animal he might be devouring. I almost open my eyes to see if he's left, but then I feel him shift closer and the temperature of my body begins to dwindle as his body hovers over mine, barely touching, yet each one of my nerves attach to him.

"I feel guilty doing this to you," he whispers against my neck. "I feel guilty doing it to anyone really, but you have this really curious, naïve look in your eyes that makes it really hard to say no." I feel his lips brush my neck, soft and moist, and the sensation seeps down into my skin, spilling into my body like liquid ecstasy. Under no control of my own, I fall back against the steps. An arm quickly winds around my waist, his hand cups the back of my head and he holds me up. I want to open my eyes and look at him, but my eyelids are sealed shut.

"There's this thing," his lips graze my collar bone and warmth centers to my heart and stills it, "that not all vampires can do that's called *venenatorum osculum.*" The way the words roll off his tongue sounds sexy. It makes my thighs tingle and my body arch up against his chest. "I can manipulate things inside you." He kisses the hollow of my neck and my entire body stills; paralyzed with a yearning for him to fill the massive hole in my heart, which seems to have enlarged severely over the last few seconds.

"I can put feelings in there; make you feel things you never knew existed," he whispers and his mouth lingers above my chest. I want it on my chest. I want him on me. I want so much at the moment. His voice lowers and grows ragged. "Or I can take it away."

"Please don't take it away," I nearly beg as he pulls the collar of my shirt aside. I curl my toes preparing for whatever he's going to do, hoping it will fill up the void inside me.

But then I feel him tense, his fingers and mouth move away from me, along with his body. My eyes open as he guides me upright. He isn't looking at me, but at the front door, which is wide open and Alex is standing just outside of it.

He looks pissed. Well, pissed is kind of an understatement. He looks infuriated; his face red, his fists clenched, his eyes dark and his arms crossed so tightly in front of his chest that the lines of his muscles are showing. "Are you two having fun out here?"

It's one of those moments where I know it's best to lie. "Not really. We were just—"

"Oh, I know what you were doing." He jogs down a

few steps and Laylen rises to his feet. "Having fun teaching her about vampirism? I guess you two skipped right past the introductions."

"Technically, we already know each other." Laylen is a little taller than Alex and his legs and arms are lankier. "And maybe, if you would have explained it to her, then I wouldn't have had to. She doesn't seem to know anything about our world."

"You know why that is." Alex shuffles forward and I can feel the tension in the air like a viral disease; I feel bad for putting it there. "She's not supposed to know."

"She knew I was a vampire," Laylen points out. "And she had questions, so I answered them."

Alex's fists tighten and his jaw twitches. "More like showed her and broke a ton of rules."

Laylen leans forward and anger flashes across his face, which is mixed with pain and anguish. "Those are the Keepers' rules and, since I'm not a Keeper anymore, I don't have to follow them."

Alex grits his teeth and Laylen steps around him, his long legs skipping over a few steps as he heads for the house. I remain on the steps, unsure of what to do. Should I follow Laylen? Go inside? Stay here?

I start to move for the house when Alex turns and looks at me, or looks through me anyway.

"Go inside," he says quietly and even though I'm not a fan of his bossiness, I obey because it looks like he'll crumble if I so much as utter a word.

CHAPTER
ELEVEN

N O ONE SPEAKS as we make our way down the hall. Alex lollygags at the rear and Laylen towers in front. Alex is clearly irritated about the incident he walked into on the porch. I'm still unsure what happened. Now that I've gotten some space from Laylen, I realize how foggy my head had been when I was close to him. Not to mention, how much my hormones are bonding with my thoughts. Is that what Laylen can do? Make me horny?

Laylen heads into the room I left earlier. I'm about to walk in when Alex grabs my sleeve. He doesn't give me time to turn around as he drags me back down the hall and around the corner into a foyer with black tile floors and a mirror hanging on the wall. There is also a small table that has pictures of Laylen and Aislin together at various different places. *Are they a couple?*

Alex steers me around by the shoulders so I'm facing him and then he backs me up against the wall.

"What are you doing?" I protest as I step forward.

His hands come down on the wall and he restricts me between his arms. "I was going to ask you the same thing."

"I wasn't doing anything wrong," I state as his hands slide down the wall and stop just above my shoulders. "Just talking."

"You do know what he was doing to you, right?"

"I asked him to do it."

He arcs an eyebrow and bends his elbows so he can move in closer and it galvanizes my body. "You *asked* him to manipulate your feelings? Considering what you've went through, I would assume that'd be the last thing you'd ever want."

"I just wanted to see what a vampire could do. It isn't that big of a deal." I pause. "And why does it bother you so much?"

"Because . . ." He locks his elbows to give us distance. "Look, you're new to this whole aspect of life and I don't want your curiosity to get you into trouble. Because it can. Trust me."

"You keep saying that . . . trust me." I lean forward, lessening the space between our faces. "Yet, I know nothing about you. How can I trust someone I don't know? I mean, I've known Laylen for like twenty minutes and I already feel like I know more about him than I do about you and I've known you for a few weeks."

He isn't intimidated by my take-charge attitude. He welcomes it, moving in even closer so our foreheads are converging. "That's bullshit. I've told you things about me."

"And how do I know any of that's true?" I ask. "After everything, after the sheer fact that you were around me for days upon days acting like everything was normal. Being able to act like that and omit the truth can only come from practice."

He pushes back from the wall and shakes his head.

"Believe whatever you want, Gemma. See how far it gets you."

With that, he leaves and I have no idea what he means. I have no idea what anything means anymore. I'm a mess. A giant, erratic, emotionally driven mess that is supposed to save the world.

IT TURNS OUT that Alex and Aislin still can't get ahold of anyone, so there is a heavy amount of friction in the room. I sit at the table and watch Alex pace the floor with his hands crossed behind his back. He does it for so long I think he is going to wear a whole in the floor.

Aislin is in the end chair messing around with her phone while Laylen searches the bookshelves as a way to busy himself. I think there may have once been something going on between Laylen and Aislin because they haven't once looked each other in the eye.

Aislin drops her cell phone on the table and slumps back in the chair. "Maybe we should just go looking for them."

Alex halts and unfolds his hands from his back. "That's easier said than done, Aislin, since we have no idea where to look for them."

"I'm just trying to help." She frowns and scoops up her phone. "You don't need to be rude."

"Did you guys ever consider that maybe they don't want you to get ahold of them?" Laylen slides a book onto the shelf and walks over to the table. He hasn't spoken in an extent amount of time and his voice seems to make Aislin and Alex edgy, but I like the sound of his voice. He grips at the back of the chair next to mine. "That maybe they're hiding from you."

Alex shoves up his sleeves and tosses his phone aside. "Why the fuck would they be hiding from us?"

Laylen lets go of the chair and stands upright. "You tell me. I've been out of the loop for a few years now."

"Yet, there's an underlying meaning," Alex retorts, striding to the table, "written all over your face."

Laylen crosses his arms and so does Alex. They stare at each other like two dogs ready to rip each other's throats apart. Aislin and I trade an uneasy glance, but we're both afraid to intervene.

"You want to know what I think?" Stretching his long legs, Laylen makes a path around the table toward Alex. "That it's not just a coincidence that Stephan, Marco, and Sophia are all unreachable when hell breaks loose. I mean, for all we know, they could be working with Demetrius and the Death Walkers."

"Why would you think that?" I interrupt. "I thought the Keepers were good."

"Gemma, just ignore him." Alex prowls toward Laylen with a cocky sway in his walk. They're closing in on each other and their chests are heaving with their rage. "He's full of shit."

As the two of them reach each other, I scoot the chair back from the table and stand up. "All of you are strangers to me, so I'm not sure *who* or *what* to believe."

Laylen cinches his lips together, holding back a grin as he looks at me. "Smart girl."

I want to say thank you, but the look on Alex's face shuts me up. His eyes are flaring and his fists are balled so firmly his knuckles are chalk white. It's like he thinks I'm supposed to straight up trust him. For the last few weeks, I've thought he was just a normal guy, who I happened to share some electrical bond with, and I thought that was because I was going insane.

"I'm sorry, but I'm confused and I don't want to trust anyone at this point." I lower myself into the chair. He keeps his eyes on me and it makes me want to cower under the table. There is too much power and control in those eyes; it melts my inhibitions.

"Maybe we should go back to Laramie and check up on things," Aislin speaks and cuts through the tension in the air. "There might be something back at the house that could help us figure this out."

"Are you crazy?" Alex asks, tearing his gaze away from me and focusing on her. "There's no way we're taking Gemma back to Wyoming. You saw how many Death Walkers showed up at the cabin. It's too dangerous."

"I'm never going back? Wait. Why? I have a home there and a . . . ." I stop because what else do I have there? A bed. Classes. Emptiness. Nothingness. Pieces of meaningless memories that are more weightless than dust.

"You can't go back when the Death Walkers know where you are." His brow arches upward. "Does that upset you or something?"

"No," I admit, "but where am I going to live? And what about my stuff?"

Alex puts his hand to his neck and pops his neck. "That's a question only Stephan can answer *because,* right now, I have no fucking clue what the hell's going on or what the next move is. No one prepared us for this."

"Prepared you for a Death Walker invasion," I joke and then choose to keep quiet after Alex's gives me a death glare.

"I think sometimes, your moods get a little confused," he says. "Because a lot of them don't fit the situations."

"Yeah, but at least I have an excuse," I retaliate. "You're just moody for unknown reasons."

"Oh, he has reasons." Laylen slaps Alex's shoulder roughly and Alex winces. "He just won't admit them."

Alex glares at Laylen's hand. "That's not what this is about."

Laylen steps back, shaking his head. "Yes, it is. All this," his eyes flit to me, "is about wanting what you can't have."

Alex raises his fist and targets it at Laylen's jaw. Laylen does nothing but stand there, embracing it, as if he wants to feel the pain. I start to jump from my chair, but Aislin beats me to the punch, literally. She's in between them before Alex can sling his fist forward.

She thrusts her hands out to the side of her and pushes both of them back. "Stop fighting. Fighting has never done any of us any good. In fact, it's the main reason why we haven't talked to each other in the last few years." She looks at Alex, then at Laylen, and then her hands fall to her sides. "Now, we need to focus on the problem and come up with a plan." Her shoulders rise and fall as she lets out a deep breath. "What we could do is leave Gemma with Laylen while you and I go back to Laramie and see what's up. Check their houses, see if anyone is there or if anything gives us a clue to where the hell they disappeared to."

Alex's eyes narrow at her. "There's no way in hell I'm leaving Gemma alone with him."

Laylen laughs, but it was underlined with hurt. "Am I not even considered a person anymore?" Alex doesn't respond and Laylen shakes his head.

"Here's a thought," I chime in. "It's my life, so I think I should have some say in this. And I say I'm comfortable with staying here alone with him."

Alex snorts a sharp, derisive laugh. "I'm sure you are. I got a full view of how comfortable you two are with each other when I walked out onto the porch."

Aislin's forehead furrows and she looks at Laylen for an explanation. "Wait, what happened out on the porch?"

Laylen looks guilty and starts to open his mouth, but Alex cuts him off.

"Don't worry about it." Alex pulls out a chair to sit down. He looks tired; there are bags under his eyes and they're bloodshot. Positioning his elbows on the table, he lowers his head into his hands, looking defeated. "Aislin, how quickly can you get us to Laramie and back?"

She poises her chin up as she rounds the table and collects her phone. "As quick as you need me to. You know that. I'm good to go if there are only two people. It's when there are too many that things get complicated."

"Then we'll leave Gemma here." Alex raises his head and stabs a finger in Laylen's direction. "But if anything happens to her, it's on you."

He rolls his eyes and sits down at the table. "Nothing's going to happen to her. As much as you hate me, you know I'm perfectly capable of fighting off some Death Walkers."

"Not in large numbers," Alex says. "No one's capable of that unless they have the Sword of Immortality, and no one's seen it for a few years."

"I have to go back into the library and grab my candle and crystal first," Aislin announces as she heads for the door. "Then we can go. The sooner we get out, the sooner all this will be over. I don't like not knowing what's going on. I'm a very structured person."

Laylen and Alex trade a glance and there is laughter in their eyes. For a second, they look like friends.

"Yeah, that's you," Laylen comments sarcastically as he turns a chair backwards and sits down in it; letting his lanky arms dangle over the top. "Miss Organized and Structured."

She turns around. "Hey, don't be mean!"

Alex is tracing his finger along his palm absentmindedly. "He's not being mean. He's just stating a fact everyone knows." His eyes flicker in my direction. "Even Gemma probably has caught on to how disorganized you are."

I shake my head because I don't know enough about her to pass that judgment. "I don't know that."

"Well, you should," Alex says. Aislin whisks forward and smacks him on the back of the head. His shoulders constrict and move upward. "Hey, I wasn't the only one who said it."

"Well, you were the first one in my reach." She rolls her shoulders back to straighten her posture. "Now, if you'll excuse me, I'm going to go get my Wicca stuff so I can use my awesome magic gift—which none of you have—to take us back to Wyoming." She starts toward the exit, but slams to a stop and smacks her hand against her forehead. "Shit! Shit. Shit. Shit."

I'm starting to realize that maybe I'm not as crazy as I've always thought. Maybe everyone is crazy. Maybe crazy is actually normal.

Laylen nibbles on his lip ring as he works to restrain a smile. "What's wrong?"

She turns around and pouts out her lip. "The Death Walkers' ice ruined my crystal. We were lucky we even made it here." She makes her way back to an empty chair. "This sucks. Now what are we going to do?"

It gets so quiet I can hear everyone's hearts beating.

Thump, thump, thump, thump. They sound like tiny drums.

"What kind of a crystal was it?" Laylen inquires. "The gold-leaf one?"

"No, it's the one made of amethyst." She props her elbow on the table and lets her chin fall into her hand.

"The Vectum Crystal?" Laylen asks and she bobs her head up and down. Laylen hooks his finger over his shoulder and points at the window. "There's this place in Vegas—Adessa's Herbs and Spices."

Alex cracks his knuckles. "I'm thinking that Las Vegas probably isn't the greatest place to go. There are all kinds of dark creatures there. Vampires. Werewolves. It's too dangerous."

My eyes amplify as I stare out the window at the twinkling lights in the distance. They have to be the city's lights. "There's Werewolves?"

Alex points at Laylen with a bored look in his face. "There're vampires. Of course there are werewolves."

I shake the image of a dog howling at the moon out of my head. "Do they bite?"

Laylen lets out a soft laugh as he twirls a set of keys he's taken out of his pocket around his finger. "You sure are fascinated with biting."

My cheeks flush because I really am. There's something about getting bitten that enthralls my emotions and I want to experience it in real life.

Daggers shoot from Alex's eyes as he glares at Laylen and then his attention centers back to me. "It doesn't matter what they do. All that matters is that you're safe and sound here, far away from them."

"I don't think I'm really safe and sound anywhere," I say. "Besides, don't you have like a box of weapons to protect me or something?"

He struggles not to laugh at me. "Weapons or not, it's too dangerous. If an inhuman—and maybe even human—creature gets close to you, they're going to want to get closer."

"Why?" I ask.

"Because they will," he responds. "You have this . . . thing about you."

"Then stay here with her," Laylen proposes as he leans back in the chair and places his hands behind his head. "Or, I'll stay with her and you take Aislin. There's a ton of solutions, so stop getting your panties in a bunch."

Alex stares impassively at him. "I'm not getting my panties in a bunch. I'm being careful."

"Careful about what exactly?" Laylen wonders. "Gemma getting hurt, or you hurting Gemma."

"What?" Aislin and I say simultaneously.

Aislin glances at me and then at Alex. "What's he talking about?"

"Let him explain it to you," Laylen says with an accusing tone.

"There's nothing to explain." He shoves his chair back from the table and rises to his feet. "You promise we'll just go straight there and straight back. No stops or anything."

Laylen stares at him incredulously with his hands spread out to the side of him. "Are you kidding me? Where else do you think I'll take us? McDonald's? Walmart? Oh wait, I do need to make a quick stop by the cemetery."

I snort a laugh, but it quickly dissipates at the fury blazing in Alex's eyes. "You think this is funny? Do you think getting killed is funny?"

I shake my head. "But what he said was."

Aislin grimaces and drops her head down on the

table. "Can we just get going already?"

Alex's hands wring the back of the chair. "Don't underestimate the Death Walkers, Gemma. They'll kill you if they get the chance."

Fear capes the humor inside me. He's right. It isn't funny. The prickle lets me know that I need to get things in check and take things seriously. It soothes me with each stab. "I know that. And I'm sorry. I won't laugh at inappropriate things again."

He is stunned by my apology. "Well, good."

After a lot of arguing, a decision is finally made. We would all go to Vegas with the stipulation that I will stay in the car and there will be no stops except to get the crystal. Including cemeteries and Walmart.

I have blood all over my clothes and Aislin insists I need to change before we leave. She informs me that she has clothes stashed in the house. We go into a room with a white four-post bed covered with tons of fluffy pillows. There is an oversized armoire in the corner and Aislin marches up to it and throws the doors open.

"The only problem is you're about five inches taller than me." She taps her finger against her chin as she evaluates the selection of clothes hanging up. "But I guess we'll just have to make something work."

I take a seat on the bed. "Do you come here a lot? You must if you have your own room."

She pulls out a pink T-shirt and tosses it on the bed. "Yeah, this house actually used to belong to Laylen's parents and we used to come up here to take a break from everything." She throws a glittery scarf onto the bed. "Things change, though." She sighs, staring down at a pair of jeans in her hands. "We haven't been up here in a really long time."

She starts delving through the clothes again. Shirts, jeans, skirts, and dresses begin to form a pile on the bed beside me. The room smells fruity and it matches the frilly theme of the bed. There are photos all over the walls, so I get up and amble around to look at them. I find photos fascinating because they capture a moment of emotion, whether it's fake or real.

Some of the photos are of Laylen and Aislin and there are others just of Laylen. There's one taped to the dresser mirror of Laylen standing out in the desert with his arm wrapped around Aislin. Alex is next to Laylen and there is an attractive blonde girl cuddled up against him. They're smiling. *Happy.* It makes my heart hurt. Have I ever been happy? I search through my limited memories and come up hollow.

"That was taken a couple of years ago," Aislin remarks as she wiggles a hanger out of the sleeves of a sweater.

"Oh, yeah?"

"I think I was about eighteen." She balls up a shirt and tosses it back into the armoire. "So, like, five years ago."

I do the math. "That would make you . . ."

"Twenty-three." She interrupts as she chucks a skirt onto the bed. "And Alex is twenty-four."

"No wonder he seems to hate school," I note. "He's old."

Aislin laughs as she hooks the hanger back on the bar. "He's not that old, Gemma. Only a few years older than you."

I pick up a handmade ceramic heart that's on the dresser and turn it over in my hand. Her room is so different from mine, decorated and full of items associated with memories. "How about Laylen? How old is he?"

"Well, he would've been twenty-five, but after he got . . . um . . ." She trails off as tears pool in her eyes. She's hurting thinking about the past, something I understand. It's right then that I realize Aislin isn't a bad person. She's nice and has a lot of emotion in her, just like me. "But, yeah, he's stuck at twenty-two now." She dabs the tears away with her fingertips, chucks a white lacy shirt onto the bed, then comes over and stares down at the pile of clothes with her hands on her hips. "Now, see if any of these will fit those long legs of yours."

NOTHING FITS. ALL the pants are too short and all the shirts are baggy in the chest area. I flop back on the bed, wearing a pink shirt that shows off my stomach and jeans that barely reach the lower region of my ankles. "I think I might have to just wear my clothes." I drape my arm over my head.

She picks up my shirt that has blood on it and discards it in a hamper in the corner. "No way. You did hear Alex when he said vampires could be there. He wasn't kidding and they're not like Laylen. They'll bite you."

There's that word again. *Bite.* "Okay, then what do you suggest?" I peek out from underneath my arm. "Because I look ridiculous."

She glances around her room and when her eyes land on a trunk at the foot of the bed, her face lights up and she claps her hands. "Oh my God. I have the perfect outfit." She kneels down in front of it, flips the latches, and raises the lid. "I have no idea why I didn't think of this before." She sticks her head in and begins digging around. I sit up as she shuts the lid. She springs to her toes and extends her arm in my direction. "Here you go. One outfit that will fit not only those long limbs of yours, but it'll also help you blend in."

I take the piece of fabric from her hand and hold it up in front of me. It's a strapless, black leather dress with a lace-up section on the back. "Where did you get this?"

She twists her golden brown hair up as she makes her way over to the porcelain vanity. "I had a friend who wore it for Halloween one year and she left it here."

I run my fingernail down the red ribbon on the back and twist it around my finger. "It's a Halloween costume? For what? A slut?"

Aislin opens a drawer and takes out a compact and a makeup brush. "She was supposed to be a sexy witch, but she did end up looking more like a slut."

I unravel my finger from the ribbon. "And now you want me to wear it?"

She clicks open the compact. "Trust me; you'll be thanking me when we get to Vegas. It'll help you blend in." She begins powdering her nose.

I glance down at the leather dress in my hand. "*This* will help me blend in?"

She nods. "You'll see when we get there. In Vegas, anything and everything exists. Walk around looking normal and you're the one that stands out."

I get to my feet and head for the door, grabbing my boots on the way out. "Where's the bathroom?"

She turns in the chair and points to the right. "Third door to your right." I start to leave and she calls out, "Oh yeah, and Gemma, wear your hair down. You have such pretty hair."

Sighing, I leave her to primp and go into the bathroom, fully aware that I'm going to look ridiculous. I might not know much about myself, but I know enough to comprehend that a tight, leather dress isn't going to look good on me do to my lack of curves.

I carefully slip out of the shirt and jeans and then step into the dress. I shimmy it over my hips and then have to take off my bra because the dress is made to go all-la-natural. I lace up the back the best that I can, but it's loose. Then, I slip on my boots before yanking the elastic out of my hair and letting it fall down to my shoulders. I'm not used to wearing such a limited amount of clothing; I feel naked and ridiculous.

I splash some cold water on my face in a pathetic attempt to bring myself out of this dream because vampires, witches and secret groups who save the world aren't supposed to exist.

But after I pat my face dry and open my eyes, the same navy blue walls of Laylen's bathroom still surround me. I glance into the mirror hanging above the sink and sigh at the sight of my freakish violet eyes that collide against the glass; like my hair does with my pasty complexion. Add the gothic dress, as well as the boots, and I look like a character straight out of the Addam's Family.

There's a knock on the door. "Gemma, are you ready to go?" Aislin asks.

I blink one last time at my reflection, then turn away from it, throw open the door and step out. Alex and Laylen are with Aislin, standing next to a table decorated with a vase of wilting flowers. Aislin has changed into a simple grey dress with matching flats and her hair is pinned up. Laylen has the same outfit on; black jeans, a black tee and black boots; it's a hell of a lot of black. Alex has changed into dark jeans, a long-sleeved, fitted, black shirt and there are leather bands on his wrists.

I give an animated swing of my arm. "All right, throw in a hand that walks around and a creepy Victorian house, and I'm good to go."

All three of them look at me at the same time and then they go quiet as they stare at me.

Great, I look sillier than I originally thought. "It's a joke. About the Addam's Family," I say, tugging at the hem of the dress. "I should change, right?"

Smiling, Aislin shakes her head, while Laylen coughs into his hand. "No, you look great." She walks up to me as she digs through her purse. "You just need this." She draws her hand from her purse and moves a black pencil toward my face. I wince as she traces a line around each eye and then steps back, putting the lid back on the eyeliner.

"She kind of looks like one," she says with a tilt of her head as she studies me. "You know that?"

Alex steps up beside her with his eyes fixed on me. There's a raw animalistic look in them that makes the blood rush to my cheeks. "She does, which is good. Maybe they'll leave her alone."

I rearrange the top of my dress higher because it's slipping down. "Look like what?"

"A Black Angel." Aislin tosses the eyeliner back in her purse and zips it up. "They're really pretty, but really dangerous."

"Is that like a Fallen Angel?" I ask.

"Not exactly," she says. "They're hypnotic and powerful. They have this way about them that draws people to them and if you get too close to one, they can possess your mind."

I gape at her. "Possess your mind and make you do what?"

Alex steps forward. "Whatever they want, which is why we have to be careful and stay away from them."

"Are there a lot where we're going?"

Alex wavers. "It all depends on the Wicca store. If there's black magic there, then yes, a Black Angel might be there or maybe even something worse. And it's good you're dressed up like that." His eyes scroll up my body. "Maybe everyone will try not to get too close to you. And we can keep your identity hidden."

"From the Death Walkers?" I ask. "Or from Demetrius?"

"From everyone." He moves nearer and blows out a breath. "No one can know who you are, Gemma. If the wrong person finds out who you are—what you are—then word will get back to Demetrius. Or they might try to use the power for themselves." He pauses. "You're very valuable."

Valuable to whom? I let out an uneasy breath and tug at the top of my dress again, wondering what I'm getting into. "I can't get the ribbon to fasten very tightly. I'm worried it's going to fall down."

Alex makes a circular motion with his finger. "Turn around and I'll tie it."

I obey and hold my breath as he steps up behind me. Sweeping my hair to the side, he hooks his fingers through the bottom cross of the ribbon and gives it a gentle tug as Aislin and Laylen wander down the hallway toward the front door.

He doesn't utter a word as he deliberately traces his finger to the next section. I suck in a breath as he pulls on that one too and his breath hits the back of my neck. I try to remain calm as he fastens the next one by pulling it so securely that the leather clutches my ribs.

I put my hands just below my breasts and work to get air into my lungs. "It's tight enough I think."

His chest brushes against my back as he laughs and gives the ribbon another tug. "Not tight enough. We don't want them falling out."

I bite down on my lip. Hard. And a little blood pools out. "I'm sure they'll stay put. I can barely breathe."

His knuckles graze between my shoulder blades as he ties the ribbon into a knot. He's breathing erratically and his chest collides with my back with each inhale. "I know, but I want to make sure." There's an elongated pause and then I feel his lips touch the back of my neck.

I stay still as he rolls his tongue along my skin and gives it a little suck, sending shivers all over my body. I want to crumble to the ground and let him catch me, but he pulls away and the feeling evaporates as he heads down the hall with a swagger in his walk. All I have left is a warm sensation on my back and I'm not sure if it's from the kiss or the prickle trying to whisper a new emotion to me.

Either way, I stuff it down and follow them out the front door, knowing I have to get my feelings under control, so I can think clearly and keep myself alive.

Because that is the whole point of life. Isn't it?

CHAPTER TWELVE

L AYLEN DRIVES A 1960s Pontiac GTO; black with white racing stripes down the middle. *Another sexy car to add to my list. And a sexy driver.* With his long fingers curled around the steering wheel, Laylen speeds off down the dirt road toward the city.

I'm in the backseat, watching the stars streak by as the car zooms down the road. Alex is next to me and is being really quiet. His knee keeps jiggling up and down as if he's centering his nervous energy into that one leg. It's making the air stifling and I can still feel where he kissed my neck, like a lingering chill.

"You know if you keep bouncing your leg like that, you're going to get a cramp," I say, when his nervous energy starts to spread to me.

He ceases jiggling his knee and looks at me. "Is it bothering you?"

"Kind of," I admit and fan my hand in front of my face. "You're making it very hot in here."

"Maybe it's just my hotness that's making *you* hot and bothered," he jokes with a smirk.

Annoyance overcomes me and I slap his knee, kind of

roughly. "That's not what it is."

He rubs his knee with a half-smile on his face. "You're vicious."

"And you're arrogant."

"That's been a given from day one." He pauses and then glances up front at Aislin who has her eyes shut and her head resting against the window. He scoots over in the seat and leans in toward me. He smells like cologne mixed with soap and I breathe in his intoxicating scent. "You need to be careful while we're in the city. Stay by me at all times."

"Yes, boss. Any other orders you need me to follow?" I'm joking, but the look on his face is dead serious.

"There's a ton of orders I'd love for you to follow," he says and reclines back with his jaw set tight. "But I'd break a lot of rules if I ever gave them to you; and unlike some people, I don't break the rules." He glances up at Laylen and then directs his focus to the road ahead. In the darkness of the cab, his eyes look like coals and his face is a shadow; he looks haunted.

There's a brief confirmation from the prickle that lets me know I feel bad. Only hours ago, in the cabin, I'd been rubbing up against him, feeling the most amazing feelings ever and then I went and did whatever it was that I did with Laylen. I'm working up a mild apology when the city rises into view and my thought process hits a screeching halt.

Lights blink against the blackness of the night in vibrant colors and giant billboards light up the sides of the road. In the distance, where the hills fade out, buildings stretch toward the sky. I sit quietly, craning my neck from left to right to take it all in. Everything's so flashy and shocking. The shock only grows when we reach the heart of the city, where the sidewalks become packed with mobs of people and the air buzzes with excitement. There are people dressed in costumes; drinking, laughing and I even see one man strip off his clothes.

I pinch my arm to make sure I'm not dreaming and wince from the sting I undeniably feel. "Holy shit."

Alex tucks a strand of my hair behind my ear and whispers, "What? Did you think you were dreaming?"

I rub my arm. "Maybe. It wouldn't be the first time I wasn't sure if I was awake or not."

He gives me a strange look. "What do you mean?"

I shrug and fix my gaze on a man dressed as a gladiator, handing out flyers to pedestrians. "I mean exactly what I said—sometimes I can't tell what's happening in real life and what's just a dream."

"How long has this been going on?"

"For most of my life. Or, well, since I started feeling, which, to me, was kind of the beginning of my life."

He looks at me and, I mean, really looks at me as if I'm really a person and not a star or a strange girl. "What kinds of dreams? Were they the one's with the Death Walkers?"

I nod. "Yeah, the Death Walkers were in some of them. And you." *And sometimes Laylen.*

The lights from the street mirror in his eyes. "And what was I doing in these dreams?"

"Umm . . ." Thankfully it's dark because I'm pretty sure my cheeks are bright red. "Stuff."

It doesn't take him very long to catch on. "Oh." His forehead scrunches and he covers his mouth, then puts his hand on his lap; uncertain of what to do with himself.

After that, it gets quiet. I would feel stupid, but I have bigger problems to worry about than Alex thinking I'm a pervert. I focus on the scenery; a glass pyramid, a giant pirate ship and a small replica of the Eiffel Tower. At the end of the taller buildings, Laylen veers to the right and the lights fade with the crowd. The buildings shrink into smaller, worn out houses and the gutters lining the streets are littered with garbage and cigarette butts. When we pass a corner where a group of people are shuffling around, beating the shit out of each other, Aislin locks her door.

"You do realize it's almost one o'clock?" Aislin informs Laylen as she checks her watch.

Laylen flips the signal light on. "Yeah, so? You do realize that this is Vegas, right? Most places stay open all night."

"Yeah, but the later it is, the more the weirdoes are going to be out and about." She adjusts the strap of her dress, which has slipped off her shoulder.

"Weirdoes make the world interesting." He flashes a smile at her as he parks the car up against the curb.

She shakes her head and tries not to smile. "That's a great way to look at things."

Surrounding the car are abandoned buildings. The windows are boarded up and there are no lights on inside any of them. The only proof of human existence is a guy wearing a black hooded jacket, cargo pants and army boots, who scurries down a dark alley when he sees us.

Laylen silences the engine and the radio, and then shuts the lights off. It gets quiet and very dark.

"Are you okay?" Alex asks and his low voice sends vibrations along my skin. "You look freaked out."

"I'm fine," I lie, clicking my seatbelt loose. "I've been chased by a pack of Death Walkers for crying out loud. It can't get much worse than that."

"Yeah, it can, Gemma. Things can get a lot worse," he states definitively.

I'm not sure if he's trying to scare me, but he is making me uneasy. "Like how?"

"Don't worry," he says in a husky voice. "I promise I won't let anything happen to you."

"You say that all the time," I state quietly. "And I'm starting to wonder just how bad things are; how much protection you think I need."

He keeps his lips close to my earlobe. "It's not about things being bad. It's about me making a promise."

I tilt my head a little and my cheek touches his lips, but he doesn't move. "I reiterate, sometimes it feels like you're speaking in code."

Aislin clears her throat. "Um, guys? I think we should go in and get this over with."

Her voice breaks the connection and we both move away from each other; Alex returns to the other side of the car.

Aislin surveys the buildings. "So what's the game plan? Just go into the place and get the stuff? Where is the Wicca shop anyway, because these places all look abandoned?" When Laylen stares silently out the window, Aislin rotates in the seat to face him. "Laylen, did you hear me?"

He lowers his hand from his lip ring and mutters, "The Wicca shop isn't inside any of these buildings."

"What do you mean; it's in none of them?" Alex asks. "What the fuck's going on?"

Laylen vacillates. "I needed to stop here first before we go and pick up the crystal."

There's a split second where I can feel the heat of hell breaking loose and then Alex scoots forward in his seat.

Even though his movements are slow, they're full of warning. "I thought we all agreed no extra stops." His voice is so controlled it sends a chill down my spine.

Laylen slides the keys out of the ignition and keeps his voice unvarying. "Before you start getting your panties up in a bunch, hear me out. Trust me; you'll want what's here."

"Trust you?" Alex lets out a cynical laugh. "Are you kidding me? I already trusted you and look where it got us."

Laylen thrums his fingers on top of the steering wheel. "The Sword of Immortality is here . . ." He points at the closest building. "At the Black Dungeon."

Alex balls his hands into fists and a vein in his neck bulges. "And why is it at the Black Dungeon?"

"I lost it during a poker game a few months ago," Laylen answers evenly. "I thought I had an unbeatable hand. Turns out, I didn't."

"So, let me get this straight." Alex is livid. "You stole it from the Keepers just so you could lose it in a poker game."

"I stole it for a good reason," Laylen replies. "I didn't want to leave it in the Keepers' hands after I became immortal. You guys made it very clear about your feelings for me when I changed."

"We wouldn't kill you." Aislin presses her hand to her chest, flabbergasted. "Laylen, how could you ever think that?"

"Because it's the truth," he says simply, not meeting her eyes, instead he's staring at the street sign.

Silence takes over. Dogs howl in the distance. Tension pollutes the air. It's at that moment that I realize just how out of the loop I am. They have history, they understand the secrets of the world; the one's no one believes in because believing in them is too terrifying for the average person.

"I'm sorry, but what exactly is the Sword of Immortality?" I finally dare to speak.

"Exactly what it sounds like—a sword that can kill an immortal," Alex says, tapping his fingers restlessly against the console. "And it would have been really useful back at the cabin. Then maybe we'd have been able to kill a few Death Walkers, instead of running like a bunch of pussies."

My fingers curl around the edge of the seat and my nails dig into the leather. "So, right now, at this very moment, if the Death Walkers show up, we can't kill them?"

"All we can do is run." He pauses and I can hear the fury lacing each huff of his breath. "So what's the big plan, Laylen? Because now that I know it's up there, there's no way we're walking away until we have it."

"I haven't really gotten that far." Laylen points at a two-story brick building with a crooked rain gutter and a rickety sign on the roof. "All I know is that it's up on the second floor, in a secured display case." He glances at Aislin. "A display case secured by black magic."

"Black magic's not my specialty," Aislin utters softly. "You know that."

Laylen holds her gaze. "Do I?"

She nods and averts her eyes to the window. "You know my father would never allow it."

He reaches over and delicately touches her arm and I see a glimpse of their history; the ones in the pictures. "I'm sure, if you think really hard, you can figure out a spell that would get us in."

She's quiet for a while and when she speaks, her voice

is barely audible. "I could do an *effrego alica*. It'll remove the Black magic around the case long enough for us to break it, but, if there are alarms . . ." She looks at Laylen with sadness in her eyes as she draws her arm away from his hand. "That I can't help."

Laylen pulls his hand away and rests it on top of the shifter. He looks even sadder, if that's possible. "If there are alarms, then we'll run."

Alex shakes his head. "That's the stupidest plan I've ever heard. Besides, how are you going to even get up there? From what I can remember, there are guards all over the bottom floor and the stairway, which is the only way up to the second floor, without flying."

"I'll pretend that I'm going upstairs to feed off Aislin," Laylen says flatly. "It's the only reason they let people up there."

"And what if one of the guards or someone like Draven goes up there?" Alex asks in a clipped tone. "Then what?"

"Who's Draven?" I wonder. "And what the hell is in this Black Dungeon?"

"Lots and lots of evil," Alex mutters as his gaze traces the lines of the nearby buildings.

"Draven is the owner of the club," Laylen explains, staring off in deep thought. "And someone will have to stand at the bottom of the stairway . . . You and Gemma can do that and send a text if something is about to walk up. I'll go up with Aislin and stand guard at the entrance of the room. I'm more than capable of protecting her."

"And then what? You hide? Run?" He frowns. "There's only one way out of there."

"Look, I'm not the one who is in desperate need to get the sword back," Laylen points out. "We can either leave, Aislin and I can go in blind and try to get the sword, or we can all go in and watch each other's backs and have a better chance at getting in and out undetected."

"We need that sword." Alex flops back in the seat, bumping my shoulder. "And what about Gemma? She's going to stand out like a sore thumb down in that crowd."

I run my hands along the front of the dress. "I thought you guys said this would help me blend in?"

Alex shakes his head. "You're innocence is written all over you; they'll eat you up."

"Literally?" My voice cracks.

His gaze slides to me and he analyzcs me through hooded eyes. "It depends on what literal we're talking about, but to clarify, I mean they're going to want to get their hands and teeth all over you."

I don't know what to say to that, so I keep quiet.

"She could pretend she's one of them," Aislin suggests. "And you know how they view Black Angels that aren't locked up—they're like goddesses to the Immortal."

"She can't pull it off," Alex states bluntly. "She's too reserved and weak."

I slug him in the upper arm. Not to prove a point, but because he's pissed me off. "I'm not weak. I've put up with a lot of shit over my lifetime."

He winces a little and then his fingers cover his arm. He scans up my legs, my dress, my neck and lips, finally stopping at my eyes. "You really think you can go in there and pretend like you're a powerful, domineering, Angel from hell."

I nod, even though doubt floods my body. "Ycs."

It is such a lie, but he buys it. Or maybe he just decides not to care so much about me and care more about the sword. "Fine. We'll hang out on the bottom floor in the club area, next to the stairway. Aislin and Laylen you'll go up and get the Goddamn sword." Laylen starts to open the door when Alex reaches forward and snags the collar of his shirt. His eyes go dark and his voice comes out in a low growl. "If you're up to something, I'll get the sword myself and use it on you."

Aislin's eyes widen and so do mine. Laylen stares at Alex inexpressively and then nods his head once. Only then, does Alex release him. As I climb out of the car, I know I'm in over my head. Vampires. Witches. Werewolves. Hell's Angels. No matter how many supernatural books I've read, it's a hell of a lot different than real life.

THE MOON ILLUMINATES against the alley and lights up the puddles on the ground. The air reeks of mold and wet dogs, and the garbage cans ooze filth onto the ground that crunches beneath my shoes.

Laylen stops in front of a rusty door at the back end of a warehouse and holds his fist to the door. "Is everyone ready for this?"

"Probably not." Alex gestures his hand at the door. "But let's get it over with."

Laylen lets his hand fall against the door. A couple of seconds later a small flap at the top of the door glides open and a pair of dark eyes peer out. "What's the password?"

Laylen elevates his forearm up to the flap. The flap slips shut and is followed by the sounds of several locks clicking. The hinges creak as the door swings open. Behind it is a man shorter than me with bony arms and greasy black hair. He's dressed in black jeans, a jacket and across his neck is the same tattoo as Laylen has on his arm.

"What does that mark mean on his neck," I whisper to Alex.

He leans toward me, keeping his voice low and his arms crossed over his chest. "It's the Mark of Immortality."

I'm shocked, but I know I have to remain centered. I'm supposed to be in control, strong, and dominant. I straighten my posture and cross my arms, like I'm the toughest girl . . . Angel in the world.

Laylen greets the man by nodding once. "Doug. How's it going, man?"

Doug mutters an unfriendly, "It's goin' good. Haven't seen you in a while." He takes the three of us in with a skeptical look. "Who are they?"

Laylen plays it cool with his gaze steadfast on Doug. "They're with me."

Doug raises an accusing eyebrow. "They got the mark."

Laylen braces his arm against the wall. "Look, I know you let people in here without the mark. In fact, there's a feeding ground upstairs."

Feeding ground. I'm definitely in over my head. Alex must have sense my apprehension, too, because he laces his fingers with mine.

"I don't know what you're talking about." Doug steps back inside and starts to shut the door.

Laylen sticks his hand out and slams his palm against the door, holding it open. "You can't have double standards Doug. I know you let mortals in."

Doug narrows his eyes. "Let go of the fucking door, before I break your arm off."

I start to laugh because the idea of a tiny man like Doug breaking Laylen's arm off seems ludicrous, but I stop when Laylen lowers his arm swiftly and darts back.

Doug begins to shut the door again when Aislin marches forward.

"Somno iam!" she exclaims as her arm snaps out in front of her.

Doug groans as he clutches at his heart and then his eyes roll back into his head. "You . . ." His body goes rigid, his shoulders jerk upward and his knees lock. His body aligns in a perfectly straight line before he falls backward and hits the floor.

Aislin lowers her hand back to the side and a huge grin expands across her face. "See, we're going to be okay."

Laylen nods his head and his eyes widen. "Well, alright, I guess that works."

Aislin hops over the unconscious Doug and Laylen follows after her. When he is inside, he bends down and hooks his arms underneath Doug's. Then, with a grunt, he drags him inside and Alex and I walk freely through the doorway. Once we are all in, Laylen slams the door and fastens the locks.

"Okay," Laylen says and heads toward a brick archway on the other side of the room. "Let's make this quick before someone either finds him or he wakes up."

We walk down a slender hallway extending from the archway, Laylen and Aislin in front, Alex and I in the back. I notice the metal lanterns that hang on the stone walls have the Immortality mark on them. I'm catching on that this is an all-exclusive Immortal club with a feeding ground upstairs, but, even with that concept, nothing could ever prepare me for what I walk into.

At the end of the hall, the area opens up into a large, but crowded room. Lanterns dangle from the ceiling, fueled by fire, not electricity. The red ceiling lights sparkle across the marble floor and there's a balcony above with a spiral staircase twisting up to it and connecting the two floors. That's the easy part to take in. It's the lower half that is intense.

There's a dance floor in the middle of the room and it's crammed with people, swaying hypnotically to the low beat of *Deftones* "Change." They're tall, short, fat, and thin; some have pale skin and other's scaly skin. There are fangs coming out of people's mouth and fur growing on their bodies. They are touching each other, drinking; some are half naked, shirts off, wearing clothes that barely cover any skin.

In each of the four corners of the room, there are life-size, iron-rod birdcages. Trapped inside the cages are the most beautiful women I've ever seen. Their legs are extensive, their skin smooth and their lips a pale blue. Black-feathered wings sprout from their shoulder blades and a whip curls up their arms. Each has a black leather dress on that resembles mine and their hair is as black as ash. They are twirling around a pole in the center of the cage and with each movement, I feel a pull towards them; they are hypnotic. Several people around the room seem mesmerized by them, like they feel the pull too.

"They're Black Angels," I say over the music as I turn to Alex. I'm surprised to find that he's watching me intently. "Aren't they?"

He nods once. "They are."

I peer over my shoulder. "I don't know why you guys think I look like them. They have wings and they move so confidently, like they own everyone. They're so . . . beautiful."

"The one's that walk outside their cages don't have wings." He sketches a line between my shoulder blades and my body counters with a shudder. "And the last part you'll be fine with. It's the middle I'm worried about." He waits to see if I catch on to his hidden meaning.

I do, but remain composed because that's what I'm supposed to be doing.

"We should get this over with," Laylen says, removing his cell phone from his pocket. "If anything at all happens, we'll text each other."

Alex nods and then Aislin and Laylen start to head across the dance floor, but Alex catches Aislin by the arm. "Wait, how are you guys going to get it out without being noticed?"

Aislin's eyes twinkle and she snaps her fingers. "It's called magic."

He lets her go and she follows Laylen as he shoves his way through the crowd and onto the dance floor. Seconds later, the crowd swallows them.

Alex immediately snatches ahold of my hand and steers me toward the bar that's next to the dance floor and off center with the stairway. We can't see the bottom because of all the people, but I can see the rest of it. I keep my eyes glued to it, even when people run into me; trusting Alex to lead the way. When I see Laylen and Aislin emerge onto the midsection of the stairway, I relax and allow myself a quick glance around the room.

There are people and creatures in booths eating dinner, at the bar ordering shots. A lot of attention is magnetized toward me; quick glances from some of them, but others rudely stare. I adjust my shoulders higher and move to Alex's side because it seems like a domineering move. We walk up to the bar together and Alex pulls out a barstool for me.

I sit down, swing my legs to the front and rest my arms on the transparent countertop that shows the alcohol bottles lined up underneath it, along with a vat of red, thick liquid. I pretend I'm okay. Completely in control. Until the bartender strolls up and I'm reminded just how naïve I am.

"What can I getcha?" He's tall with wide-ranging shoulders and there is a tiny mole just above his lip that I can't take my eyes off of.

All my innocence shines through. "Umm . . . What are the choices?"

"Two shots of vodka." Alex pats his hand on the counter.

The bartender nods and swings a rag over his shoulder as he backs away. He doesn't take his eyes off me until he's at the back counter and has to turn around to collect the glasses.

Alex leans over in the stool. "Just knock it back quickly and try not to choke."

I bend my body to the side until our heads are touching. "Can't I just *not* drink?"

Alex shakes his head and gives a quick glance at the stairway. "Act tough, remember?"

Drinking is tough? Or maybe he wants me to do it for another reason? Sighing, I turn toward the counter and then jump when I come face to face with the creepy bartender. It takes a lot to shove down the scream in my throat.

His face is only inches away from mine. "You one of them, ain't ya?"

"Wouldn't you like to know?" My voice comes out steady and I do an internal happy dance.

"I very much would like to know." He relocates back just a little and sets two tall shot glasses down on the counter. They're filled with a clear liquid that smells like

195

gasoline. "In fact, I'd put money on it." When I say nothing, he backs away with a sly grin on his face.

I swivel in the barstool, freeing a loud breath. The music is loud enough that it goes unnoticed, though. "What a weirdo."

Alex picks up a shot glass. "Take a look around Gemma. This place is full of nothing but weirdoes." He raises the glass to his lips and angles his neck back, sucking out the drink in one long gulp. His neck muscles move as he swallows it, then he lowers the glass and sets it back on the counter.

As weird as it is, I've never drank before. I put the glass to my lips, hold my breath and tip my chin up, letting the drink spill into my mouth and flood my throat. It feels like acid ripping away at my esophagus and stomach muscles. I seal my lips shut, forcing myself to choke it down as I drop the glass down on the counter. I can't breathe. Can't think. My blood and my heart flare with potent heat. "Why the fuck did you have me drink that?" I mutter through a soft gag.

"Breathe," he whispers, glancing around the room with his arms crossed. "Or you're going to black out."

I inhale through my nose and it makes my lips stutter. The choke and burn propel up my throat and I start to lean forward to hack. Alex meets me in the middle, rendering me motionless with a touch of his hand on my arm. He pushes me upright, makes me sit up straight, then he bends forward and suddenly his lips are on mine. At first, I think he's trying to hurt me because his mouth is pressed against mine so hard it feels like the skin is going to bruise. He's strong. And fierce. His hands come down on my hips and he jerks me forward as his tongue slips into my mouth. The taste of him inside my mouth smothers the alcohol and I still can't breathe, but for a whole different reason.

He continues kissing me, grabbing at strands of my hair so he can tip my head back and devour my mouth, but as quickly as it starts, it strikes a dead end as his lips leave mine without forewarning.

"Let's dance," he breathes demandingly and I'm confused because I thought that I'm the one who's supposed to be domineering.

I don't protest, though, as he guides me to my feet and directs me toward the dance floor. I try to stay next to him, but the tightness of the dress limits my legs' mobility. I also feel dizzy and my limbs are kind of heavy. Walking suddenly seems to be the most complex thing in the world and, after a lot of staggering, he finally wraps his arm around my back to support me.

As we reach the crowd, I tuck in my elbows, but then put them back out, not wanting to seem intimidated. He shoves through the people that smell like sweat, as well as rust, and when we finally arrive in the middle, he stops. There's a blond girl to my right with fangs poking out of her mouth and she's dancing with a guy that has pointy ears. To my left, is a woman with purple hair made of thick strands that have heads with eyes at the end.

"I *did* see someone with snakes for hair." I utter to Alex. "That night at the cabin."

He stands in front of me with his eyes fastened on the stairway just over my shoulder. "Yeah, you shouldn't have been able to see that."

"Why not?"

"I'll explain why in the car." There's a silent cautioning in his eyes, so I zip my lips and shuffle closer to him as I'm elbowed in the back and the side. It's overwhelming;

too many people and too many sexy moves going on. I'm struggling to remain collected.

Luckily, the song switches to a slower, more sensual beat and everyone mellows to grind against each other. I'm not sure what to do or why we are out here, but Alex takes the lead. He puts his hand on my hip and lures me to him with his eyes on me. He slides his hand slowly up my side, along my ribs and to my shoulders where it starts to drift downward. His skin is searing hot against my arm and when he arrives at my wrist I practically die from the heat. He grips my wrist forcefully; pressing his fingers into my skin, then lifts my arm up and positions my hand on top of his shoulder.

My body is very much alive, awake and in tune when he does the same thing with my other arm. I can't hold back the moan of pleasure clawing up my throat. I let it out because there's nothing else to do.

The muscles in his jaw twitches as he places his hands on my hips and entices me toward him until our bodies are connected. He begins swaying us to the music and rubbing against me with each movement. His green eyes are black below the inadequate lighting and his lips are blood red. He inches his mouth toward my ear and breathes against my skin. "The bartender was on to you. I had to find a way to get you out of there."

"By kissing me?" I ask, breathless.

His fingertips knead my hips. "That was to get you to stop choking." He pulls back a little. "And the dancing is to get you into the crowd and away from wandering eyes. You stand out way too much."

I glance at the blond girl with fangs and she's nipping at pointy-eared guy's neck. He lets out a groan similar to the one I let out just seconds ago. "I think I blend in pretty well," I say.

His brow teases upward. "Oh, yeah?"

"Yeah." I slip my hands farther up his shoulders and down to his back. When my palms are covering his shoulder blades, I dig my nails in and pull him closer. "In fact, I think I have this whole Angel thing down pretty well."

He shakes his head, grinning haughtily. "You'd be screwed if I wasn't here to guide you through."

"If you weren't here, then I wouldn't be here." My head is getting hazy and uncensored words are slipping out of my mouth.

He frowns. "I know that."

He grows quiet, takes a step back to add room between us, and his attention leaves me as his eyes drift to the stairway. It bugs me because I want them on me. I want him to look at me. Touch me. Be only about me. I'm becoming very needy and the feeling consumes me.

I hook a finger underneath his chin and make him look at me. "I thought you brought me out here to dance?"

His eyebrows dip together. "No, I brought you out here to keep you hidden and to keep an eye on the stairway."

I shake my head and scratch him with my nails as I draw my hand away. "I want to dance, just like everyone else."

His eyes go squinty as he scrutinizes my facial features and eyes. "Are you drunk?"

I shake my head with sureness even though I have no idea what being drunk feels like. "No, I'm perfectly sober."

"Good because you only had one shot."

"Obviously."

He shakes his head and I clamp down on his shoulders and force him to diminish the space he's put between us. His eyes enlarge and his lips part in shock. Without another thought, I bend my head forward and collide our lips. The music is loud and drenches my body in lyrics as I bask in the taste of him. My head spins with vapor as I suck his lip into my mouth. He groans loudly, and I bite down on his lip and let my hands trail down his back with my nails aiming downward so I'm gently scratching his skin.

"Gemma," he murmurs as his hand moves from my hip to my back, then creeps downward. He cups my ass and crushes my body against his. I'm drowning in blackness and he is my air.

I seal our lips together and his tongue willingly slips into mine. I feel his breath enter my mouth and the compulsion for more takes over me. My hands glide up his back and I fasten my arms around his neck. I taste him thoroughly as I stand on my tiptoes and climb on top of him. His breath hitches in his throat as I hook my legs around his midsection, allowing his hardness to press against me. It's stimulating and makes my body crave more, so I cling onto him and writhe my hips up and down, rubbing up against him.

A deep, throaty groan escapes from him and he reciprocates by pushing his body closer to mine. His hand slip between my legs and his eyes are shut, but mine refuse to close. I can see everything. Feel everything. I'm high. I'm centered. I'm in control.

People are dancing recklessly and it's like we're in a movie that's stuck on fast forward; none of it can be real. Alex is kissing me, feeling me, touching me and making me feel like I've been starved. My arms begin to tremble and when I glance down at them, my skin is covered in black veins like tar has replaced my blood. The veins are crawling across my skin and I start to scream. I'm falling.

Floating. What am I doing?

Alex jerks back and his lips are moving, but I can't hear what he's saying. I unhitch my jaw to speak, but my voice is noiseless. My eyes roll into the back of my head and my limbs go limp. I begin to sink to the ground and I'm not sure how far down it is before I hit.

Or, if I'll ever hit anything.

Maybe I just fall and fall and fall.

CHAPTER
THIRTEEN

I'M DROWNING IN a black ocean and the clouds above rain ash. The water is hot and my skin is covered in blisters. It's burning me alive and filling my lungs with venom. I'm dying. I'm . . .

"Can you hear me?" Alex's voice floats through my dream of death.

My eyes roll into the back of my head as my eyelashes flutter open. My head is resting on Alex's lap and the streetlights outside highlight the concern on his face. He has a bite mark just below his lip and long red marks on his neck.

"Where am I?" My voice is hoarse.

He lets out a sigh of relief. "Thank God."

"Is she going to be okay?" Aislin asks.

I realize we're in the backseat of the GTO and that she is in the passenger seat. There's a scratch on her forehead, two holes in her neck and her hair has fallen out of the pins.

"Why do you have bite marks on your neck? And why does Alex have those red lines on his?" I begin to sit up and my brain throbs against my skull. I press the heel of my hand to my forehead and wince. "Ow."

"Lie back down," Alex insists and guides me back down onto his lap. "Don't try to sit up until we know you're okay."

"What happened?" I ask, situating my head into his lap. "And where's Laylen?"

"Laylen went into the Wicca shop to check things out before we all go in." He brushes my hair away from my forehead. "And what happened is someone slipped you a sensualis augendae."

"What the hell is that?" My voice cracks. "A date rape drug?"

He shakes his head and then hesitates. "Not a drug, but a spell."

"So someone put a date rape spell on me? I bet it was the bartender."

"It could have been a lot of people. There was too much attention on you and . . . well, like I said, you radiate innocence. I should have never brought you in there."

"How did you get me out?"

"Carried you . . . Can't you remember? You put up quite a fight."

My eyes enlarge as my mind sifts through the cloudy images of what happened. I'd been all over him, practically attacked him. "I scratched your neck, didn't I?"

He covers the lines with his hand. "Yeah, but don't worry about it."

"I'm so sorry." I reach out to touch his neck.

He lowers his hand and lets my fingers graze the lines. "I said, don't worry about it. Trust me. It wasn't bad." The look in his eyes and the huskiness of his voice makes me wonder if he thinks it was good.

I fix my attention to Aislin and the holes in her neck.

There's dried blood around each one and the skin has a ring of red around it. "Did you get bitten?'

She sighs deeply. "Yeah, we ended up running into Draven. Luckily, it was after I made the sword invisible with a charm, but, still, there are consequences for me being up there."

"Because you're human?"

"Because I'm a Keeper."

"Oh . . . So he bit you as a punishment?" I summon my energy and drag my body upright, sliding my feet off the seat and onto the floor. I feel like it's partially my fault for not being able to play a good Black Angel and getting poisoned. "Aislin, I'm so sorry."

She covers her mouth and clears her throat, squirming uncomfortably. "It's okay. It wasn't that bad."

I glance back and forth between Alex and Aislin; finally Alex explains, "Vampire bites are intoxicating to mortals. The only punishment from a bite is that you'll want more."

My mouth forms an 'o.' Aislin nods, then faces the front of the cab and stares at the small, brick building with a crescent moon outlined by a black star painted on the window. I notice that there is the same mark on the back of Aislin's shoulder.

"What is that on your shoulder?" I ask. "A tattoo, or a mark, like Laylen's?"

"It's doesn't represent the same thing as Laylen's." She sketches the outline of the tattoo with her finger. "But it is a mark—the witch's mark. After I became a witch, it appeared there." She lifts her foot onto the console and flips the ceiling light on. On her ankle there is a ring of golden flames that trims a black circle. "And this one appeared because I have Keeper blood inside me."

"And they just all of a sudden show up?" I ask, gripping my head. "Out of the blue?"

"My Keeper's mark appeared when I was about twelve, which was also about the same time I really started learning about what it means to be a Keeper." Aislin returns her foot to the floor. "And my witch's mark showed up when I was about fifteen, which was when I first found out I possess Wicca magic."

"So everyone has their own mark?"

"Oh yeah, there are a ton of them. One for vampires, pixies, fey, Foreseers . . ." She trails off as she takes in the shocked look on my face. "Oh, yeah, I guess I should have started out by explaining that, yes, those things do exist."

I nod as I lower my hand from my head. "I just didn't realize how true it all is."

Alex leans forward to capture my gaze. "How true what is?"

I turn to face him. "Everything I've read. I thought all of the creatures were just made up."

His lips tug up into a small smile. "Books are like a gateway to real life."

"I guess so." I bend my neck and rest my head on the back of the seat. "So how many marks do you have?"

He eyes me perceptively. "I just have the Keepers' mark."

I tuck my hair behind my ear, remembering how I saw it when he answered the door shirtless back at his apartment. "Oh yeah, the one on the side of your ribs."

He brings his leg up on the seat as he turns his body toward me. A sly grin spreads across his face. "If you need a refresher, I can show you it again."

"Okay." I blame the eager response on the remains of the Rufi magic spell inside my body.

"Alex," Aislin hisses. "What are you doing?"

"Get out of the car if you don't want to see," he says without taking his eyes off me.

"No way," she refuses. "If I get out, you two will probably screw each other on the backseat."

In the snap of a finger, Alex goes from hot to cold. He slumps back into the seat and his Adam's apple bobs up and down as he swallows hard. I come to the conclusion right then that maybe Alex suffers from a bipolar disorder. He's so emotionally erratic. First, he hates me. Then, he kisses me, touches me, and makes me moan. Sometimes, I irritate him. Sometimes, he's teasing me.

Aislin heaves a huge sigh of relief. "Oh good, we can go in."

I track her gaze to the front of the store and Laylen is beneath the entry waving us in. None of us speak as we climb out and enter the store, which fortunately doesn't have any costumers but us.

The air smells like sage, as well as oregano, and the black and white checkerboard floor has the witch's mark painted in the middle. Glass counters border the walls that display jewelry, candles, and incense. On the shelves, behind the counter, there are creepy, almost disturbing objects. The worst is a statue of a naked man and woman kneeling down in front of each other. Extending out of the woman's back is a large spider with a set of fangs aimed at the man's head.

Aislin browses the room, trailing her fingers along the glass. "Where's Adessa?"

"She'll be down in just a minute." Laylen relaxes against a display case and his eyes wander to me. "You doing okay?"

I nod, feeling embarrassed because he knows—

everyone knows—that I basically tried to rape Alex in the middle of the club. But Alex didn't seem too eager to stop me either.

I walk around the room, wondering what it means. Had he been under a spell or did he really just want me? I come across a small glass ball filled with violet ribbons positioned in a stand. I peer down inside it, curious if I'll see my future. Maybe I'm a Foreseer, although that can't be true. I don't have a mark.

"If you're not careful, you might get stuck inside that." Alex suddenly appears by my side and I jump, startled. "It's a Foreseer's crystal ball."

I throw my hand over my accelerating heart. "Jesus! You scared the shit out of me." I catch my breath and glance back at the ball. "So, this is what they look into to see the future."

He nods and flicks his fingers against the crystal ball. "But they have to go inside to see the future. So please be careful. We don't want you getting stuck in one."

I lower my hand from my chest. "But I'm not a Foreseer."

"Yeah, but you're . . . different. I'm afraid the power inside you might set it off." He raps his fingers on the crystal ball again. "In fact, you probably shouldn't touch anything in here at all."

"Including the floor," I say with acerbity. "Because that seems like it would be very tricky."

"That does sound pretty tricky." He leans in toward me and drops his voice. "I think you know that's not what I meant, so quit being a smartass."

"Why? You're being an ass." I inch forward and invade his personal space and am rewarded with gratification when he jolts from the sparks that overwhelms us.

"I don't understand. One minute you're being nice to me and the next you're being a jerk."

"That's because I'm conflicted," he states, touching the scratches on his neck.

"About what?"

"About doing what I want and what's right."

I'm about to ask him what he wants to do, but a woman stoops through the beaded entryway and steps into the room. She's around thirty-years-old or so with cat-shaped eyes and her black hair flows to her waist and curls up at the ends. She wears a blue velvet dress, large hooped earrings, an array of metal bracelets, and her skin is the color of honey.

"It's so nice to meet you all. I'm Adessa, the owner of this store and a second generation witch." Her voice is smooth like silk. "Laylen told me that one of you is a witch yourself and is looking for a Vectum Crystal." Her eyes land on me. "And I'm guessing it's you?"

I shake my head and point at Aislin. "No, not me . . . her."

"Hmm . . . that's interesting." She assesses me for a split second longer, and then turns to Aislin. "So, what particular one are you looking for, my dear?"

"Well, I've been using the purple amethyst." Aislin rearranges her golden-brown hair so it will cover up the bite marks on her neck. "But since we have to travel a long distance, I think maybe the gold-leafed one would work better."

Adessa twists the chain of her necklace around her finger. "How long of a distance is it?"

"I think about 500 miles," Aislin says. "Give or take a few."

Adessa unravels the necklace from her finger and

walks behind the counter. "I think I have something that will work even better than the gold one." She tips her chin up and draws an invisible rectangle in the air with her finger. One of the shelves flattens into the wall and disappears. My mouth drops agape as a door appears in its place. Adessa flicks her hand and the door swings open.

"After you," Adessa says to Aislin with a motion of her hand.

Aislin bites down on her lip and tentatively steps inside. Adessa follows her, then a red light beams throughout the room and the door slams shut.

I'm teetering somewhere between fascination and terror. "Magic blows my mind."

"If you think that's fascinating, then wait until you start traveling to other cities and worlds." Laylen strolls up beside me and rests his arm on the countertop.

I hop up onto the counter and cross my legs. "Other cities and worlds?"

He unfastens the clip on his leather watch and resizes the band. "Yeah, like the City of Crystal. The Underworld."

"The Afterlife." Alex strolls up on the other side of me with a look of possessiveness in his eyes.

"The Afterlife?" I ask, tugging the bottom of my dress down. "Like, The Land of the Dead."

"Kind of." He slides his arm along the counter until it touches my hip. I guess he's conflicted again, but I wonder if he's doing what's right, or what he wants. Maybe the Keepers are making him get close to me. The thought nearly strangles me. I want him to want me, just like the song says.

"There are a lot of worlds for the dead," Laylen says and hops up onto the counter beside me. He lets his long legs dangle to the floor as he nudges me playfully with his elbow. "One day, I'll have to explain them all to you."

Alex unexpectedly places a hand on my thigh and he draws me closer to him. "If she has questions, she can ask me."

Laylen gives him an innocent look. "What's the matter, Alex? Afraid she'll hear the truth?"

Alex grinds his teeth and grips onto my leg harder. Laylen looks amused as he hops off the counter and then walks toward the other side of the room. "That's what I thought," he calls out.

Alex keeps hold of my leg, but stays quiet. I try to pretend that it isn't making me think dirty thoughts, but there are so many sensations running between my legs that I'm pretty sure I could have an orgasm at any moment.

I need a distraction. "Why did Adessa think I was the witch?" My voice sounds raspy.

Alex gives me no relief as he slips his hand higher onto my thigh. "Probably because of your eyes."

I absentmindedly touch the corner of my eye. "Are they that weird?"

"They're weird," he says as his hand brushes the hem of my dress. "But in a good way." His fingers slip underneath the leather. "They're mesmerizing."

Sparks kiss my entire body, from my toes to my legs to my neck, and my back begins to curve forward. I think it will stop him, but instead he glances over at Laylen who is distracted by a box on one of the shelves. Then he delves higher until his fingers touch the edge of my panties.

"I can't stop with you." There's a plea in his voice, like he's begging me to make him stop. Like I have that kind of control of the situation. I'm helpless as my legs uncross and my body begins to recline back on the counter. It's disturbing because Laylen is right there and I don't care.

All I want is for his fingers to search a little bit higher.

Alex makes this funny noise in the back of his throat and then my back brushes glass. The crystal ball rolls underneath me and I feel a current rush up my spine and slam into the nape of my neck.

Alex's eyes bulge as his nails plunge into me. "Noooo!"

I feel my body being pulled into pieces, each limb disconnecting from my center, as I'm sucked away into a blanket of darkness.

CHAPTER
FOURTEEN

I 'M FALLING, DEEP and fast into an unknown place. Maybe it's an abyss and I'll never reach an end. Fear consumes me as I realize that I might spend the rest of my life falling.

A white light abruptly appears below my feet. As I plunge closer, it begins to shimmer like glass hitting the sunlight, brighter and brighter until it becomes so vibrant I have to shut my eyes. I tuck my knees to my chest as warmth swathes me. Then, I suck in a breath as my knees slam into the ground and plunge into moist dirt and grass.

My body flips forward and my face lands in the grass. My knees feel bruised, but I leap to my feet and take in the scenery. Orange and pink leaves skip across the grass, which stretches for miles until it reaches the trees. There's also a lake and the water shimmers in the sunlight. The place is strangely familiar, but I can't quite figure out why. It's the same sensation I had when I drifted to the field with the mother and daughter. Was that what that was? A vision, like this? There hadn't been a crystal ball, though.

I check to make sure my stitches are okay when a streak of purple whizzes by and I jump back with my hand against my heart. A little girl, wearing a purple dress, runs up to the shore of the lake and spins in the sand. She's around four or five-years-old with long brown hair flapping in the wind. She kind of reminds me of the girl in the field. Her face is distorted by a haze.

"Don't get too close to the lake," a voice calls out from behind me.

I whirl around just as a boy runs past me with his arms stretched outward. He looks to be a few years older than the little girl. He has dark brown hair and his face is blurry also.

"You need to be careful," he warns. "You don't want to fall in."

"Don't worry," the little girl replies, teeter-tottering at the edge of the water. "I'll be careful."

"Please, just move away," he begs with his hand extended out to her. "You don't know how to swim."

She takes ahold of his hand and he leads her away from the lake. "You always save me."

"I don't understand," I mutter.

"You two, get over here right now!" The sound of a man's voice makes the color of the land around me dim and the hairs on my arms stand on end. He's tall, husky, with jet-black hair similar to Marco's. He wears a black button-down shirt, grey slacks and has a gold chain around his neck. And like the children, his face is also obscured.

He marches with confidence, each stride firm and in control. He's intimidating and disturbs my nerves. "It's time to go," his voice ices out at the children. "Get your asses back to the castle."

"Where are we going?" the girl asks as she clutches onto the boy's hand.

"That's none of your business!" the man bellows. "You never ask me questions. Do you understand?"

I hear the soft tread of approaching footsteps and then a slender figure dashes by me. She has long brown hair and she's wearing a floral dress. I think it might be the mother and daughter from the field.

She scoops the girl up in her arms and hugs her protectively. "You stay the hell away from her!" she shouts at the man.

Her presence brings warmth to the darkness the man instilled and the two combine to create a recipe of emotions that makes me nauseous. I squat down to the ground, feeling like I'm going to throw up.

"This is not your decision," the man snaps and, in two long strides, is standing in her face. "You knew when she was born that this would have to happen one day."

"Mommy, I'm scared," the girl whispers as she buries her head into her mother's shoulder.

The mother smoothes back the girl's hair and kisses the top of her head. "It's going to be okay, sweetie. You don't need to be scared. I promise I won't let anything happen to you."

"I'd like to see you try." The man turns to the boy and points his finger at a hill. "Go inside, right now."

The boy glances from the man to the girl, torn on what to do. "I don't want to."

"Don't you dare mouth off to me!" the man shouts and the skin on his neck tints red. "Now, get your ass inside!"

"Sorry, sir." The boy's voice shakes as he bows his head and trudges up the hill toward a grey stoned castle with lofty towers and a peaking roof that stretches high into the clouds.

The man reels back to the woman. "Now, we can do

this the easy way or the hard way."

She stands defiantly, holding her daughter in her arms as she steps back. "You aren't taking her anywhere. She's my daughter, not yours. You don't own everything in this world."

"Bullshit I don't." He pauses and the woman continues to back away. "So it's going to be the hard way, then." He lunges at the woman and steals the little girl from her arms, even though the girl kicks and hits at him.

The woman screams as she reaches her arms out toward her daughter, but the man draws out a knife from his pocket and she freezes.

"You wouldn't dare," she whispers with her fists balled at her sides. "You need her too much."

The man aligns the sharp point of the knife closer to the girl's neck. "Hurting her won't make her useless, just scarred."

"Don't hurt her," the mother begs, clasping her hands in front of her.

The girl hovers back from the knife. "Momma, help me."

Keeping a hold of the knife, the man reaches into his other pocket and pulls out a small black bag. "Or, if you want, I can use this?" He tips his head down at the girl. "Hey, sweetie, how would you like to go for a swim in the lake?"

The girl shrinks back. "But I can't swim."

"You'll be fine," the man coaxes as he begins to untie the bag. "Someone will be there to help you."

"Knock it off!" the mother screams and storms towards them. "She's just a little girl. And—and if you put her there, then you can't get her back."

The man laughs, throwing his head back, and shoves

the woman back. "There are ways to get her back when I need her. She would probably be better off down there, anyway, until it's time."

The woman stumbles, but quickly stands back up. "Please don't do this. *Please*."

"Oh, I won't; just as long as you get into the lake yourself," the man says. "I'm giving you a choice. It's either *you* or her."

I leap to my feet. Go in the lake! Why!? Was he going to try and drown her? Fighting down the vomit burning at the back of my throat, I walk towards them.

"You'll never get away with this." Her voice is edging toward hysteria. "I know the real reason why you want her and, sooner or later, someone else is going to figure it out. You'll never be able to get away with it."

"Oh, I highly doubt it. I have everyone wrapped around my little finger." He sets the girl down on the ground, puts the knife out in front of him, and points his finger at the castle. "Go inside now."

She crosses her arms and elevates her chin. "I'm not leaving my mama."

"Go!" the man hollers and crows caw from the trees.

The girl steps forward, getting closer to the man. "You are a very, very bad man."

The man targets the sharp side of the blade at her face. "You think so?"

"Go on inside, sweetie," her mother says and gestures her daughter to go. "It's alright. Everything will be okay."

It takes the girl a second, but she finally lowers her arms, and heads toward the castle. My heart breaks for them, knowing somehow that it will be the last time they'll see each other. The girl will grow up motherless. There will forever be an empty hole in her heart and all she'll want is to feel love, but maybe it will never be possible because this moment will shatter her.

There are so many similarities between the little girl and me, and I wonder if that's why I'm seeing this vision. Am I going to meet the girl one day? Am I supposed to help her?

"Now it's time to deal with you." The man lets a pause drag out as birds caw in the distances and circle above our heads "Get in the lake."

I shake my head. *No.* This can't be happening. I don't want to see this, yet, I can't seem to stop running toward them.

"You've been planning this all along, haven't you?" Her voice quivers as she backs toward the shoreline and the man matches her every step. He has the knife in one hand and the bag in the other. "Every single word that's come out of your mouth has been a lie."

"You know me well. Now quit stalling and get into the lake. Otherwise, I'll have to force you in and that will make the situation unnecessarily painful."

"You're wrong about not getting caught." She reaches the brink of the lake and the waves roll against her ankles. "There are people who you don't have wrapped around your finger."

"Then, I'll have to take care of them as well." He scoops out a handful of what looks like ash from the bag and then sprinkles it into the lake. It makes the water murky and still.

"Don't think you've won." She holds her chin high and submerges her legs into the lake. "Someday, it will all catch up with you."

The water rises to her waist and the lake goes dead calm, like before a storm. The wind stalls and the birds become silent. It's as if every part of nature knows something bad is going to happen. Like me. My legs fight to reach her, but I hear a *swoosh* and then the water splashes up. She plunges under the water, her arms flailing before they disappear. I let out a blood-curdling scream that ripples through the stillness. The man turns his back on the drowning woman and strolls away, whistling some funky tune that sounds like a mix between "It's a Small World After All" and "Twinkle, Twinkle, Little Star."

Without even thinking, I jump into the lake, forcing my legs against the pressure as the cold water ascends higher upon my body. When it reaches my chest, I freeze, suddenly remembering that I can't swim.

I'm about to backtrack when I feel a set of bony fingers wrap around my ankle and I'm jerked beneath the water. I gurgle as water floods my lungs and mouth. My legs and arms battle to find the surface, but the hand pulls me down into the ice-cold water and keeps dragging me deeper until I can't hold my breath anymore.

CHAPTER
FIFTEEN

I GASP FOR air as my eyes shoot open. The first thing I see is Alex's worried face and then Laylen's. I'm lying on the cold, tiled floor of Adessa's store. My skin is dry and my lungs aren't waterlogged. I can breathe again.

I scramble to my feet and then grip the counter when the blood rushes to my head. "What the hell just happened?"

"You touched the Foreseers' ball after I told you not to." Alex's voice shakes slightly. "And you went into a vision just like I said you might."

"It was an accident . . . I was distracted by you trying to . . ." I trail off when I notice that Laylen is listening intently. "Whatever. It doesn't matter." I place my other hand on the counter, trying to control and bury all my emotions; but I can feel each one, like nails being inserted into my heart. He killed her. He made her drown and the girl was left in his hands. What did he do to her when he went back to the castle?

"I can't breathe," I pant as my chest rises and falls violently. "Oh my God, I can't . . . I can't . . ."

"Gemma, look at me." Laylen's voice envelops my

body.

I tip my chin up and meet his eyes, which look like deep pools of water. "If you want me to, I can calm you down." He glances at Alex, checking.

I look to my side and Alex steps into my line of vision. He examines my eyes and he must see something horrifying because he nods at Laylen. "Go ahead, but only this one time."

I turn back to Laylen and he nods, then places a hand on my shoulder. "Are you okay with it?"

I'm not exactly sure what he's going to do to me, but it has to be better than the invisible nails in my heart. "Go ahead. Please."

He rests his other hand on my other shoulder and then positions his body in front of me. He slides his hands up my neck, rests them on my cheeks and hunches over so he's at eye level with me. "It'll be just like on the porch, only . . . less sensual."

I swallow hard. "Okay."

He wets his lips with his tongue and shakes his head so his bangs are out of his eyes. "Now close your eyes."

Giving one last glance at Alex, I let my eyes close. Images of water and the woman drowning instantly overpower my head, but they fade as tranquility flows down my body. It's like I'm being kissed all over and those kisses erase every single place the vision has taken in my soul. I'm being healed, sewn back together again. My emotions belong to me.

"Let your heart settle," Laylen whispers. "And your body relax."

I give into his instructions and my knees start to buckle. His hand winds around my back and he braces me against his chest. I feel his lips brush my hair and then he says, "Take her to the car."

I don't know who he's talking to, but, seconds later, an arm slides behind me and I'm being scooped up into someone's arm and a current drowns me. I relax against his sturdy chest and let him take me wherever. I'm calm. I'm all right.

I hear the bell go off as we exit the store, and then cool night air hits me. The car door squeaks open and he stops moving, leans forward and sets me gently onto the backseat. The leather is cool against my skin and I roll to my side, ready to go to sleep.

The seat sinks next to my feet and the door slams shut. I know he's in the car with me, but he remains silent. "Are you going to be okay?" he finally asks.

I open my eyes, even though I don't want to. I haven't slept in ages and I want to sleep. "I think so."

His gaze is consuming, even in the dark. "Can I . . . Can I ask you what you saw? In the vision?"

Sighing, I push myself up and put my feet on the floor. There's a gap between us and I don't try to reduce it. I give him a recap of every detail I can remember from the vision and Laylen's magical touch keeps me at peace through the entire journey.

"You know you were really lucky, right?" Alex mutters when I finish.

I'm perplexed. "Lucky how?"

He props his boot up on his knee and stares ahead at the street. "For one thing, I've heard stories about people getting stuck inside visions and never returning; and, for another, because you didn't get captured by the Water Faerie."

"Water Faerie?" My dress is crooked and I raise my hips to realign it back into place. "Okay, that needs explaining."

He glances at my hips as I lower my ass back to the seat. "It's what pulled you and the woman down in the lake. Water Fey are the Guardians of the Underworld."

"The Underworld?" I ask. "As in, the place where the Greeks believed people went after they died?"

"Close." He seems hesitant to embellish. "But it's not exactly the same." He takes a deep breath and keeps his eyes ahead. "The Underworld is the land of the dead. It's also a prison. After the Keepers capture someone like, say for instance, a vampire that has been on a killing spree, we sentence them to a life in the Underworld as a punishment."

I question why he uses a vampire as his example, perhaps as a jab at Laylen. "But why wouldn't you just kill them instead? It makes more sense that way and it seems like a far worse punishment."

He shakes his head. "Trust me. Death is an easier punishment than getting sent down there. Most go insane from the torture within a few weeks."

"Wait a minute." I pause, drinking in the knowledge he gives me and I connect it with what I know. "Does that mean the woman I saw get dragged into the lake is going to end up in the Underworld?"

"Maybe," he answers with unwillingness. "The Water Faeries usually don't kill the people. They are under strict orders to take whatever they catch straight to the prison."

"But, why do they want prisoners?"

"Because they feed off the prisoners' fear. It's what keeps them thriving, even in their dead form."

I hug my arms around myself. Nausea is starting to mix with the tranquility Laylen put in me. "So, if the vision I saw really ends up happening, then the woman's going to end up being tortured down in the Underworld."

"Maybe." He sighs, and then moves his foot off his knee and to the floor. "I'd like to believe the future can be changed, especially since we're trying to do that with the star and the portal."

"What if it doesn't change?" I whisper. "Then what?"

"Depending on how strong she is, she could survive the torture for up to a few years without it driving her mad. But once she loses her mind, the Queen will have her killed."

"What Queen?"

"The Queen of the Dead. She's in charge of everything that goes on in the Underworld. After a prisoner goes insane, they no longer produce the right kind of fear for her people to feed off of, so she gets rid of them."

I feel like banging my head on the window, but my body is too drained to move toward it. "That's the most ruthless thing I've ever heard."

"You have to understand that most of the creatures we send down there have committed horrible deeds," he explains. "The kind of crimes that haunt people's nightmares."

"Well, considering the Death Walkers have killed me over and over again in my nightmares, I can understand that comparison," I say.

His head gradually turns toward me, but he doesn't look at me. Instead he looks over my shoulder at the window. "You never mentioned before that they killed you."

I sit up straight and move my face into his line of vision, trying to get him to look at me. "I didn't think I needed to give you the details."

"I always want you to give me the details," he says and closes his eyes. "Always."

Why won't he look at me? "You don't think my nightmares are visions, do you?"

"No, that's not even possible for a Foreseer to do." He opens his eyes and continues to stare over my shoulder at the window. "They have to have the power of the crystal to channel the psychic energy. But Gemma, I'd really like you to give me the details of the nightmares you keep talking about."

He's acting strange, like it hurts him to look at me and be in the car with me. "Well, I want you to give me details, too. About you."

He glances at my face, but then swiftly looks back at the window. "There's not that much to know."

I inch toward the edge of the seat and place myself in his line of vision. "I don't believe that for one second and I have a great idea. You can start off by telling me why you won't look me in the eye."

He blinks several times and finally meets my eyes. "Because I don't like the calm, sleepy look in your eyes."

I rub my eyes with my fingertips. "I'm just really tired. I haven't slept in over twenty-four hours."

"It's not from tiredness." He sighs. "It's from Laylen. He put the look there and I don't like it because you look content and you hardly ever look content."

I drag my bottom lip into my mouth and press my knees together, avoiding his accusation. "Alex, I want to know something about you. Something real. Like maybe why you're so hot and cold all the time? It confuses me."

He shakes his head. "I can't tell you that yet."

"Then tell me something real." I practically beg, because I need things to feel real at the moment, instead of feeling like I'm drowning in a sea of illusions.

He places his hand beside my leg, not touching me,

but close. "The first time I saw you, I was scared."

That isn't what I expected. "You seemed pissed."

"I was pissed, too." He scoots forward and our knees brush. "But pissed at myself for feeling the way that I did—the way that I do." His jaw tightens and then his hand moves to my hip. "I was taught not to feel that way."

My muscles constrict beneath his touch and every ounce of the comfort Laylen put in me singes into ash. "To feel what way?"

His lip part, then he shuts his eyes tightly. "Out of control. Lost. Confused. Terrified. I'm not supposed to let those things get to me." His eyes open and I suck in a breath at the rawness they emit. "You want to know something real about me, Gemma? I'm empty. Dead. Completely numb inside, except for when I'm around you. I'm hot and cold because I try to fight my feelings, because that's what I'm supposed to do—that's the right thing to do."

I think about what he said earlier: *what's right and what he wants.* "Do you want to feel those things though?"

"I want to feel a lot of things." His fingers burrow into my hip and I shudder as heat caresses my skin. He bends his elbow and with one hand pulls me across the seat toward him. When I'm near enough, his free hand grabs my waist; he lifts me up and sits me down on his lap so I'm straddling him. My chest heaves erratically as he traces his finger up my cheekbone and tucks a strand of my hair behind my ear.

His lips dip toward my neck. "Whenever I'm around you, I forget everything else." He doesn't explain if that's good or bad, and I don't get a chance to ask him because his teeth nip at my neck and I forget how to speak.

I bring my hands up to the back of his neck, then slide

them up and tangle them into his hair. His mouth opens and his tongue rolls along my neck. I draw his face closer and lift my hips up and his mouth nears my collarbone. I'm completely ready to go back to the feeling I experienced on the bed in the cabin. I want him to explore me further. I want him to touch me all over, but he gives me a quick kiss and then pulls back. I'm about to object when he picks me up by the waist and I nearly smack my head on the ceiling of the car as he lays me down on the seat. Then he covers my body with his and kisses me hard, stealing my breath away.

When our bodies can't take it any longer, he pulls away and looks down at me as we both pant. I can feel it, just like he said, the numbness in me when I'm not with him being filled and I need more. I move my hands up his muscular arms and the longer I touch him, the more I let go because I let my emotions own me. When I reach his back, I try to force him to me, but he shakes his head in protest.

I frown. "What's wrong?"

His eyes shadow over with a look that sends my body into a fit. He kneels up and grabs my arms roughly. I let him because I want to and that's all that matters. In one quick motion, he pins my wrists together and restrains them above my head. Then he lowers himself back on me as his hand glides down my body. When he reaches the top of my dress, he jerks it down and my breasts spring free. Moments later, his mouth is devouring my nipple, licking it and biting it gently. There are too many emotions inside me; need, want, hunger, panic, fear, connection, serenity. It's potent and amazing to the point of overwhelming.

I arch my back up as my nipples harden and then let my legs fall open. His hand immediately slides down my stomach to the bottom of my dress, then his mouth moves upward, his breath soft on my skin and his lips wet. His other hand keeps my arms pinned up above my head as his fingers slip up my inner thigh. I want to grab him, dig my nails into him and let it all out, but I'm helpless and can only cry out.

"Oh my god." My neck arches as my body curves into him.

He moves his lips from mine and looks me in the eye as his fingers graze the trim of my panties. For a faltering second, I almost tell him to stop. I've never done this before. I've never done anything at all, except with him. I'm deprived in every area of human affection and it's terrifying to think that he's going to be inside me. As he slips his fingers beneath the fabric, the fear and doubt are immediately replaced by this need to find out what it feels like to be alive and connected. He waits long enough for me to stop him before he slides a finger inside me.

"Fuck," he groans and he lowers his mouth to mine as he begins to move his finger.

My nipples brush against his chest with every ragged breath I take and I find myself wishing he had his shirt off so I can feel his skin touching mine. I moan and bite at his lips and he bites back at mine. It feels so good and my hips start to move against him. I can feel it again, the sense of freedom from a world of pain. It's almost within my reach. Right as I'm about to reach it he slips another finger in me and his mouth leaves mine. My lips part as my neck arches and my head tips back. He watches me fall blindly into a feeling I've only experienced with him and I want to stay there. Forever.

As I come back down, he slips his fingers out of me and releases my wrists. I leave my worn-out arms above my head as he props up on his elbows, one on each side of my head. I work to regain control of my breathing and he smoothes my hair back from my damp forehead.

He studies my eyes carefully with a small, smug smile on his lips. "There, now I can look you in the eyes again."

My lips turn upward, but I'm too tired, overwhelmed and drained to speak.

The smile erases from his lips and he lets out a slow sigh. "I'm completely fucked."

I'm not sure what he means. "Why? Because of me?"

He traces my cheekbone with his finger and I will my eyelids to stay open. "Because I wasn't even supposed to become friends with you."

I've yet to understand what the term friend means on a personal level. "Is that what we are? Friends?"

He lets out a soft laugh as his hand strays to my jawline and then to my neck. Repositioning his body slightly to the side, he traces a delicate path down my collarbone to the curve of my breast and then the pad of his thumb grazes my nipple. "We're not even close."

My body quivers underneath his touch and he begins to lower his lips to mine again. God knows what the hell we would have done next if the damn bell on the store's door didn't ding. He jumps off me like I'm made of fire and grabs my arms to aid me upright. I reach for the bottom of my dress to pull it back over my legs and he grabs the top and covers my breasts.

I'm combing my fingers through my hair when the passenger door swings open and the interior lights click on. Aislin climbs into the car, carrying a petite silver box with delicate flower engravings on the frame of it.

"Okay, so we . . ." She trails off when she catches sight of us. "What are you two doing?"

"Sitting here, talking," Alex answers with a nonchalant shrug. "We had a bit of an incident inside and needed a time out."

She eyes me over with accusation. "Gemma looks flushed."

"That's because the accident involved her," Alex says with a blasé attitude and I realize just how good of a liar he is.

"Oh no." She sets the box down on the console. "What happened?"

"I went into a vision," I say, noting the lingering breathlessness in my tone.

"What!" she exclaims so loudly a dog from one of the nearby yards starts howling. She lowers her voice. "You're a Foreseer."

I shrug, but Alex shakes his head. "I don't think so. I think it was the star's power that set it off. You know the divination crystal runs off energy."

"Yeah, but does the star radiate that much power through her? I thought it was controlled inside her."

"Who knows how it works, Aislin. You know nothing's ever happened like her. She's basically a mystery."

The moment of bliss I experienced just seconds ago vanishes as everything catches up with me again. I'm reminded of what I am, what I used to be. I'm reminded of the pain, the desolation, the betrayal. They continue to chat about me like I don't exist and, after a while, I kind of wish I didn't.

Laylen climbs into the car and then we're on the road, heading back to the house. I rest my head against the window and allow exhaustion to take my body as I shut my eyes. I drift to sleep, wondering what my dreams will hold.

CHAPTER
SIXTEEN

I'M PLUMMETING DEEPER into the murky lake; the water smothers my lungs and blinds my eyes. I kick my legs, trying to fight my way to the surface. I refuse to drown. I refuse to die.

"Gemma." A voice floats up from beneath my feet. "Hang on."

I kick harder and paddle my arms, attempting to doggy puddle.

"No, Gemma, down here," the voice comes from below me and I'm overpowered by a comforting feeling. I know whoever it is won't hurt me. I'm supposed to listen to it . . . I'm supposed to go to it. My legs and arms go limp and my dead weight carries me down to the bottom of the lake where tall grass encloses me.

"Good," the voice entices. "Now, I need your help."

For what? I think.

The voice responds inside my head. I need you to save me.

How?

Just trust me.

I trust you. Bubbles float from my mouth.

Good. Now, whatever you do, don't panic.

Why?

A set of fingernails stab into my ankles and I'm being hauled downward again. I panic and claw at the water, but I'm drowning; useless, becoming part of the dead. For a brief, yet very important moment, I don't care.

SOMEONE SHAKES MY shoulder. "Gemma, wake up."

My eyelids snap open, I spring upright, and my head smacks into Alex's. "Don't touch me!"

"Fuck, Gemma." Alex surrenders his hands up in front of him and I pant loudly and hug my legs to my chest. "Calm down."

I eye his hands, then glance around at the vacant front seats of the GTO and then at the shelved walls of Laylen's garage. The interior light is on and the car door is wide open.

"Where are Aislin and Laylen?" I stretch my arms above my head, curl my back in and stretch.

"They're already inside," he says as he reaches around the seat and flips the lever. "Getting things set up for Aislin's spell."

I yawn. "How long have we been sitting out here?"

He pushes the seat forward. "Awhile."

"Why didn't you just wake me up?"

"Because I knew you were tired and I thought I'd let you sleep. In fact, if you want, you can go lie down in one of the spare rooms." He ducks out the door and climbs out of the backseat.

"I think I will." I scoot toward the door and he offers his hand to help me out, but I decline, moving around it, and put my feet onto the cement floor.

"You're mad," he states. "At me?"

I cross my arms over my chest. "Why would I be mad?"

"I have no idea," he says as I proceed towards the steps. "That's why I'm asking."

I twist the knob and push the door open. "I'm not mad. I was just painfully reminded of what and who I am to you."

His fingers encircle my elbow and he stills me. "And what do you think you are to me?"

I look directly into his eyes and utter the truth. "A star."

His fingers prod deeper into my arm, but he presses his lips together, not denying it. I feel my heart fracture down the middle and a tiny fragment chips off. Where it will end up, I don't know.

AFTER I CHANGE out of the leather dress and back into my clothes, which Aislin washed, I go to sleep like Alex suggested. He makes me keep a knife on the nightstand next to the bed in case something happens while he's gone. I find images of cloaked monsters, a glacier world and an eerie lake haunting my head as soon as I shut my eyes and, soon I'm wide awake.

I lie in bed for a while before I force myself to get up. It takes me even longer to decide to go find Laylen, but, finally I tuck the small knife into the back pocket of my jeans and step out into the hall. The house is enormous and it takes a while to find him. He's in a small room with black walls, no windows and a corner lamp. There is a trivial bookshelf in the corner and a stereo is on top of it, playing the soft tune of "Into the Ocean" by Blue October. In the center of the room is a red sofa where Laylen is lying down, reading a book. I feel uncomfortable just walking in so I stand in the doorway, deciding the best way to interrupt him.

He's fully engaged in the book and doesn't seem to notice me. I start to back away, deciding to let him be when he turns the page and calls out, "You can come in, Gemma. I promise I don't bite." He glances at me with a sparkle in his blue eyes. "Then again, maybe I should say that I do. That might entice you to come in."

I press my lips together and step over the threshold. "I'm not that fascinated with biting. Just curious."

He smiles, shuts the book and sets it down on a rectangular table in front of him. Then he sits up, lowers his boots to the floor and pats the spot beside him. I take a seat and he studies me, like I'm a foreign creature.

"What?" I run my fingers through my hair and wipe my face self-consciously. "Do I have something on my face?"

He shakes his head and sucks his lip ring between his teeth. "No, it's just that you look so much like her."

"Like who?"

"Like your mom."

Every single one of my nerves unites with my heart; it bounds in my chest and dispenses eagerness through my body. "You knew her?"

He nods as he pushes up the sleeves of his black shirt. "I did and you look so much like her. Except for the color of your eyes. Hers were blue."

I picture a woman with long brown hair like mine, lengthy limbs and eyes as blue as the sea. "What was she like? No one's ever told me anything about her and I can't remember a single thing."

"She was really nice and she was one of those people who you knew you could trust," he says it like it's the simplest thing in the world to tell me and I decide Laylen might be the one person who can teach me what the term *friend* means. "You really can't remember anything about her?"

I shake my head, bring my feet up onto the couch, and bend my legs to the side of me. "But I was only one when she died."

"No, you weren't," he says with a pucker at his brow. "You were four. Who told you that you were one?"

I pierce my fingers into the palms of my hand until the skin splits open. "Marco and Sophia."

"Why would they do that?" Laylen reclines back in the sofa, pondering. "Why would it make a difference whether you were one or if you were four?"

"Maybe to torture me?" I flop my head on the back of the chair and stare at the ceiling with my hands lifelessly at my side. Is there anything in my life that isn't built on a lie? "I've never understood them or much of what they did, other than they seem to really hate me."

His fingers graze the inside of my wrist. "I'm sorry, Gemma."

I elevate my head and look at him. "You don't need to apologize. It's not your fault it happened."

"That's not completely true." He lets out a stressed sigh and his muscles flex as he folds his arms. "I knew what the Keepers were doing with you and I didn't do anything to stop it."

"You were like, what, eight when all this was going on?" I say. "Besides, it had to be done to me, right? So the world can be saved and all that; or, whatever the fuck the point was?" I loathe the bitterness that drips into my voice.

He's lost in thought, nibbling on his lip ring and making these soft sucking noises. "Maybe, I guess . . . Gemma, what has Alex told you?"

I give him a quick recap of what I've been told. The one thing I keep quiet about, though, is the electricity and what it does to Alex and me. That's just too complicated. And too personal.

"I don't even know what to say," he says when I finish. He gives me a sympathetic look and I feel pathetic. "I'm so sorry. I didn't realize how bad things were for you."

"Again, it's not your fault," I repeat, plucking at a loose string on the armrest.

"You know, Stephan made this big plan to keep you from feeling or whatever," he expresses. "But what I never got was how the plan actually worked. How Marco and Sophia were supposed to make you become emotionally detached."

"Alex told me it was because if you raised someone to never know what happiness and sadness and love are, then they wouldn't know how to feel them. It was working great, too, until a couple of months ago when I snapped out of my zombie trance."

"And you don't know what caused that?"

I shake my head. "I have no idea, other than the fact that I remember it felt like someone was watching me right before it happened."

He contemplates everything for a concise moment. "None of this makes sense." He brushes his blue-tipped bangs out of his eyes with his fingers. "It's like when your mom disappeared. Not much about that made sense, either."

My heart strikes in my chest as my eyes enlarge and I verge on a panic attack. "I—I thought she died? I was told my mother and father are dead." My voice squeaks at the end.

"They figured she must have died because of what happened." He scoots closer so we're huddled together, places a hand on top of my thigh and my heart settles. "I overheard my parents talking about how Jocelyn was pissed off when she found out you had to go live with Marco and Sophia so the star could be protected and she was planning on running away with you. As soon as Stephan found out he went to stop her. I guess he found you standing up at the top of this hill in the forest, but he couldn't find your mom. The Keepers looked for her for about a month, but they never found her." My blood boils. "So they just *assumed* she died because they never found her?"

A look of loathing shadows his face. "That's how the Keepers are—secretive and confusing."

"But that's bullshit!"

"A lot about the Keepers is bullshit."

I clutch at my chest as I hunch over, trying to breathe normally. "What if she's not dead and she's out there somewhere . . . alive?"

"That's the exact same thing my parents thought," he says and runs a hand down my back to comfort me.

I take a few deep breaths and then sit back up. "Maybe we could talk to your parents and try to get more details."

His eyes dim as he lounges back in the chair and rests his arm on the armrest. "My parents are dead, Gemma. They died in a car accident a few months after your mother disappeared."

Me and my Goddamn uncensored mouth. "Oh my God. I'm so sorry."

"Don't worry about it. It was a long time ago." He acts like it isn't a big deal, but he can't even look at me.

"Does Alex know about any of this stuff?" I change the unpleasant subject. "About my mom and how she supposedly died?"

"The thing about Alex is . . . he's kind of been brain-washed." His voice carries hesitancy. "He's got it in his head that the Keepers can do no wrong, but, yeah, I've mentioned it to him and he didn't believe me."

My mind is spinning. There's so much I don't know and so much Alex hasn't explained.

"Hey, I have an idea." Laylen rises to his feet and tugs down the sleeves of his shirt so they cover his arms and mark. "Why don't we take a break from all of this deep talk and go into the kitchen and get you something to eat?"

I nod and follow him out of the room, wondering what to do next and who I can trust. It seems like the world is full of unsolvable mazes and liars trying to direct me through them.

I MIGHT HAVE been witnessing the strangest scene I've ever come across. A vampire/Keeper is making my break-fast and it's nothing simplistic, either. He's cooking ba-con, eggs, French toast *and* pancakes because he says I need choices. No one has ever cooked me anything before and I'm in awe.

I'm sitting on one of the barstools that border the is-land, breathing in the fresh scent of cinnamon, bacon and the aroma of a brand new experience. We haven't talked much, but I'm enjoying watching him move around the kitchen. The way every time he ducks his head and his hair falls in his eyes, the way his limbs stretch as he walks and the way he keeps sucking on that lip ring of his.

"So, I've been thinking," he says as he turns the pieces of bacon over with a fork and the grease in the pan sizzles. "About your emotions and or should I say lack of emotions."

I inch the stool forward and the legs scrape against the tile. "Okay, what about them?"

He twists the knob on the stove, adjusting the temperature of the burner. "I'm thinking that sounds an awful lot like magic."

"Magic?" I prop my elbows onto the countertop and rest my chin on top of my overlapping hands. "Like Wicca magic? Or like black magic?"

He grabs a plate from the cupboard. "It could be either, really, or something else entirely different from Wicca magic. There's a ton of things that can wipe out a person's ability to feel."

"Wait, you think they *wiped* out my emotions?"

"It's possible." He scoops up a spoon full of eggs and piles them on a plate. "In fact, it makes a lot of sense. I mean, I knew you when you were a kid and you were fine then; happy, healthy and kind of bossy." He flashes me a grin.

"I wish I could remember you," I say as he slides the plate of eggs across the counter. "It kind of seems weird that I don't."

"That could be because of your emotions." He turns off the stove and grabs a rag that sits next to the sink. "I mean, think about it. You were emotionally detached from life—from everything, right? And emotions play a huge part in why people remember things."

"I guess that makes sense." I take a bite of eggs and they taste delicious. "But maybe, that could come from magic, too?"

"Good point." He finishes cooking the rest of the food. "But the question is, why? I mean, I know it's supposed to be because of the star, but what if it's because of something else."

I choke on my eggs. "You think I was made emotionally numb for another reason?"

He sets a pan in the sink and turns on the faucet. "Gemma, at this point, I have no idea what's going on. I've spent three years in the dark, never hearing a word from any of the Keepers." He speaks loudly over the running water. "And then Alex and Aislin show up with you and say that the Death Walkers suddenly found you after years of you going undetected."

Strangely, he's making sense. What if there's more? Why have I just assumed that the story Alex told me was the correct story?

He turns off the water and begins piling French toast, pancakes, and bacon onto the plate. When he's done, he sets the plates on the counter in front of me. Then he hops onto the counter and watches me as I eat.

"You're not eating any?" I ask, pouring syrup over a few slices of French toast.

He shakes his head. "I don't eat food."

"What . . . oh." I feel so stupid. Of course he doesn't. He's a vampire. I point my finger at him and click my tongue. "Gotcha." I dig into my food, struggling not to act too uneasy at the fact that he seems to be fascinated by my chewing.

"So what do you eat?" I break the silence.

He shrugs. "Nothing, usually. I'll eat food sometimes when I'm bored, but it's never out of hunger."

I drag the fork across the eggs, deliberating. "Laylen, can I ask you a question?"

"You can ask me anything."

"Anything?" I ask and he nods again. I take a bite of the eggs and chew. "How exactly did you get turned into a vampire?"

His face contorts with confusion. "I can't remember."

"Is that how it normally works when a person goes through the change, or whatever you call it?"

"It's called the transition." He hops off the counter and strolls around the island toward me. "And no, something else caused the memory loss." He pulls out a stool and sits down beside me. "The only thing I can remember about that night is coming out of a club and hearing someone come up behind me. When I turned around, everything went black. When I woke, I had a bite mark on my neck and blood all over me." He holds up his arm and tracks a finger along the Greek symbols that are on his forearm. "And, of course, I had this lovely little thing right here."

"Was it hard to deal with?" I set the fork down on my plate and rotate in the stool so I'm facing him and our knees are touching. "I mean, changing like that? It had to be hard."

He nods. "My Keeper's blood helps me control my cravings for blood, but it doesn't mean they're nonexistent."

"So, you've never bit anyone—ever?"

He scratches at his wrist and shifts uncomfortably. "I didn't say that."

My heart skips a beat. "So, you have."

He stares at the wall in front of us. "I've had a few

slipups, but I never killed anyone."

"Do they . . . Do you . . ." I have no idea why I'm asking the question, only that I'm curious and need—and I mean *need*—to know. "How does it feel?"

His eyebrows shoot upward as his head whips in my direction. "How does it feel when I bite someone?"

I nod. "And how does it feel for them?"

"Why are you asking?" he asks me inquisitively.

I decide to be honest. "Curiosity, and the fact that I can't seem to keep my damn mouth shut."

His lips tug up to a miniscule smile. "You really want me to tell you how it feels to sink my teeth into another person's neck?" I start to apologize because I think he's upset, when he leans forward. "How it feels to suck hot blood out of someone's vein?" I swallow hard at the animalistic look in his eyes as he dips his head toward my face. "How it feels to hold someone in my arms, knowing I can do *anything* to them?" His voice purrs across my skin. He puts a hand on each side of me, slants his body and moves closer. "You really want to know, Gemma?" He breathes on my neck and I choke.

"I don't . . . I don't . . ." I trail off as his lips brush against my skin and my eyelids shut on their own accord.

"What if I told you it was terrible?" he whispers against my neck. "Would you run?"

"I don't know . . ." I begin to fall backwards on the stool and grab ahold of the edge of the counter.

"What if I told you it felt mind-numbingly good?" He kisses my neck and my shoulder shudders into him. "Would you let me bite you?"

My mind has melted into wax and air has gotten trapped in my lungs. "Would you bite me, if I said yes?"

"What do you think?" His lips part and I feel his teeth

nick my skin. I don't move because I want to know. I want to stay right here.

As I'm entirely letting go to my curiosity and my body's need for an answer, his tongue slides out and he licks me like a dog. My eyes snap open as he pulls away and there's a huge smile on his face.

"I would never bite you, sweetheart," he says with humor in his eyes. "You're too innocent and pure and that makes for a bad addiction." When I pout, he touches his finger to my bottom lip. "And besides, I'd never be able to forgive myself if I bit you." I let my lip return to its rightful place as he gets up from the stool and makes his way to the window. "And I'm not a fan of feeding. I've only done it a few times and it makes me feel guilty afterwards." He draws back the curtain and lets the sunlight inside. "So, what do you want to do next—"

The window explodes, sending shards of glass through the air, like deadly raindrops. Laylen ducks down as a wave of ice rushes through the broken window and curves down to the floor. It slithers towards my feet and spirals up and attaches to the ceiling, forming thick beams.

"Laylen!" I jump from the stool and it topples over. "Are you okay?"

As I round the corner of the island, he stands up. My brain barely registers his movements as he races over to me at an inhuman speed and grabs my hand. The next thing I know, we're racing down the hallway and the ice is chasing us.

"What the hell was that?" I pant as I force my legs to take longer strides.

"Death Walkers." He veers us to the right as one of the rooms' doors blows from the hinges and flies towards our heads. The rest of the doors follow and he hunkers down, pulling me down with him. He shields my head with his arm and glances up and down the hall. "I have no idea how they fucking found us."

Ice crawls across the floor, along the ceilings and glazes the walls. Snow whirls in the air as the house begins to crack down the center of the floor. It's petrifyingly cold and I have flashbacks to the night in the woods, being chased, watching the Death Walkers take out the cabin with their ice.

My heart hammers in my chest as I tuck my head into his shoulder. "What do we do?"

His chin brushes the top of my head as he turns his head from left to right. "Come on. Follow me. And keep your head down."

He moves his body away from mine and keeps his head low as he gets down on his hands and knees, crawling toward the front door. I follow; the ice on the floor burns against my palms and the wintery cold air crisps my eyelashes. Beams are forming in bulks, creating a jail cell with no way out.

I continue to follow Laylen, sliding from left to right out of the beams, but fog starts to seep through the open doors and windows, filling up the entire house. Before I know it, I can't see a damn thing.

"Laylen?" I cough against the plunging temperature in the air. "Laylen, where are you?" He doesn't answer. "Laylen, please."

The dead silence is terrifying, but I try not to panic. I crawl on my hands and knees until I find my way into a room that's clear from the murky fog. I jump to my feet and remove the knife from my back pocket; noting the blue tint of my skin and the tremble and tightness of my frozen limbs. The fog is getting to me and I need to move fast before I get hypothermia.

"What the hell should I do?" There are no windows in the room, just a few empty shelves and a door. I quickly run over to it, but it comes crashing down and flies straight at my head. I drop to the floor, flat on my stomach, and the blade of the knife grazes my hand and slices my palm open. With my uninjured hand, I begin to push myself up when something steps up in front of my face. Black fabric circles its feet and ice cracks out from under it.

I kneel up and tip my chin up to the Death Walker standing in front of me. It's sickening to look at up close; dry peeling skin and blood oozing from the visible muscles. Its eyes are hidden underneath the hood, but the glow is blinding.

I skitter backward on my knees, poising the knife out in front of me. Without warning, it charges, sending ice dispersing from the walls and ceiling. The shards are as sharp as glass and each piece that hits me rips at my skin. I manage to swing the knife at the monster, knowing it won't kill it, but hoping it will wound it. I only slice the fabric of its cloak, though, and seem to piss it off. I dodge to the side and try to get my feet steady beneath me, but it floats over my head and lands behind me. I whirl and aim the knife at it again, but I'm way off goal and I stab at the air.

My feet slip against the slick floor as I try to spin back around to run, but it grabs ahold of my arm and lifts me up until my legs are dangling below me. I open my mouth to scream, but a dense cloud puffs from its fleshless lips. Cold air enters my throat and steals the sound away.

Bits of ice and frost crackle across the inside of my mouth and down my airway. The Death Walker tips its head back, lets out a blood curdling scream and countless shrieks echo throughout the house. Its fingers leave my arm and I crumple to the floor, clutching my neck as I roll onto my back. The Death Walker cries out again as my body stops falling, each limb dying. The ice spreads down into my lungs, wrapping around each bone, contracting them and I can feel the skin shriveling from the pressure. I listen to my heart still as the Death Walker leans over me. As it opens its mouth again, my heart goes silent. Then everything goes black.

CHAPTER SEVENTEEN

"SOMETIMES I THINK it'd be better if I were dead," I say to Alex as I walk around the trees and head further into the forest.

He catches me by the arm, jerks me back and twirls me around to look at him. "Why would you ever say that?"

I stare at the lake that's peeking through the brim of the forest. "Because then, I wouldn't have to feel the pain anymore."

He hooks his finger under my chin and makes me look at him. His green eyes glisten in the sunlight that is flickering through the branches of the trees. It looks like he's about to cry and I don't understand why. "If you couldn't feel the pain anymore, then you wouldn't be able to feel how great it feels when it leaves you. Without pain, everything else wouldn't matter to you. It would all be the same."

"Sometimes I think that'd be better."

"Better than love?"

I swallow hard as tears puddle the corners of my eyes. "I don't know if I know what that is and I'm not *sure I ever will."*

He embraces my cheek with his hand and grazes his thumb just below my eyes. "Yes, you will. You'll know because for a moment, that pain will be gone."

"GEMMA, CAN YOU hear me?" Alex whispers. "Gemma, wake up."

I feel myself being lifted and then arms coddle me closer to a tepid chest. Electricity webs through me and the ice in my body shrinks and melts. I'm no longer cold, but feverish. I tuck my head in and let the heat take me over as light gleams around me.

"Whatever you do, don't go to sleep," he says. "Keep your eyes open."

I'm trying, but it's hard. I can't . . . Suddenly I can't feel the pain anymore.

I WAKE UP confused and with an earsplitting headache. My hand is bandaged up, I'm lying in a log bed, and there's a blanket over me and a pillow under my head. The walls are made of the same logs as the bed and so is the nightstand and the dresser. There's an antique vanity in the corner and a window next to it, which shows the extensive scenery of mountains that are submerged in snow.

I clutch my head as I sit up and blink my eyes, trying to piece everything together, but my memories are a bit foggy. "Am I back in Wyoming? Holy fuck, have I been dreaming the entire time?"

"Depends on where you think the dream started from?" Alex's voice wraps around my body and makes me remember the dream I'd been having. It also makes me remember all the things Laylen and I talked about.

He's by the doorway, looking comfortable as he leans against the doorframe with his arms folded. He's wearing a black t-shirt, faded jeans with a tear in the thigh area, different from the clothes I saw him in last time, and his dark brown hair is damp.

I lower my hand from my head. "How long have I been out?"

"A little over six hours," he answers simply. "You were pretty out of it."

"Six hours?" I start to get up, but the soreness in my head sends me straight back to the bed. "What happened? Because the last thing I can remember is the Death Walker breathing on me, then it felt like I was dying."

He uncrosses his arms, walks across the room and sits down at the foot of the bed. "You should have been dead. The Death Walker breathed the Chill of Death on you and it's lethal, but somehow . . . somehow you're alive."

I check over my arms, which have fingernail-size cuts all over them. "How did I survive?"

He shakes his head and the muscles in his arms go stiff. "I have no idea. All I can figure is it has to do with the star being inside you."

The star. I wish he'd stop reminding me. I throw the blankets off me and move my legs over the edge of the bed. "Where are Aislin and Laylen?"

He rubs his hand down his face and sighs. "Aislin couldn't transport all four of us out of the house at the same time, so she had to make two trips. When she transported back to get Laylen, she never came back."

"What!" I exclaim and begin to put weight on my feet, despite my wobbly knees. "Well, we have to go back there and get them. I mean, the Death Walkers were there and they—"

He grabs my arm and gently steers me to the side so I fall onto his lap. "Calm down, my father called not too long after and said they were fine. That Aislin's crystal had shattered, but they were able to make it to the car and drive to the city."

I remember the conversation Laylen and I had in the kitchen. "So they're okay?"

He nods. "Yeah, they're okay—everyone is okay. Everything is going to be okay. God, it's nice to be able to finally say that."

Why does it feel like there are pieces of the story missing? "Did you talk to them yourself?"

"Who? Aislin and Laylen?" he asks and I nod. "No, I tried like a thousand times before my father called, but their phones went straight to voicemail."

"Then, how did your father get ahold of them?"

"They called him from Adessa's."

"And where are they now?"

He eyes me over suspiciously. "They're all headed here. Why?"

"And what about Marco and Sophia?" I say, cradling my bandaged hand as I tip back. "Where are they?"

"I'm not sure, yet," he replies with a dash of annoyance. "When we went back to Laramie, we couldn't find anyone."

None of this makes sense and it's frustrating because he doesn't seem to care. It's like he's blind—brainwashed. "And what about your father? Where was he this entire time?"

"He was out in Magia Terra." He takes my injured hand in his and traces the folds between my fingers.

"Magia Terra?" My body responds elatedly to his touch, but I tell it to shut the hell up.

"It's like this wasteland where useless or broken magical objects are dumped," he explains as his finger roams to my palm where the knife entered. "He does work there a lot and there's no reception whatsoever. I don't know why I never thought of it before."

"But he's back now?" I frown as he brings my hand to his lips and he delicately kisses the bandaged area. He's being weird. Too affectionate.

He nods, then picks me up by the hips and turns me around to face him. "He's headed here now, so relax." He kisses my neck as his fingers sneak up between my legs and he spreads them open so there's one on each side of him. "Everything's fine."

Everything isn't fine. I have no idea where we are, what happened, or what exactly was said when Stephan finally called. I've missed a lot while I've been out and the only person that has been completely honest with me isn't here.

His fingers travel up the top of my leg and he kneads my thighs with his fingers. "Relax, everything's okay."

I crane my neck and glance back out the window at the snow-covered land. "Where are we?"

"We're in one of the Keepers cabins in Colorado." He fixes a finger underneath my chin and makes me look back at him. "Can we stop talking about this now? I'd really rather be doing other stuff," he says in a demanding tone and then he leans forward and kisses me freely.

It's completely out of character for him. Usually, he's either out-of-control or trying to restrain himself and the last time we talked, he made it pretty clear that he thinks of me as just the star. He's too comfortable, as if he suddenly thinks it's okay to kiss me and touch me. I need to stop him and get some answers.

"I think we should . . ." I begin to protest against his lips, but I trail off as his tongue determinedly enters my mouth.

His hands slide up to my waist, leaving a trail of heat on my stomach as they touch my bare skin. Turning us to the side, he winds one hand around my back and covers my body with his as he lays me on my back. He spreads my legs open and positions his body between my legs and we fit perfectly together. At least for a moment, but as his hand wanders up the front of my shirt and cups the outer layer of my lacy bra, I remember how powerful his touch is and I scream at my brain to snap out of it.

It works. I wiggle my arms between us and, with effort, push him back. "Is there any way I can take a shower? I'd like to wash off all my cuts."

He pants, his green eyes glossy as he studies me. Then, his hand leaves my shirt and sneaks between my legs. "You want to take one right now," he says, rubbing me.

My body quivers for his fingers to be inside me, but I fight against it, and remain in control. I nod because I need a second to clear my head and try to figure out what's going on.

He sighs and then brings me with him as he stands to his feet. He tugs my shirt back over my stomach and tucks a few pieces of my hair behind my ear. Then he laces his fingers with mine, leads me across the room and scoops up a bag near the doorway. "While we were in Laramie, we stopped by your house and picked up some of your clothes and stuff."

"Thank you," I say and take the bag from him.

He leans in and kisses my cheek. "You're welcome."

If it wasn't for the flow of electricity, I'd think he's the mirage because Alex is not affectionate. Hot, intense, irrational, maybe even a little bipolar—yes. Loving and caring—no.

He shows me where the bathroom is and then makes a joke about taking a shower with me before leaving. I'm lost and I don't know what to do. Jump out the window and run through the mountains? Trust Alex? Trust Stephan?

I strip off my clothes and let the water run hot before I step in and close the curtain. Rinsing off my body feels like I'm rinsing off the last few days. By the time I step out, I feel a little bit better. Not trusting, but better.

The room is overflowing with steam and I can barely see. I feel around for a towel and then wrap it around me. When I head to the counter where my bag is, the steam parts open and reveals a figure standing near the door.

I step back and tighten the towel around me. "Hello?"

He takes a step forward and exposes his dark green eyes, messy brown hair, broad shoulders and an amused smile on his lips. It looks like Alex, but I can tell right away that it isn't by the lack of voltage in my body.

"Shit . . . You're the mirage." I back toward the shower, smacking my knee on the corner of the porcelain tub as I work to hold the towel together. He matches my moves, mimicking my pace, and then speeds up when I reach the stained glass window in the corner.

"And you're Gemma." His voice is soft like velvet, alluring even. "Beautiful, confused, poor, broken Gemma." He trails his fingers along the top of the towel, just above my chest. I bend my knee to kick him, but he bends his own and his knee caps restrain my legs against the wall. His hand drifts toward my neck and I let out a scream as I smack his hand away.

He slaps his hand over my mouth, snatches ahold of my wrists, and twists my arm in a very awkward position. Then he spins me around so my back is pressed against his chest and his arms snake around my midsection. I raise my foot and fling my leg back to kick him, but he hops away and dodges my endeavor. His arms constrict around my arms and his skin is warm against mine, but not in the same way as Alex's. He has a strange smell to him, like lilacs mingled with freshly fallen rain. The smell is pungent and makes me nauseous.

He covers my mouth with his hand as he directs us toward the door and I bite down on his skin. "Dammit." He slaps the back of my head as he curses and I swing my head back; making us lose balance and we slam into the toilet.

As he works to get us both to our feet, without letting go of me, the door comes crashing in and Alex rushes inside. The blood promptly drains from his face. "What the fuck?"

The mirage laughs disdainfully as his arms wrap back around me. "Hello to you, too, old friend."

"Old friend?" My eyes widen and I freeze. "Alex, you know him?"

Alex shakes his head, looking as perplexed as I feel. "Who are you?"

The mirage shakes his head. "I'll be the one asking the questions."

Alex glances at me for an explanation and I shrug. He cautiously takes a step further inside the room, closing in on us. "Why? You have no place to go."

The mirage laughs again. "I think you're forgetting what a mirage is and how we travel. I can be out of here quicker than you can blink, if I want to."

"Fuck." Alex stops moving and clenches his fists as he battles to contain himself. My body lets out a terrified shudder. I've never seen him worried. Usually, he's the man with the plan, but he looks helpless and lost.

The mirage's mouth moves next to my neck and a floral scent whelms my nostrils. "Shudder again and I might just take you back to my house instead of where I'm supposed to take you. I could have a lot of fun with you."

I angle my head to the side and cringe. The towel is slipping loose and he has himself pressed up against me in every strategic place. "Back off, pervert."

"If you touch her, I'll break off all your fucking fingers." Alex dares another step into the room so the only thing between us and him is the sink. "And since I'm pretty sure you know what I am, after all, you seem so dead set on being me, then you know what I'm capable of *and* just how good I am at breaking bones." He pops his knuckles and neck.

The body of the mirage begins to quiver and vibrate. The possibilities of what he could be doing spin a web of disgust through my body, but Alex seems pleased by whatever he's doing. He continues to shake and shiver faster and faster, until he conclusively lets out a jolt that lurches us both forward.

"Nicholas Harper." Alex crosses his arms and a patronizing look arises on his face as the mirage skims his arms down to my waist.

I slant my head back to look at the mirage. His hair is no longer brown, but a sandy-blonde and his eyes are as golden as the desert sand. He's shorter than Alex and a little thinner, but probably around the same age. It creeps me out to see him in real form, not because he's bad looking, but because I realized he's basically a shape-shifter and he can be anyone.

"You know, it's really fun messing with your head," he says and his real voice is higher. "And that scene in the forest was priceless. I'll never forget the scared looks on your faces."

Alex shakes his head. "I'm not sure why I'm surprised. I always figured you'd end up with something like the Death Walkers. Tell me, when did you decide to switch sides?" He's acting arrogant and condescending which I normally hate, but, at the moment, I'm thoroughly entertained.

"I didn't switch sides," he says with irritation. "I was merely having fun with this lovely girl right here and the Death Walkers just happened to show up at the right time. It couldn't have been better timing if I planned it myself."

"That was all it was about?" Alex doubts with a frown. "To simply fuck with our heads?"

"There's always a purpose." His shoulders lift up and then descend as he shrugs. "But, it doesn't mean I have to divulge it to you."

"What about the other time?" I question and Alex looks at me for clarification. "The one in the parking lot? Where you were pretending to help me with the Death Walker?"

"Mind manipulation. Foreseer's are excellent at it." His breath stings at my nose and I almost gag at the floral scent. It's so powerful, like he's recently eaten rose petals. He strengthens his hold on me, arms tightening as he urges me closer to his chest. His heart beats through his chest and against my back, slow and rhythmic like a drum. "She's a beautiful thing, isn't she?"

I scrunch my nose and make a face. "Let me go." I try to kick him, but miss again.

"I'm the one calling the shots here," he says, then sniffs my hair as his hand drifts down my stomach to the base of the towel. Alex starts to move forward with a vein popping out in his neck. "Which means I can do whatever I want with you."

I wiggle my arm enough that I can jab my elbow into his stomach. "Fuck you."

His stomach muscles tense. "Feisty. I like it," he whispers in my ear and I slam my head straight into his nose.

"Shit!" His hands leave my body and I dash over to Alex, meeting him in the middle of the room. He grabs my arms and swings me behind him. Prodding me with his elbow, he drives me toward the door as he reaches for his pocket.

"I wouldn't do that if I were you," Nicholas calls out, still clutching his nose. There's blood running down his arm and dripping onto his grey t-shirt.

Alex pulls a small knife from his pocket and flips the blade open. "Gemma, go."

"Go and there will be even bigger consequences." Nicholas pinches the brim of his bleeding nose. "And since you're a Keeper and know all the laws and rules, I bet you can guess what they are."

"Foreseers can only punish Foreseers," Alex states as he poises the knife out in front of him.

He removes his hands from his nose and there's blood all over his face. "Which is exactly what she is."

My jaw nearly slams to my knees. "Excuse me."

Alex turns his head and puts his finger to his lips,

shushing me. "Listen, there's been a misunderstanding."
He looks back at Nicholas. "Gemma, she's . . . there are
things about her that make her different, but she's not a
Foreseer."

He grabs a towel from off the hook and begins to dab
the blood off his face. "Did she see a vision?"

Alex wavers with his arm bent at the elbow and the
knife stationed in front of him. "Yeah, but there were spe-
cial circumstances."

"Look, I don't give a shit what she is or what the circumstances are. You know the law and the law says if a
person sees a vision, then they belong to the Foreseers."
He wipes his hands off with the towel and tosses it onto
the counter. "Gemma saw a vision; therefore, she belongs
to *us* and she's going to the City of Crystal with *me.*"

"I know what the fucking laws say," Alex snaps. "But,
like I said, she's . . ."

"Different." Nicholas throws his head back and
laughs. "It doesn't matter. She has to go back with me.
She can try and plead her case when she gets there, if she
wants to." His gaze drinks me in. "She can even wear the
towel."

I pull a disgusted face, secure my hand onto the towel
and then cower back behind Alex. "Can't you make him
go away?" I hiss.

Alex shakes his head over and over again and then he
pounds his fist against the countertop, causing perfume
bottles to topple from the cabinet into the sink. He kicks
the cupboard and punches a hole in the wall, breathing
furiously and with deep, ravenous heaves of his lungs.
After a long dragged out pause, he finally utters, "Fine,
she'll go."

"What!" I cry, jumping in front of him. "Are you

kidding? I'm not going anywhere with him to some city with a bunch of future seeing weirdoes."

He sighs heavily and adjusts the towel higher up on my chest. "You don't have a choice, Gemma. Laws are laws. If we break them, we'll pay and you'll still end up having to go down there."

I lock eyes with him and give him a silent plea. "Can't you do something, like beat him up? Or, stab him with your knife?"

Alex smashes his lips together like he's trying not to laugh at me. "As much as I would love to do either, I can't. Technically, he hasn't done anything wrong."

"He was with the Death Walkers," I argue. "And he's been fucking with my head . . . he made me think I was going crazy."

Nicholas lurks towards us with a smirk. "Now, that wasn't entirely me. Some of that stuff was conjured up from your own head. I was just trying to give your Foreseer ability a little nudge. You should be thanking me. Now that the gift's starting to surface, the nightmares should stop."

"Can't we just run?" I ask Alex, ignoring Nicholas.

Alex shakes his head and offers me a look of compassion. "Foreseers can travel anywhere by the power of the crystal. If he wants to find us, he can and very quickly."

Nicholas starts to laugh as he reaches the edge of the counter. "We are brilliant creatures, aren't we?"

Alex rolls his eyes and slams his hand against Nicholas's chest, shoving him back. Nicholas bumps his hip on the corner of the sink as he staggers backward, tripping over his feet. "Just so you know, I'm going with her," Alex tells him.

The humor vanishes from Nicholas's face as he

recovers his steadiness by bracing his hand on the wall. "You can't go."

"There are no laws forbidding Keepers from entering the City of Crystal," Alex informs him as he slides his pocketknife back into his pocket. "So I can go whether you like it or not."

It makes me feel a little bit better, but not much. I don't want to be a Foreseer. I already have too much on my plate, and adding the ability to see futuristic visions is going to splinter it even more. "Are you sure there's no other way?" I whisper to Alex, hoping.

There's definitiveness in his eyes. "I'm sorry, but don't worry, I'll make sure you come back with me. You won't have to stay there."

Can I believe him? Can I trust him? What other choice do I have?

He licks his lips as he stares at my mouth, and then increases his voice so Nicholas can hear. "The Keepers have much more weight than the Foreseers and, in the end, we all know how this is going to turn out."

Nicholas's eyes smolder like embers as he glowers at Alex. "Nothing's changed. You still do whatever the hell you want."

"Yep," Alex replies coolly as he leans in and kisses my cheek possessively. "I absolutely fucking do. There's no other way to live life."

"Whatever." Nicholas retrieves a miniature crystal ball from the pocket of his cargo pants. It's filled with red rubies and there's a glittery tint to the glass. "Go head, my little Gem," he says to me as he holds the ball. "Ladies first."

I glance at the towel barely covering my body. "You have to let me change first."

"Says who?" Nicholas questions and I want to slug him. "There's no way I'm going to leave you alone. For all I know, you'll jump out the window and run."

"And what?" I question. "Run out into the mountains and die?"

He shrugs. "From what I've seen, you could be that stupid."

I shake my head and march forward with my hand beginning to elevate to hit him. Not just for this, but for everything else; for pretending to be Alex and making me think I've lost my mind.

Alex gently touches my hand and it subdues me. "We'll step out so you can dress, but hurry, okay?"

"I didn't agree to that." Nicholas moves towards us, but Alex pushes him back again, and his shoulder slams into the wall as he fights to keep his footing.

"You don't need to be a fucking pervert," Alex says in a firm voice. "Now, step out and let her change. She won't go anywhere."

Nicholas studies me for an eternity, then his eyes dim to a deep brown as he winds a path around me. He squeezes between us and the towel rack, and heads to the doorway. "You have one minute." He goes out into the hall and Alex follows, giving me a lingering last glance before he shuts the door.

I hurry and pull on my jeans and a black t-shirt, then twist my hair up into a messy bun with a few bobby pins I find in a drawer.

"Fifteen seconds," Nicholas shouts from the other side of the door.

Panicking, I glance at the window and consider jumping out and making a run for it. Maybe the risk of freezing to death is worth it? Before I can arrive at a definite decision the door swings open and the knob bangs against the wall.

Nicholas struts inside with the crystal ball in the palm of his hand and Alex is just behind him. "Times up."

I really, really dislike this guy. "What exactly am I supposed to do with it?" I ask as I put my hands on my hips and stare at the crystal.

"Put your hand on it," he instructs as he elevates his arm so the crystal ball is closer to my face.

I glance at Alex and he nods once. I summon a deep breath and tell myself I'm not afraid, that I've lived without fear forever and that this vile, toxic feeling intensifying in me really means I'm hungry. As my fingers brush the cold glass, there's a burst of light and warmth that inundates my body. My body jolts forward as the sink, shower and mirror evaporate into light. A tunnel forms in front of my face and twists toward me. I try to back away, but I can't tell what's up and what's down. I feel my limbs disconnect, but there is no pain, only soft tugs. I fall apart and collapse into a tunnel, unsure where I will end up.

CHAPTER
EIGHTEEN

M
Y LIMBS RECONNECT with my body as I crash against a glass floor and catch myself with my hands. I quickly push to my feet and my wrist lets out a loud pop. I wince as a sharp pain zips up my arm. I cradle my wrist and get to my feet. I'm standing in a field layered with grass that glistens like gemstones. Above, the sky is blue with sharp, distinct edges that resemble the cuts on a diamond. The clouds float back and forth, thin and wispy. At the end of the field is a godly throne perched on an immense silvery podium that's trimmed with various shades and sizes of emeralds.

"What the hell is this place?" I mutter.

There's a faint *swoosh* and then Alex drops down from above, landing gracefully beside me. His cheeks are wind kissed and his hair is disarranged. He quickly puts a finger up to his lips. "Shh . . . Keep quiet."

Another *swoosh* and Nicholas appears next to me. He smoothes the wrinkles from his cargo pants and ruffles his sandy hair back into place. "That was fun," he remarks cleverly as he rubs his hands together. "It's seriously the best part about being a Foreseer—falling into the unknown and not knowing where you're going."

I shake my injured wrist until it pops back into place. "If you think that was fun, then I'd hate to hear what you think is torture."

"You, a four-post bed, and some leather straps," he says with a wink. My jaw drops and he grins.

"Can we just get this over with?" Alex rearranges his hair into place with a quick tousle from his fingers. "The quicker we get out of here, the better."

"What's the rush?" Nicholas stuffs his hands into his pockets and rocks back on his heels. "They're never going to let Gemma leave until she's trained." He winks at me again. "Which gives us a lot of time to get to know each other."

"No thanks," I tell him. "I'd rather go back with Alex."

Nicholas scowls at me and stomps off in the direction of the throne that sits a couple hundred feet away. Alex and I trail after him down a path of broken teal porcelain and past a translucent sheet of glass. Every once in a while, the sheet of glass flickers and an image of a woman flashes across it. She is doing different things each time; writing in a journal, crying in a street, dancing in a field.

"It's how they keep an eye on the future," Alex whispers in my ear. "The screen continuously shows them what's going on."

I nod as the image of the woman fades into a lake that ripples in the sunlight, and that's how it stays until we reach the throne's podium. Standing beside the throne, is a short, plump man with elf shoes and curly brown hair. Nicholas approaches him, says something in his ear and the little man nods before hurrying off through the grass.

Alex places his hand on the small of my back and says in a low tone, "And you need to be careful around

Nicholas. He's part faerie and he can't be trusted."

"Faerie," I mouth with wide eyes. He looks normal, which makes me question how many people are just people? And how many are something else disguised as humans? Have I crossed paths with some of them and had just been too oblivious to notice?

We wait in silence until an elderly man materializes from behind the throne. He's tall and lanky with pallid skin and shoulder-length grey hair. The silver shade of his robe matches his eyes and on the top of his hand is a circle wrapped around a "S." I assume it's the Foreseer's mark, although, I haven't spotted one on Nicholas.

Nicholas backs away from the throne and stands near the rim of the podium as the old man takes a seat in the throne. His thin fingers curl around the velvet armrests as he situates in the seat. "Welcome to the City of Crystal. I am Dyvinius, leader of the Foreseers." He speaks in slow, monotone syllables. "I understand that you were able to use the Foreseers' power to view a vision yesterday?"

I glance at Alex. What am I supposed to say? "I guess . . ."

"That's wonderful." Dyvinius drums his fingers. "I'm not sure if you know much about what a Foreseer does, or who we are, so I'll explain because it really is the most magnificent thing," he says and repositions the bottom of his robe so it's covering his feet. "A Foreseer uses the energy of the Divination Crystal to see what's going to happen. It helps us prepare the world for the future. Once a vision is read, it becomes permanent. There is *no* changing it."

He should probably explain that to the Keepers, since they think differently. The bigger picture suddenly opens up before me like I'm finally looking past the light and witnessing a small part of my future. Through all the chaos, emotions and secrets unwinding, I've never taken the time to see what it all means when I connect everything. In the end, I'm the key to saving the world. I will always be the star first and Gemma second.

"When a person goes into their first vision, they usually don't know what they're doing," Dyvinius continues. "Typically, a Foreseer's ability is discovered *before* they see their first vision. Occasionally, someone does end up slipping through the radar undetected. Most of the time, we find them, but sometimes, we don't." His silver eyes target on me. "We have a tracking system that lets us know when there's been an interference with the Divination Crystal. Now, it's not necessarily bad, but the vision does need to be read correctly. Otherwise, it can alter the human world." His face lights up and the wrinkles around his eyes multiply. He claps his hands and straightens up his shoulders. "And so, I've brought you down here to go into the vision again and read it correctly. That way, you can be trained as a Foreseer."

My mouth droops to a frown. "Do I have to?"

Alex snags the back of my shirt and draws me back as he steps forward. "She can't stay here right now. There are certain things that require her to stay with the Keepers at the moment."

Dyvinius's eyes glaze with ice. "And you are?"

"Alex Avery," Alex responds, positioning himself in front of me so I have to peek over his shoulder just to see what is going on.

"Is there any relation to Stephan Avery?" Dyvinius questions.

Alex reaches behind him and slips his fingers through mine. "He's my father."

"Oh, I see." Dyvinius frowns, displeased. "Tell me,

Alex, what are the circumstances that are keeping Gemma with the Keepers?"

"I can't answer that," Alex says. "Like the Foreseers, the Keepers have certain things they have to keep to themselves."

"Yes, but there are also laws we're all supposed to follow and the law states that if a person is able to use the crystal ball to see a vision, then they have to be trained in the City of Crystal by the Foreseers." His mouth sags and on his expressionless face, it looks alarming. "If Gemma doesn't stay here, then she could alter the future by accident. Or get trapped inside a vision if she tries to enter one again. Untrained Foreseers are very dangerous."

My heart races inside my chest. He's going to make me stay.

"I understand that. I really do," Alex reassures him, stroking the back of my hand. "But there has to be something we can work out."

Dyvinius considers this, running his thin fingers along the jewel patterns on the armrest. "Hmmm . . . like, maybe a bargain?" A dark look arises on his face and his grin is very Cheshire Cat. "Perhaps we can work something out. If you make a promise that she will never use a crystal ball again until she is properly trained, then I don't see why I can't let her go back with the Keepers for a while." He pauses. "Of course, after it's all done, she'll have to come back to get trained. Otherwise, I'll have to have *her* make the promise, but I have a feeling you'd rather do that."

Sensing something is wrong, I yank on Alex's arm. "Alex, what will happen if you make the promise?"

He moves his hand away from mine. "I guess a promise can be arranged by me," Alex says through clenched teeth.

"Very good." Dyvinius beams, gesturing his hands at the palace land behind us. "You understand that you're making a promise and that there are consequences if you break the promise?"

Alex nods slowly. "Yeah, I understand how it all works."

Dyvinius leans forward in the throne and looks like a greedy little thief with hunger in his eyes. "Then I need you to say the words out loud."

I try to grab Alex's arm to stop him, but he wrenches it away. "I promise."

I feel something break, like a crack in the sky, and I know that somehow he will be paying for making the promise. I want to hug him for it and hit him at the same time.

Dyvinius relaxes back on the throne. "Now that that's been taken care of, I just need Gemma to read the vision correctly and then I'll let both of you return to the human world."

I cross my arms and move out from behind Alex, shooting him a quick questioning glance, but he avoids eye contact. "I don't know how to do that."

Dyvinius responds, "Well, I'm guessing that when you went in the vision, either some clips were missing, or things might have been blurry."

"Yeah," I reply. "I could see what was going on, but I couldn't tell who anyone was because their faces were too blurry."

"That's good, though. It will make it a little easier for you to correct because all you will have to do is put their faces together," Dyvinius explains. "It's when events are missing when things become a problem."

"Okay, but that doesn't explain how I'm supposed to

put their faces together," I say, deflated. Going back into the vision is one of the *last* things I want to do because I don't want to witness the woman drowning all over again. It was too painful the first time.

"You go back and read the vision again." Dyvinius looks at Nicholas who's sitting at the edge of the podium. "And Nicholas will go in and help you."

Nicholas rises to his feet with a sly smirk on his face. "It'd be my pleasure." He winks at me and I glare in return.

This is all wrong. Not only do I have to go back into the horrifying vision, but I have to go in with the assistance of a foreseer/faerie/creepy pervert.

Dyvinius snaps his fingers and the chubby little man from earlier scurries out from behind the throne. He's carrying a crystal ball with violet ribbons swirling in the glass and it looks very similar to the one back at Adessa's. He places the ball in Dyvinius's hands and bows his head before scampering back behind the throne.

Dyvinius extends the crystal ball toward me with his fingers wrapped around the smooth glass. "Whenever you're ready, Gemma."

Sucking in a breath, I stride up to the podium and stop just short of the foot of the throne. I peer down at the crystal, seeing nothing but ribbons and the reflection of my violet eyes. "I just place my hand on it?"

"To start with." Dyvinius motions at Nicholas. "Get over here and take her hand."

Nicholas zealously snatches my hand and it takes a lot of effort not to cringe. "Orders are orders."

"Gemma, close your eyes and picture the vision you saw," Dyvinius instructs. "Then hold the picture in your mind while you place your hand on the crystal."

Ready to get this over with, I shut my eyes and focus

on the eerie lake full of painful memories. I picture the grey stoned castle with peaking towers, where the children are forced to go. I picture the trees and autumn leaves that blow from the wind as the woman drowns. I let my fingertips skim the glass and then I'm jerked forward and my body ruptures into pieces before raining into the tunnel made of light.

CHAPTER
NINETEEN

I DROP OUT of the sky, like a bird with a broken wing, with no control over my landing. My feet crash into the ground and sink into the dirt. I trip forward, my knees bending, and roll my ankle to the side.

I hop forward, trying to shake it off. "One of these times, I'm going to break apart."

"Are you alright?" Nicholas settles beside me and swiftly grabs ahold of my hand.

I tug my hand out of his and put weight on my sore ankle. Traveling by crystal is going to end up killing me with all the injuries I've been getting. "I'm fine. I'm just not very good at landing."

"You'll get the hang of it, eventually," he says. "In fact, I could give you private lessons."

I shake my head and hobble forward toward the lake that's rippling in the soft breeze. "No, thanks." I shield my eyes and turn in a circle, taking in the green grass, the leaves dancing across the land and the castle looming in the distance. "So, what do I do now?"

"You wait until the vision starts." His sneakers scuff the dirt as he hurries to my side. "You'll have to tell me when it does, though, so I can help you see it clearly."

"You can't see when it starts?"

"It's your vision, so only you can see it. That's the way things work."

I motion at the trees around the lake. "What does this look like to you?"

His shoulder presses against mine and the scent of lilacs, forest and rain invade my nostrils. "Everything looks grey," he breathes. "There's a little haze and color here and there, but most of it is distorted."

I'm about to knee him in the leg to get him to back off when a streak of purple whizzes by us. The little girl dances and spins in the sand near the lake, her long, brown hair blowing in the wind.

"Okay, it's starting." I move away from Nicholas and hike toward the shore.

"What do you see?" he calls out.

"A girl dancing in front of a lake."

"Can you see her face?"

I shake my head. "It's as blurry as it was the first time I saw the vision."

"Then you need to focus harder," he says simply, trailing behind me.

Like it's that simple. I glance over my shoulder at him. "Focus harder on what? The images?"

He gives me a look that puts me on edge and then he struts up behind me. His fingers enfold around my upper arms and I start to step forward, but he lures me back. "Right now, your mind is trying to adjust to the power of the crystal, but it can't quite figure out how to get completely there. The first thing you need to do is relax."

I try to overlook the flowery aroma and focus on relaxing. My mind searches for something that will make me calm. Laylen's face appears in my head, but then it shifts to Alex. But Alex doesn't make me calm. At all. He makes me uneasy, irrational and just plain insane. At the moment, though, seeing his green eyes settles my unstable pulse so I latch onto the image of him. "Okay, I'm relaxed."

"Good, now let your mind focus. The images are already in your head, but you haven't connected them to what you're seeing yet." His fingers creep up to my shoulders like little spiders. "Have you ever looked at one of those magic eye pictures before?"

My shoulders stiffen under his touch. "Uh, yeah, I think so? In school, once, when I was a kid."

"This is kind of like looking at one of those." He begins to massage circles on my skin. "Relax your eyes and let your mind make sense of the images."

Jerking my shoulders upward, I shrug off his hands and concentrate on the images. The boy has raced up to the girl and is guiding her away from the lake. Their faces are hazy, so I hold onto the image of Alex and it relaxes my eyes and unwinds my body. A tunnel starts to form and the trees and lake begin to blur into colors and shapeless images. Slowly, the girl's face alters like a lens on a camera. It's coming into focus—

The man strides up the hills toward the shoreline and darkness sweeps across the land. The calm drains from my body and smothers my concentration with it.

"Shit," I mutter.

"What's wrong?" Nicholas asks.

"I almost had it and then this man appeared and he ruined my concentration."

"Don't look at him then. Try to pretend he's not there."

Easier said than done. I know what the man does—how

evil he is. I return my line of concentration to the boy and cling onto the image of Alex again. The tunnel gradually shapes into a tornado, swirling around until it peaks at the bottom. The boy's features began to surface through the haze, but before I can link the image to my mind, the tunnel snaps back as the woman sprints up to the man.

"What happens if I can't do it?" I ask with discouragement. "Then, what am I supposed to do?"

"You can do it," he insists, still hovering over my shoulder. "All you have to do is catch a glimpse of each of their faces and, in the end; your mind will connect the pieces together."

"And what if I can't see all of their faces before the vision ends?"

He lets out a hushed chuckle. "Then I guess I'll have to keep you down here until you do."

Determination washes away my discouragement and I avert my attention back to the vision. The boy is heading back to the castle. Shoving anything related to stress out of my head, I relax and the tunnel develops again. Bits and pieces shift like a puzzle being put together and the haze begins to fade away. He has green eyes that match the leaves and grass, brown hair, and a sad look on his face. *What a minute. That can't be . . . no there's no way.*

As he disappears into the castle, I fling my concentration to the man, who is yanking the girl from the woman's arms. I focus on nothing else, except piecing together the girl's face. My head is pounding, but I refuse to look away. Seconds later, the tunnel spins and the blurriness crumples.

My jaw drops to the ground. Her eyes . . . The color . . . Violet. "It can't be," I mutter, slowly walking towards them. "It's not possible."

But no matter how many times I blink, she looks the same and a painful revelation slams against my chest. The girl is me. It makes no sense, though. I can't remember this happening. Besides I thought I was supposed to see the future, not the past.

The woman—my mother, starts to back down the hill to the lake, and I will my legs to move and chase after her. Suddenly solving the vision is much more important than anything else in my life.

"Hey! Where are you going?!" Nicholas shouts after me.

The tunnel zooms onto my mother's face; bright blue irises, a warm smile, snow-white skin. I think of the picture I found. As beautiful as she was in the picture, she's a hundred times more beautiful in person. It's all making sense now, pieces connecting, and the weight of it sends me to my knees.

Tears stream down my cheeks as I watch her get dragged beneath the water and the man leaves her, walking back up the hill. He has a sickening grin on his face, a scar on his cheek and hair as dark as the night sky. I grab onto every little detail I can. I hate this man, and I have to figure out who he is. I hate him with so much passion that it makes everything else inside me numb. I will kill him one day, like he killed my mom—I will make him pay.

"What the heck happened? What did you see?" Nicholas asks as the image of the man fades into the grass.

"Nothing." I suck back the tears and stare out at the dark, still water. "It wasn't important."

"It had to be something important since you're all worked up."

"I'm fine," I tell him and get my feet under me. "But can you answer one question?"

His mouth turns upward into a pleased grin. "Sure."

"Is it possible to see a vision that takes place in the past?"

"Yeah, but it's not very common, since there really isn't much point in seeing the past," He pauses, contemplating. "So I'm guessing your vision took place in the past?"

"Yeah, I think so. . . ." I trail off, recollecting everything I've seen and how much it hurts, deep inside my chest. "Can we just go back now? The vision's over."

He eyes me over with his golden eyes. "I know it is. I can see everything now that the vision is complete. It's a beautiful place, by the way. Well, minus the Keepers' castle."

"This is the Keepers' castle?" Alex had mentioned that the lake was the entrance to the Underworld, but he never said anything about the castle belonging to the Keepers. Why would he keep that from me?

He thrums his finger on his chin. "I thought you would have known that since you're a Keeper."

I disregard his question because I have no idea if I'm a Keeper or if he's supposed to think I am one. "Can we go back now?"

"What did you see?" He eludes my question and strides toward me. "Was there a purpose to it?"

"I don't know." There's a personal purpose to it, but the bigger picture is unclear. Something is tugging at the back of my mind, but it won't emerge. "Is there supposed to be purpose to every vision? Is that maybe the reason why I saw it?"

"Sometimes, but not always. Normally, Foreseers use the crystal to see a vision that has a purpose." He tucks his hands into the pockets of his pants. "But your vision was started by accident, so maybe there's a reason you saw it, and maybe not. And maybe that's why you saw a vision from the past."

I know there's a reason I saw it. It's not just about me watching what happened to my mother. I'm remembering it too, when it first happened, something I've never been able to do before. "Please take me back." I hold out my hand for him to take.

"Are you sure you want to go back? We can stay here a little bit longer . . . Get to know each other a little better." He moves toward me and I back away toward the trees.

"What the hell is your problem?" I ask as my back brushes against the trunk of a tree. "Don't you know when someone's not interested?"

"Oh, come on, Gemma." He reaches above me and his hand comes down to the side of my head. Autumn leaves fall from the branches and shower down over our heads. "Let's stay here for a while and enjoy the seclusion."

I maintain a firm voice. "There's no reason for me to stick around here. Now, please, take me back."

His mouth curves into a devious grin, then as quick as a flick of a firefly he leans forward and presses his lips to mine and his hand comes up to my breast.

I shove him back and slap him across the face. "Don't you ever touch me without permission again."

He rubs his cheek. "Feisty." He grins.

I march forward and lean into his face, stabbing my finger roughly against his chest. "If you don't take me back now, I'll show you how feisty I can be."

"Relax. I'll take you back." He lowers his hand from his face and there's a handprint on his cheek. He links arms with me and steers me back toward the hill. "But can I just say that you're a little nervous for a Keeper?"

But I'm not a Keeper. I'm just a confused girl stuck in a world that doesn't make sense. I feel the now- familiar pull bringing me back to the normal world; I shut my eyes and let myself go.

A LITTLE GIRL laughs as she runs around a tree and her fingers snag at the leaves on the low branches. "You can't catch me. You can't catch me."

A little boy with green eyes and dark brown hair chases after her. "Wanna bet?"

They both laugh as the girl runs out from behind a tree and sprints across the grass into a field of violet flowers. Her violet eyes blend with the flowers in the field and there's freedom in the way she runs, like she has no burdens bearing down on her shoulders; no fallen star, claiming hold of her heart. The boy dashes after her, moving faster. As he nears her, she stops in the center of the field and reels toward him. Her eyes sparkle as she considers something, then she races toward him and throws her arms around his neck.

He catches her and they both laugh. "You're really on one today, aren't you? But that's okay. I'm having fun."

She smiles brightly. "You're my best friend in the whole-wide world, Alex."

WHEN I OPEN my eyes, my feet are planted back on the podium in front of the empty throne with Nicholas at my side. The sky above looks a little darker and the blades of glass a little sharper, like the scenery has slightly altered. Or maybe it's my perception? Alex is sitting at the foot of the throne and a thousand emotions rush across his face at once as he rises to his feet. "Are you okay?" he asks me.

I look into his eyes that match the little boy's eyes in the vision. *You've known all along.* "I'm fine."

Nicholas frees my hand from his sweaty grip, saunters up next to the throne, and takes a seat in it. "Everything looks smaller from up here."

Alex rolls his eyes. "That's just what the Foreseers' need—someone like you in charge."

Nicholas props his foot up on his knee, grips onto the armrest and raises his chin. "I think it would be one of the smartest moves they could ever make."

"I'm ready to go," I interrupt them. "I don't want to be here anymore."

Nicholas shakes his head as he stands up from the throne. "And if I was in charge, I would have never let you go." He steps down beside me. "Because you have a lot of power, Gemma. You just don't know it yet."

I don't know a lot of things yet, but I have a feeling I will, soon enough, because the truth is catching up with me, like a rushing wave ready to crash onto the idle sand of a beach.

CHAPTER
TWENTY

I HAVE IT all planned out. I'll make Alex tell me what's going on—why I can suddenly remember things about my past. Why we once spent a day running around in a field, playing. Why we knew each other so well, but now we don't. But most importantly I need to find out what he knows about that day. The day my mother was killed.

As soon as we land in the cabin, he goes into protective mode. Suddenly, he's all about me and making sure I'm okay. He gives me very little time to react.

"What did he do to you?" He places his hands on my shoulders and maneuvers me down the hall toward the couch in the living room.

I stare into his eyes and I mean really stare, past the spark, the power and the undying lust that always floods my body whenever I look at him. The scary part is that all I can see in his eyes is me.

He slows down when we reach the coffee table and cups my cheek as he watches me meticulously. "Did Nicholas . . . He didn't try anything, did he?"

I cringe at the revolting recollection of the kiss and the grope. "Besides being a pervert? No. But I'm really wondering how you know the guy . . . faerie . . . Foreseer or whatever the hell he is."

Alex shrugs and his hand leaves my face and falls to his side. "Sometimes the Keepers will get together with the Foreseers and he would come over."

"To the Keepers' castle."

"You know about that?" His eyebrow crooks.

I nod. "Yeah, I saw it in the vision, remember?"

He shifts his weight and stuffs his hands in his pockets. "Were you able to see more this time?"

"You really want to know?" My eyes narrow as I cross my arms and push past the wall of control between him and me. "I'm going to ask you some questions, and I want you to tell me the truth. I mean it this time. None of your bullshit, omitting the truth."

He claims my gaze, mimicking my assertiveness. "What's your question?"

I take a deep breath, preparing myself for the worst possible answer because a question like this only ends with a bleeding heart. "Has my memory been tampered with?"

The grandfather clock in the corner ticks maddeningly loud in the background and the snow splatters at the windows. The beams above our heads creak and somewhere in the house a faucet is dripping.

He stares at me indifferently and unmoving, as if time has immobilized and I know that it's true.

"What the hell is wrong with you?" I cry as my heart splits open and bleeds out. "Just answer me."

He flinches at the sound of my voice and time seems to move again. "Why do you think that?"

My voice shakes uncontrollably as I close the distance between us so he can see me bleeding from the inside.

"Because the little girl in the vision was me."

His eyes widen and he looks genuinely shocked. "It was you? How's that even possible? I thought visions were of the future."

"Nicholas said it happens sometimes," I snap. "But don't pretend like you didn't already know that. The whole time in the car, when I was babbling my heart out about the woman drowning in the lake, you pretended you didn't know what I was talking about."

He shakes his head and his hands leave his pockets. He reaches for me, but then decides against it and pulls back. "I swear, I didn't, Gemma. The first time you told me was the first time I ever heard a story like it." He pauses, making sure to maintain my gaze. "But what I don't know is why you think the little girl is you."

"Because her eyes were violet." The prickle stabs at the back of my neck and all my anger channels to him. I shove him, just to make myself feel better. To feel something that's real. "And the woman in the lake . . ." I can't finish because saying it out loud makes her death even more real.

He doesn't stumble back, doesn't flinch, and doesn't move. He's an indestructible statue that I wish I could break and crumble so he'd be broken like me. Then maybe he could understand and tell me how to take the pain away. "The woman in the lake was your mother." He whispers to himself.

My mother is gone, to a world full of evil torture, where she's either dead or insane, and I'm feeling like I'm in that world too.

"You really don't remember?"

He shakes his head and his voice and eyes soften. "Gemma, I don't even know what to say. I'm about as confused as you." He's quiet for a while, considering something, and then he lets out an uneven breath. "You think your memories been erased?"

I nod, gripping the edge of the coffee table and trying to breathe. I've lost all control. The prickle is stabbing at the back of my neck. I'm breaking apart, dying, and I wish it would all just end. "Do you remember when we were in the cabin and I was crying?"

"Yeah, I remember." His voice is a whisper through the blood roaring in my ears.

"The reason I was crying is because I saw something . . . something that was kind of like a vision," I say, going back to the peaceful place. "I was in this field and it was at night and there was a little girl and a woman there, too. They couldn't see me and I couldn't see their faces. I thought that I was dreaming, but it felt so real and familiar. Familiar as in a lost memory." I stand up straight. "Familiar as in I was four-years-old when my mom died and I went to live with Marco and Sophia. Familiar as in I'd lived it before."

"How did you find out you were four?" He doesn't even try to deny it.

"Laylen told me," I fume. "He told me a lot of things—truthful things. He isn't a liar like you."

He shakes his head and fury flashes in his eyes. Before I can react, he picks me up, lays me onto the couch and encloses his body over mine. He situates his elbows next to my head and presses his chest close to mine so my hands are caged.

"Get off me," I complain. "I can't breathe."

"You need to hear me out." Alex's voice shakes as his emotions begin to flee from the box he usually keeps them in. "And listen to the whole story before you over-react."

I continue to cry and it makes me feel weak. I need to stop crying. *Stop crying!* "Then, what did you do?"

"I didn't do anything," he assures me. "I just knew about it, which to you is probably equally as bad, but it had to be done."

I sob silently as the possibilities of what happened swirl in my head. "Please, just tell me. I can't take the dark anymore."

"You remember the prophecy I told you about?" he asks quickly and I nod. "Well, I left out a few parts of the story."

"Important parts, I'm guessing."

"That's usually the case when parts are left out." He transfers his weight, giving me a little breathing room as he continues, "While Stephan was trying to figure out a way to keep the prophecy from happening, your mother disappeared—or, if what you say is correct, was thrown into the Underworld." He pauses, staring down into my eyes, but he isn't looking at me; he's remembering. "You were extremely emotional . . . Crying all the time."

"I had just lost my mom," I snap and twist my body beneath him. "Of course I was emotional."

"I'm not saying it was wrong. I'm just trying to explain why Stephan did what he did," he says, breaking out of the memory. "A lot of Keepers are born with gifts, some more useful than others. The one Sophia has is called *unus quisnam aufero animus,* or one who removes the soul."

The prickle taunts the back of my neck, embedding deeper into my skin. "You took my soul away!" Strength overcomes me and somehow, I manage to get my arms in between us to shove him off and he actually falls to the floor.

He's stunned. I'm stunned. And, for a moment, we both remain frozen in place. Then I snap out of my trance and leap up from the couch. "This is worse than the star. At least that can be construed as adding life, but taking away my soul is like ripping away the very essence of my humanity. I'm nothing but a shell of a girl. There's nothing inside me!" The room sways and my vision spots as the truth sinks into my skin like acid. I grasp onto the back of the sofa, gasping for air. "Holy shit! I'm not even a person . . . I'm not anything . . ."

Alex moves up behind me and places his hand on the small of my back. "Calm down, okay? That's not what I'm saying."

"Get—away—from—me," I gasp between shallow breaths, jerking my shoulder upwards, trying to shrug his hand off my back. "Just leave me alone."

"You need to listen to me," he begs. "We didn't take your soul away. It was something different—something less drastic."

"Then, just say it," I demand. "And stop tiptoeing around the details."

"Come sit down with me and I will." He smoothes his hand down my back.

"No." I lower my body closer to the couch and cling onto it. *Please let this be a dream. I want to wake up.*

His arm wraps around my side. His hand slides under me and onto my stomach. Then he draws me back, gets a hand under my knees and scoops me up. He sits down, bringing me down with him, so I'm sideways on his lap and my legs are on the armrest. "I need to finish this, Gemma. You need to know—deserve to know."

"If that's true, then why didn't you just tell me from the beginning?" I wipe the tears from my eyes with the sleeve of my shirt.

"Because I'm not a nice person, Gemma," he states bluntly. "And I'm sure, after I tell you; you're going to hate me."

"And you can live with that?" I choke. "Me, hating you forever?"

"I'm not sure." He inhales deeply and shuts his eyes. "But I need to get it out of me because I can't take it anymore." He opens his eyes and hunts for something in mine. I don't know what he's looking for; the truth about my feelings, whether I will hate him, or just how much pain is in me. It doesn't really matter, though, because nothing is in me, but heartache.

"Tell me." My voice is like dandelion seeds in the wind, defenseless against the power.

He nods, moves his hand up my back and holds onto me. "The *unus quisnam aufero animus* is mostly used as a form of punishment, but we weren't trying to punish you. You were just a little girl and Jocelyn's daughter. So, Sophia did something a little less severe. She detached your soul from your emotions. Since emotions have such a huge connection with memories, it made it so you couldn't remember anything about your past."

An annoying buzzing develops inside my head, like a hive full of bees stabbing at my brain. Alex inspects me attentively, trying to anticipate my next move, but all I can focus on is the buzzing.

"After your soul was detached, you moved to Laramie to live with Marco and Sophia so they could keep you hidden from the Death Walkers," he continues, putting a hand on my shoulder. "There's something about the cold that made it difficult to track the star's energy, but I'm not exactly sure what." He gives me a shadow of a smile. "Your soul is still in you, though, along with your memories. You just can't connect with either of them. Or . . . couldn't." He gives me a look that makes my skin hot and fiery, and it isn't just the electricity. It's something else—something deep within my core; a wick trying to ignite. Maybe it's my soul trying to reunite with me. Or maybe it's just a feeling that will eventually simmer out.

I slow my breathing before I speak. "Why did I start to feel again?"

"No one knows the answer to that." He shuts his eyes and massages his temples with the tips of his fingers. "And you've become immune to Sophia's gift."

Breathe. Just breathe. "She tried to do it again?"

He opens his eyes and his pupils shrivel to pin dots. "She tried it a few months ago, after you started showing emotions again. You don't remember because she did it while you were asleep."

"You mean she snuck into my room, while I was sleeping?" I sit up, rotate my aching body and kneel up on his lap. "That's the sickest and most twisted thing I've ever heard."

His fingertips delve into my hipbones as he detains me from getting up. "I doubt that, but yes, it's kind of twisted."

I shake my head, put my hands on his shoulders, and push away from him as much as I can. "So what's your' brilliant plan now? Keep me locked up here until it's time for the portal to open?"

There's an indication of pity in his bright green eyes. "There's someone else with the same gift as Sophia that's heading here right now. He's supposed to be more powerful than Sophia and Stephan seems convinced it'll work."

My hand collides with his face and my palm strikes

his cheek. His eyes widen. Mine widen. I'm trembling from anger, regret and the deep slashes he's put in my heart. I have no control over myself anymore, but I never really did. So I let the windstorm take me away as I get to my feet and head toward the hallway.

"You say it like it doesn't matter, but it does." I pick up his pocketknife that's on the table and he jumps to his feet as I flip the blade open.

"Gemma, don't," he warns, winding around the couch to get to me.

"Don't what?" I ask rounding around the table. I stretch my arm out in front of me and put the tip of the blade to my wrist. "Don't hurt myself or don't feel the pain? Which one is it, Alex. Which one really matters to you?"

He stops on the other side of the table as I drag the knife down my forearm. My arms and hands shake as blood spills out and streams down my arm. It hurts, but not as much as my heart. "I'm a person. I breathe, I have blood inside me." My voice trembles as I toss the knife onto the floor. "I'm not just a fucking star!"

He doesn't utter a word. He just watches the blood drip onto the floor and stain the wood. I suck in a sharp breath as tears drift down my cheeks and then I turn my back on him and storm into the bedroom. I think about jumping out the window. I could run and live and breathe. I could feel whatever I want. Be whatever I want. I could find love and be whole. I could find out what I really want.

But deep down, I know that I can't. It's bigger than me and no matter what I do the problem will always be there. It's either my emotions or the world. So I stay in the room and throw myself on the bed where I cry and cry until I my eyes are dry. Then I lie quietly and let myself bleed.

CHAPTER
TWENTY-ONE

"**K**ISS ME," I whisper beneath the stars. "Please. I need it now."

"Gemma, I can't," Alex says, but I can see his self-control withering. "I want to so bad, but I've already done it too much."

I clutch onto his shoulders, still fixated on the stars. "Please, I want to feel what it's like just once before it's gone. I want to know what it's like to forget for just one second—what it's like to completely connect with someone."

He sketches his finger along my collarbone without speaking and I look away from the stars. There's blackness in his eyes like the darkness in the sky, but within the depths of his pupils there's a spark that matches the stars.

He leans in and kisses me. Slowly at first, but then as the electricity takes over, his lips and tongue become rougher. He begins to rip my clothes off and I want him to because I want to feel the last part of being human—the most powerful feeling that ever existed.

Love.

And maybe this will be the way I finally find it.

MY EYES SHOOT open to the bedroom ceiling of the cabin as the feelings of the dream kisses my skin and makes me want to breathe. My cheeks are damp with tears; my neck and wrist ache. There's a hand on my wrist and a warm body very close to me. I tilt my head to the side and find Alex kneeling on the bed, winding gauze around my self-inflicted injury.

"You know, if you keep it up you're going to be one big bandage." He snips the end with a pair of scissors and then chucks them on the nightstand. Then he slides his legs out from underneath him and sits down on the side of the bed. "Gemma, what the fuck were you thinking? You nearly cut your vein open."

I turn my back to him as I roll onto my side. "I wanted to show you that I'm a real person, that hurts, and bleeds just like any other person. I wanted you to understand that I'm not just a Goddamn star."

The mattress springs up as he shifts from the bed and I think he's leaving, but then the mattress concaves as he sits down beside me. "I don't know what to say to make you feel better and I'm probably the worst person to try, but I'm going to try anyway." His arm moves over to my side and in his hand is a locket, shaped like a heart. There are floral engravings in the silver, along with a violet stone and carved on the back are the initials "G. L."

"Those are my initials?" I touch the front of it with my fingertips and a memory flashes in my mind. "What is this?"

"It used to be yours before the Keepers took it away

because they were afraid it would . . . it would resurface your memories." He pauses and slips his fingers through the chain of the necklace. "Your mom gave it to you."

I sit up on the bed and face him. There are dark circles under his eyes and my blood is all over his shirt. He looks defeated, a tree with a split trunk about to break apart and fall over. He looks how I feel.

"Why are you showing it to me?" I ask, trailing my fingers up the thin chain until I reach his fingers.

"I have no idea," he says with mystification. "I just can't—I don't have any control over anything when I'm with you and, honestly, I'm sick of fighting it."

I coil the chain around my finger. "So if I asked you to take me away—save me from the Keepers and let me keep my emotions, would you?"

He forces a lump in his throat down. "I have no idea and I'm begging you not to ask me because, if I say yes, then everything will end and, if I say no, you and I will end. There's no right answer."

I want to ask him. I want to know just how much he feels for me because I'm reaching my end and I want to understand everything that I can. I want to feel what I felt in my dream. I need to do everything I can before my time is up. "Can I wear the necklace?"

He nods and then motions for me to turn around. "I'll put it on you."

I turn in the bed, tuck my legs under me and sweep my hair to the side. "I have to ask you something."

He moves up behind me. "Okay . . ."

I tap my fingers on my knee, unsure why it even matters. "Do you feel bad? And I mean, *really* feel bad for hurting me; for lying to me?"

His breath feathers against the back of my neck.

"Gemma, I can't . . . I'm not . . . We shouldn't even be talking about this. I was never supposed to tell you."

My fingers wrap inward and my nails scrape a layer of my skin away. "Fine, please put the necklace on."

He doesn't move and I dig my nails in deeper because the physical pain suffocates the emotional hurt. "I made a promise to you once that I would never do anything to hurt you," he finally speaks. "When we were kids, and I meant it more than I've ever meant anything in my life." He pauses and we both take in a breath. "So if you want to know, if I feel bad for breaking my promise and letting you hurt for the last seventeen years, then, yes, I do. It kills me every day."

I'm not sure how to respond and he doesn't give me time, clearing his throat as he hooks the chain around my neck. "I can't quite get it to hook right."

I bite down on my lip and shut my eyes as I nod. "It looks pretty old."

Seconds later, his fingers graze my neck. "Well, shit. I guess I was wrong."

I glance over my shoulder at him and his eyes look a little watery. "Wrong about what?"

"About you being a Foreseer." He gently touches the back of my neck. "You got your mark."

I glance around the room for a mirror, but there isn't one. "Is it a circle, wrapping an 'S'?"

"How did you know that was the Foreseer's mark?" he questions.

"I saw it on Dyvinius." I turn back around so he can put the necklace on. My shoulders slouch as his arms put pressure on them. "So this means I'm actually a Foreseer and it's not the star causing the visions?"

"Probably, but I don't know how." His fingers

repetitively brush my neck as he fiddles with the clamp. "I thought it was just the star's power setting off the crystal because usually the Foreseer ability is inherited."

I let my chin touch the hollow of my neck so he can get the necklace fastened. "My mother wasn't one?"

The clamp clicks and then his fingers move away from my neck. "Jocelyn was just a Keeper."

"What about my father?" I ask, shutting my eyes as his fingers tangle in my hair. "Maybe he could be one."

He tugs at the roots and pulls my head back. What is he doing? "Maybe, but I can't say for sure since I don't know who he is."

"You don't know who he is?" I raise my head up and he lets go of my hair, then I turn around and face him. "How is that possible?"

"Because Jocelyn would never tell anyone who he was." He kneels up on the bed in front of me. "For some reason, she insisted she had to keep it a secret."

"So I'm alone in the world?" I say and blow out a breath at the truth. "I mean, really alone?"

He shakes his head and gives me a sad smile. "No, you're not."

"Yeah, I am," I disagree. "I have no mother or father. No memories. No friends." He starts to protest, but I cut him off. "And I understand that soon the pain connected to those will all be gone, but right now it hurts more than the Goddamn cut on my arm." I pause as I worked up the courage to ask a question I haven't even so much as dared to think until now. "Can I ask you something?"

He looks wary. "It depends."

I ask him anyway. "What happens after I stop the portal from opening? Then what?"

He shakes his head as he stares at the corner of the

room and, for a fleeting moment, he looks like he might cry. "I really don't know."

I could press him further, but there's no point because I know there are only two ways it could go. I live or I die. I will have a life or I won't. I will end empty and unknowing, or finally be free. I wonder how people do it. Face death when they know it's coming? Seize the day when there are minimal days left?

I crash to the bed, my head falling to my hands as I begin to sob. For once, I want to do exactly what I want when I choose and feel every single part of the moment, without holding back or being afraid. I want to live in the moment.

"Gemma." Alex places a hand on my back. "Please calm down."

I shake my head as tears stream down my cheeks. My chances are going to end soon. My emotions are going to be ripped away and they may never return. I may never get my moment to feel happiness, love, peace, freedom. And I need one that's mine.

I sit up and give him no time to respond as I crash my lips into his. I clutch onto his shirt as he kisses me back until my lips swell and my lungs need air. Then he grabs my shoulders and breaks us apart.

"What are we doing?" His breath is ragged. "We can't."

My chest heaves wildly. "Yes, we can. *Please.* I just want to feel before it's gone."

"Gemma, I'm sorry." There's sympathy in his eyes and my heart prepares for rejection. "It's not that I don't want to, but I can't."

"You've kissed me before."

"I know and it's getting harder and harder, but I'm

afraid if I start I won't stop this time. There's just too much . . ." He takes a deep breath. "There's just too much meaning and that makes everything more complicated. I'm going to lose control and I can't."

I wonder if it would hurt as bad if someone else said it, because it hurts like a knife to my heart, coming from his mouth. I know there are reasons why it shouldn't matter, but it does because he's the one that hurt me. He's also the first person I've felt something for. What the emotion is, I don't know yet. It could be hate. It could be lust. It could be love. There is a very thin line between all three.

I start to climb off the bed as the moment leaves me when he grabs me by the arm and pulls me back to him. He licks his lips and his elbows bend in a little as he lures me closer. Then without warning, that loss of control takes over and he's kissing me violently. I wrap my arms around his neck as he scoops me up and lays me on my back. His fingers knot through my hair while his other hand travels down my neck, my breast, all the way down to the top of my jeans. I don't care that it's wrong after everything that has happened. What I care about is having the moment before I'm gone. I want it more than I've ever wanted anything. I want him to slip his fingers inside me and feel me like he did in the car. I want to feel the peace inside my body. I want to feel connected to someone wholly and completely, even if it's for a few irrational moments.

His tongue slips into my mouth as his hand slides under my shirt. He snags the hem of it and his other hand glides around to my back. Holding my weight up, he yanks my shirt off in one swift motion and then he unhooks my bra. My chest heaves as I lean up, grab his shirt and begin to take it off because I want to see him and feel him like he's seen me.

I get it stuck on his head and he lets go of me to reach behind him and finish tugging it off. I immediately slide my hands up the front of his chest that's carved of muscles and imprinted with a black circle and a ring of flames—his Keepers' mark.

He covers my hands with his as it nears his neck. Fire blazes in his eyes as he brings my wrists together in front of me. He's careful not to put pressure on my injured wrist as he moves his body forward and forces me down onto my back. Then he lets me go and compels our chests together. I shut my eyes and inhale in the closeness, the contact, the human connection. Our skin statics as our bodies join and our hearts thud against each other's chests. I lie there letting the feelings overtake me, consume me. I'm flying, falling, spiraling out of control. The prickle is going wild and a ravenous need I never knew existed jerks me forward. I grab onto his face and seal my lips to his. There's no hesitation on his part as he kisses me back with every part of his body. I keep thinking I need air because I'm not breathing, but my lungs somehow find a way around that. I stop needing air and I'm free.

My fingers travel up his back and his skin is scorching underneath my palms. His back is stimulated by my touch and he slips a hand under my neck, gripping my skin, demanding me closer. He takes my uninjured arm and my elbow bends as he pins it next to my head. His tongue traces the inside of my mouth before he takes soft nips at my lips, my neck and then just above my chest. Then his tongue rolls across my nipple as he gently draws into his mouth and sucks hard, but I want him to do it harder. I want my feelings to overtake the knowledge of what lies ahead. I want him to make me feel one last time and give me something to hold onto.

Craving to get closer, I open my legs up and let his body fall between them. I begin writhing my hips and rubbing against him, but it isn't enough this time and he lets me go as he shifts away from me, kneeling up between my legs.

"What are you doing?" I pant as I rise up on my elbows.

Without saying a word, he flicks the button of my jeans and tugs them down to my knees.

"Alex." I moan as his fingers trail down the inside of my thighs.

He stops at the sound of my voice and meets my eyes. He's not in control anymore—I'm not in control anymore. Our emotions are controlling us. And the electricity. And the need to keep feeling it. Lust is definitely an addiction; like heroin, potent and controlling.

His fists clench and I hear a tear in his voice. "Gemma, I think, I should stop . . . I don't want to. You make me . . . Fuck, you make me feel alive."

I don't answer him. I just kick my jeans off, instigating a low growl out of him as he lies down on top of me again. His hands wander all over my breasts, my hips, my thighs. Ultimately, he takes off my panties and slips his fingers inside me. He feels me until I cry out and then he strips off the rest of his clothes.

I lie naked underneath him, my body sweaty and my heart racing, pumping adrenaline through my body. All I can feel is the warmth of his skin, the comfort of his body and the overriding desire to stay away from what the prickle wants me to feel because it's advising me that I should pull away. *Danger.*

When he slips inside me it hurts more than cutting

my wrist open, but I'm glad that it hurts. It makes it real, not fake, like everything else is in my life. He closes his eyes and breathes in through his nose as his head lowers like he's savoring the moment.

"Are you okay?" he whispers against my cheek.

I nod, turn my head toward him and our lips connect. He kisses me deeply as he rocks into me and I respond with an arch of my back. It hurts, but it also feels amazingly good and I want more. I loosen up the muscles in my legs so he can rock into me more easily and allow our bodies to move together. His eyes are untamed as he brings my arms above my head and even though it hurts my wrist, I let him hold me down.

When he kisses me again, I bite at his lip and he lets out a groan. With each thrust, my body and mind climb higher toward the ceiling, the sky, and the stars. When I feel myself reaching that highest point, I open my eyes and let my head fall back. I feel myself fix and then break apart again as I leave my mind and then slowly return. Somewhere along the line, I start to cry for reasons I don't understand. Not wanting him to see, I shut my eyes and turn my head.

Seconds later, Alex's movements become less rhythmic and then he stills inside me. We pant, our sweaty bodies pressed together and our hearts beating violently. He moves away and gives me a quick kiss on my cheek as he pulls out of me. I feel empty, hollow, like my heart and mind are severed from my body. I roll onto my stomach as he lies down on his back. It's quiet.

"You were right from the beginning," he says as he stares up at the ceiling with his arms tucked under his head. "You used to know me and really well. When we were kids."

I rest my hand next to my face. "I know."

He turns his head and meets my gaze. "How?"

"I've started to remember things," I say. "Like us running around in a field."

His mouth tugs to a small smile. "The one with all the flowers?"

I nod and my voice falters. I don't remember, not really anyway because they're just clips and images to me. "We seemed like we were having fun."

His smile turns sad as he scoots down onto the pillow and rolls onto his hip. "We had a lot of fun. You used to pick the flowers and give them to me all the time, even though I would tell you time and time again that guys are supposed to give the girl flowers."

I remember back in his car and how there was a dried flower hanging from the mirror. I wonder if that's why he kept it there. Maybe he has thought about me all these years. I could ask him, but I'm not sure I want to know because either answer will hurt.

His lips part and it looks like he's going to say something that will change everything. "Gemma, I. . . ." He trails off and his throat muscles move to force a lump in his throat down.

We don't say anything else as we lay face-to-face with our hands barely touching and stare at each other. It's like a silent good-bye and the moment is flawless because it's real. Part of me wishes that when I fall asleep, I'll die right there on a peaceful note.

CHAPTER TWENTY-TWO

"GEMMA, WAKE UP." Someone kisses my forehead and brings a static zap to my skin. I roll over, griping and moaning. "I'm too tired."

"Gemma, please just open your eyes," he pleads.

Sighing, I open my eyes. Alex is standing near the edge of the bed, leaning over me. He's put his clothes back on and there's a bag over his shoulder. I sit up, bringing the sheet with me to keep my naked body covered.

"What's wrong?" I ask and then curl my knees into my chest. "It's time, isn't it?"

He shakes his head, hurries to the foot of the bed and picks my jeans and t-shirt up, tossing them to me. "We're leaving."

Panic surges through my body as I grab my jeans and quickly slide my legs into them. "Did the Death Walkers find us?"

He shakes his head again as he walks over to the window and peers out. It's dark outside, but the moon is bright and the stars are vivid. "No, I'm taking you away from here."

I tug my shirt over my head and flip my hair out of the collar. "Why? What's wrong?"

He moves away from the window and adjusts the handle of the bag higher onto his shoulder. "I can't do it. I thought I could, but I can't."

I button my jeans, but pause as shock sets in. "You're taking me away so they won't detach my soul?"

He nods, stepping in front of me. "I just can't do it again . . . Lose you again."

I scratch my head, at a loss for words as I slide to the edge of the bed. "But I thought it has to be done? So the star can stay preserved and save the world . . . Alex, I don't understand?" I've prepared myself for the end and now he's saying it isn't, and I don't know what to do with that.

He releases a slow breath and then squats down in front of me. He places his hands on my knees and keeps his voice low. "I know that the world needs to be saved, but right now, I can't do it. Right now, I need you to come with me so that we can at least try to find another way to save it or get the star out of you."

"But I—"

He puts his finger over my lips. "But I need you to come now, because my father's going to be here any minute."

It's a defining moment in my life; one that I will either look back and regret or cherish. I rise to my feet and he threads his fingers through mine as panic and relief flash across his face. We exchange a look of understanding and then we run down the hall together and out into the garage.

There's an old, black Jeep Wrangler parked in the middle and he guides me over to the passenger side door. I hop in and he rounds the front while I quickly buckle my seatbelt.

He drops the bag onto the console, climbs in, and slams the door. Then he unzips the bag and takes out a sword. It has a silver blade with jagged edges and a black handle with a red stone on the end. Carved along the side of the blade is the Mark of Immortality and there are flakes of dried blood on the metal.

"Is that the Sword Of Immortality?" I ask and he nods.

He turns the key and the engine purrs to life. Then he presses on the garage door opener, rests the sword in his lap, and tosses the bag on the backseat. "It's better to be safe than sorry."

I eyeball the sword as the garage door creeps open and snow drifts in. "But I thought we were running from your father?"

He shifts the car into reverse. "We're running from everyone now, Gemma."

My eyes expand as I realize how true this is. Once we drive away, it's just him and me against a large army of Death Walkers and a group of Keepers who will do anything to protect the world.

With one hand gripping the steering wheel and the other grasping the shifter, he sucks in a deep breath. "Okay, hold on. It's going to be a pain in the fucking ass to get out of here. The snow's worse up here than it is in Laramie."

I clutch onto the handle on the roof and brace my feet against the dash. As the door reaches the top, he floors the gas, but then quickly taps the brakes. He stares in the rearview mirror with a look of horror on his face. I follow his gaze to the back window with fear in my veins, wondering if his father has arrived. There are hundreds of yellow eyes flickering through the trees and shimmering against the snow. The whole area looks like it's lit up with twinkling Christmas lights. I'm not sure if I'm more upset, or less, that it's Death Walkers and not his father. Do I want my soul more or my life?

Through the midst of the Death Walkers a tall figure steps forward and into the garage. As the light hits his face, my hand grips the door handle. The scar on his cheek, the darkness in his eyes, the evil he brings with him.

"No, no, no, no." I whisper as I flip the handle and crack the door. "It's him."

Alex turns his head toward me. He's still holding the sword and his knuckles have gone white. "Don't worry, we'll figure something out."

I let go of the door and clutch onto his arm. "No, you don't understand. That's the man who put my mother in The Underworld."

He shakes his head in denial. "No, there's no way."

I release his arm and trace my finger down my cheek. "Yes, the man in the vision had that exact same scar."

He's acting strange, torn and baffled. He reaches for the handle of the door and then changes his mind and shuts off the engine. The man enters the garage and cold air gushes through the vents of the car. "You can't be right," Alex mutters as he lowers his head onto the steering wheel.

"Alex, I'm telling you, that's him," I practically shout. "That's the man."

He raises his head and the look in his eyes takes me off guard because he looks like he doesn't know what the hell to do. "No, you don't understand. That can't be him because it's Stephan . . . That's my father."

CHAPTER
TWENTY-THREE

T HE DEATH WALKERS close in on the house, tromping up the driveway and leaving their tracks in the snow. Soon the exit is blocked by rows and rows of black-cloaked creatures, freezing the land and house. It's snowing unbreakably, veil of ice falling from the sky and to the earth. It makes it hard to see, but I can still see enough.

"What are we going to do?" I ask Alex as I kneel in the seat and keep my eyes on Stephan. "I mean, he showed up with them . . . and he did that to my mom."

Stephan is just lurking at the opening of the garage, leaning against the doorframe, like he's waiting for us to come to him. Like we're that stupid.

Alex takes the keys out of the ignition and stuffs them into his pocket. He turns his body toward the door with the sword positioned at his side. He doesn't explain as he starts to open the door.

I grab the back of his shirt and yank on it. "You're seriously not getting out, are you?"

He glances over his shoulder at me and then exhales before leaning over the console. He gathers the chain of my necklace in his hand and I think he's going to tug on it and break it off my neck, but instead, he tucks it beneath my shirt. "Whatever you do, keep that hidden. Don't let anyone know you have it."

"Wait!" I reach for him as he moves away and land on the console as he climbs out of the car. He shuts the door, leaving me alone in the cab.

I press my hand to the locket hidden under my shirt. Why did he do that? Why would he make me hide it? I think I might know, but I'm not ready to accept it, yet, because it means that he no longer wants to save me. It means that the last few beautiful moments together didn't mean anything. It means that he believes his father is good even after showing up with the Death Walkers. Alex and Stephan exchange a few words at the back of the car. Alex is talking heatedly with his hands, waving the sword around, and Stephan is a motionless conversationalist. I force my gaze off them and start searching the car for a weapon. I'm not going to go down without a fight, not just for myself, but for my mother.

I find an aged pocketknife in the glove compartment and take it out. This isn't going to end well. I can feel it through every infliction that has been done to me, but I get out of the car anyway with the knife in my hand and round to the back of the Jeep, plotting a way to kill him and wondering if I have it in me.

"Gemma," Stephan says in an eerily calm voice as I round the rear of the Jeep and come up behind Alex. "It's so nice to finally meet you."

Alex glances over his shoulder at me and his eyes go straight to the knife clutched in my hand. *Don't even think about,* he mouths and I shake my head.

"Well, Alex, you've done a really shitty job keeping her

out of trouble," Stephan says as he walks over to a shelf in the garage and rolls up the sleeves of his button-down shirt. He scans the shelves and then selects a pickaxe. "I thought I taught you better than that. I thought I taught you to be strong, not weak and pathetic." He holds the axe like a baseball bat and gives it a practice swing. My eyes never leave the blade. "I thought I taught you to never let your emotions get in the way. To turn it off and always put your obligation as a Keeper first."

Alex holds the sword behind his back with the sharp tip pointed at the floor. "I was, but I—"

Stephan swipes the axe down and sinks the blade into the wood of the shelf. It breaks apart and splinters of wood fly through the air. "I don't want fucking excuses. What I want, is a son that obeys and only follows *my* orders."

I finally understand why Alex is so hot and cold. Laylen nailed it. He's brainwashed, or at least, his father has tried to brainwash him; tried to create a soldier that only listens to him. The problem is, that the passionate emotions that grasp you and control you in the heat of the moment are far more powerful than ones that sedate you.

Stephan continues to swing the axe over and over again, ripping the garage into pieces of wood and spilled tools. He kicks at the tire of the car and slams his fist into the window. Glass covers the floor and scatters by our feet, but he doesn't stop until everything is broken.

Alex reaches back and grabs my hand as Stephan turns toward the driveway and flings the axe out at the Death Walkers. It hits one of the monsters in the chest and it lets out a deafening scream, but the rest stay motionless, the tail of their cloaks gusting in the wind as snow blows down on their heads.

Stephan stills and runs his hands down the front of

his shirt, brushing bits of wood off. "I'm not going to punish you." He seizes Alex's arm and yanks the Sword of Immortality from his hand. "But you're no longer going to be a part of this." He holds the sword in front of him and greed consumes his eyes. "Finding this, however, is the one thing you've done right."

Alex's pulse is pounding through his fingers and against my own racing pulse. His free hand sneaks around his back and he feels around for the knife. He pries my fingers off it, steals it from me, and holds it at his side. "I'm sorry."

I pull my hand from his and search for a weak spot or wide gaps between the Death Walkers that maybe I can slip through and then run out into the night. Because, I'm not going down without a fight.

Alex draws his elbow back and then his arm darts forward. It happens so quickly it takes my brain a second to catch up, but when I grasp what is going on, blood is spilling out of Stephan's chest. The knife is lodged in his chest, right where his heart resides.

A river of blood empties down his body and his skin goes white as he stumbles back, banging his elbow against one of the ruined shelves that hangs from the wall. He's killed his father! Really killed him!

"Run," Alex orders as he whirls to me. He shoves me towards the stairs that lead to the house. "He'll recover in a second."

"But you stabbed him in the heart." I trip up the bottom step.

He shakes his head. "My father's immortal, Gemma. More than immortal. Even the sword won't kill him."

Those words shake the earth below my feet and I swear to God the ground is about to open up and swallow me whole. Alex shoves a very stunned me into the house and I collapse to my knees and hit the side of the dryer. I skitter to my feet and stand up as Alex starts to shut the door.

"You're lying," I say and step towards him. "That's…no one ever mentioned anything about that."

"That's because no one knows." He reaches forward and pushes me back with strength that bruises my skin. I fall back and bang my head on the wall. "Now run. Just get somewhere and hide until I can figure this out. All that matters at the moment is that you're alive."

I'm unsure if it's a heartfelt moment where he reveals his true feelings or if he's referring to the star. I start to open my mouth to argue, but Stephan appears behind him and the door slams shut as he tackles Alex from behind. I run through the house and head for the kitchen to get a knife, but the front door blows open and is ripped from the hinges. A wave of ice rushes into the house and glazes the wood floor as a Death Walker marches inside.

I turn back for the garage door, but a Death Walker is coming in from that side. Not having anywhere else to go, I sprint for the living room and hop over the coffee table as herds of Death Walkers thunder through the sidewalls. They're stronger than I thought; using their bodies as a wrecking balls to get through the walls of the house. They're overtaking the place; their eyes lit up and their corpse fingers seeking my body.

Fuck. I need a plan. I back toward the sliding glass door, glide it open and, not giving myself time to rationalize, I run out into the forest, into two-feet of snow, with no weapon because it's the only choice I have left.

Night and the cold surround me as I swing my arms and battle the branches, fighting my way deeper into the trees. The snow is in my shoes and the cold pierces my lungs. A ways in, I make a curve and follow the moonlight, hoping I'll come out near the driveway and road. Every shadow moves and branches snap from all direction. I'm exhausted and lethargic. I can no longer feel my toes.

I hear a cackle from behind me, but don't dare look to see what it is. I attempt to pick up my knees and take longer strides; move faster. Ice crackles up behind me and I start to run again. My arms and legs are barely moving as ice spirals down from the trees. I hear a snap and another cackle, and then something heavy hits me on the head. My skull cracks and I fall face first onto the ice. I try to push back up, but I'm shoved right back down. I turn my head to the side and skim the outlines of the trees. Death Walkers are everywhere, watching me through the forest.

I have nowhere else to go.

CHAPTER
TWENTY-FOUR

THEY MARCH ME back to the house, some in front of me and some in back. They can't understand English, or at least they pretend they can't, because I try to reason with them as they close in on me. I even beg for my life and feel pathetic for it afterwards. They don't want to kill me, at least not yet, which means everything I've been told was a lie. Nothing makes sense. No one seems trustworthy. It seems like there's no hope left for clarification.

It takes a lot of energy to march one foot in front of the other. I've lost my bandage somewhere along the way and my cut has started bleeding again. My skin is pale blue and mapped with veins, and my clothes are soaked and frozen to my skin.

When we arrive at the back door of the cabin, one of the Death Walkers steps up and glides the door open even though the glass is gone. It tilts its face toward me and points its bony finger at the open doorway, motioning for me to go inside. It looks like the Reaper giving me a death omen, but I listen because backtracking means going against the rest of the herd.

The cabin is wrecked, the beams of the ceiling have collapsed, the doors are missing and there are massive holes in the walls. The furniture is shredded apart and tipped over, and the windows are in pieces on the floor. Alex and Stephan are waiting for me in the middle of the mess. Alex is sitting on the remaining piece of the couch that's intact with his hands resting in his lap and his head hung over. Stephan is near the fireplace and he has a hole in his shirt, blood on his jean, and the Sword of Immortality in his hand.

When Stephan's eyes find me, the greedy look in his eye promptly reappears. "Well, the guest of honor has finally arrived."

Alex quickly raises his head up and he looks ill as he takes in my bleeding wrist and blue skin. "What happened to you?"

The scene doesn't feel right, too formal and subdued for the circumstances. "I'm wondering the same thing about you."

Stephan walks across the room, whistling with every step. He stops when he's only a few feet from me and tilts his head to assess me. He isn't much taller than I am, but he's a lot thicker in his arms and shoulders. His cheekbones are sharp and the scar is very distinctive. "My son is no longer going to tell you anything," he says and then calls over his shoulders. "Are you, son?"

Alex avoids eye contact with me as he nods once. "Yes, Father." He seems younger at the moment and breakable. "It was my fault and I messed up, but I didn't understand the situation."

What he says aches, but so does my wound. I press my palm down onto my bleeding wrist and search the wreckage of the living room for some kind of weapon, something I can protect myself with. "What situation?" I ask, trying to stall.

"The one where you stop asking so many questions," Stephan growls and kicks a piece of table across the room. "I try and try to do everything right, but you two have made it almost impossible."

Alex rises from the couch. There's a bruise on his cheek and his nose is bleeding and crooked. "I said I'm sorry. I just got confused and forgot what the purpose was."

"Well, we're going to fix that now," Stephan says. "Before she gets any worse. I don't even want to know how far you pushed her toward humanity."

Alex glances at me and I know what he's thinking. I wonder if he can picture it as clearly as I can; how he thrust into me, pressed himself against me, kissed me and felt me because my images are quickly fading as numbness infects me.

"What are you going to do to me?" I ask, tearing my gaze from Alex and fixing it on Stephan. "Drain me dry, kill me, lock me away in a box?"

"Gemma," Alex says robotically with pity and it makes me want to throttle him. "I already explained to you what's going to happen."

I don't look at him. "You explained a lot of things to me, which make no sense now; especially, since it's been made clear what he did to my mother and that he's working with them." I aim an unsteady finger at the Death Walkers lurking near the walls. "And besides, the last time I checked, you woke me up telling me you were going to save me."

Stephan swipes the sword around and flips the blade into the air. It comes down and he twists his arm to catch it effortlessly. "I'm impressed. I really didn't think anyone would figure out what I did to your mother." He gives a dramatic pause. "How on earth did you do it?"

I expect Alex to tell him about my Foreseer ability, about the visions, about my newfound mark, but he stays silent.

"Your mother needed to go," Stephan says, pacing the length of the room. "And she went like a coward, begging me to take you instead of her. She didn't seem to understand that the world's fate depends on you and your inability to feel."

I stab my nails into my palms and let the skin split open. "If the world's fate depends on that, then why are you working with the Death Walkers?" I ask. "Because I can't see them being in a on a plan that has anything to do with saving the world. They're nothing but evil and they tried to kill me."

He shakes his head. "Kill you? They were trying to protect you."

I sink down on the couch. My skin, my jeans and my hand are soaked in blood and snow. "You can't be buying this?" I ask Alex.

Alex shakes his head and I think I see remorse hidden deep inside his pupils. "I'm sorry, Gemma."

Stephan stretches his hand in the air and snaps his fingers. "Bring me the *memoria extracto*."

The wind kicks up and spins the air with snowflakes. A Death Walker treads through the back doorway, carrying a small black box with a red eye on the lid. It walks up to Stephan and brings a chill into the room as it hands the box to him before going back outside.

Stephan bends down and sets the sword on the ground. The light casts shadows in his eyes as he stares at the box. He cups the top with his hand and pries the lid off with a requiring tug, then dispenses it onto the floor. He reaches his fingers inside and draws out a round dark object that has a sandpaper texture.

I can't help myself. "A rock?"

"It's not just a rock. It's the most magnificent thing I've ever discovered." Stephan holds the rock between his fingers and squints at it. "I found it in the Wasteland, completely intact." He tosses it in the air, turns over his hand and catches it. "It's so much better than detaching your soul because it wipes out your entire mind. You won't even be able to function anymore."

Vomit burns at the back of my throat as memories of my empty past flow through me in a line of pointless events. "You can't do that," I whisper.

Alex sucks in a breath and his hands start to shake as he joins his father in the center of the room. "You didn't tell me about this."

"That's because I can't trust you," Stephan says. "You prove that time and time again."

"I said I'm sorry. I don't . . . I don't know . . ." he trails off. The idea of pleading with Alex seems pathetic, but I spot a small window when his gaze collides with mine. "I get confused when I'm around her."

Summoning inner strength, I stagger to my feet and shuffle to him while gripping my wrist in my hand. "Alex, don't let him do this to me. *Please.* This is so much worse than detaching my soul."

His eyes hold as much agony as I carry inside me. "I'm sorry, Gemma. About everything. I should have never taken it that far."

When the angry heat sweeps through my body, I let it out the only way I can think off. By kicking him in the shin and slapping his face, arms, and chest repeatedly, but he just stands there and takes it.

But Stephan rushes forward, seizes my arm and throws me down on the ground and I land in a pile of wood that used to be the coffee table. The prickle spears at the back of my neck, liberating a feeling of irreversible hate. I never loved Alex—I understand that now—but I cared for him deeply. I trusted him against my innermost warnings; let him do things to me that no one ever had. It's my own fault for trusting him, though, and I make a vow right there that if I make it out of this, I'll never trust him again. I'll never trust anyone again.

I pull my knees to my chest and shut my eyes as the Death Walkers close in on me and build a wall of ice around us, trapping us in brick of ice. Stephan squats down in front of me, he eyes me over and then darkness possesses his pupils as he holds the rock up above his head.

"Alex, I'm going to let you do the honors," he says with a grin.

Alex's jaw twitches as he refuses to look at me. "I'd rather not."

"I don't give a shit what you'd *rather* do," he snaps. "I'm telling you, you'll do it or go with her."

Alex's fist shakes as he unhurriedly makes his way over to his father and snatches the rock from his fingers. Stephan stands up while Alex lowers himself in front of me. He struggles to look at me and I make it harder on him, not blinking or moving as I stare into his eyes, forcing him to *see* me the entire time.

"Please." I try one last time.

He doesn't answer and his hand wobbles as he places the rock in front of my face, right between my eyes. Up close, there are swirls of black that entwine at the roundest side. Those lines begin to pirouette, spin and cycle like writing a song of death and soon I can hear the lyrics.

This is it. This is the end of my short-lived life. It seems like I've done everything, yet, I've done nothing. Every moment, every emotion has been acted out on a stage made of imaginary wood that only I could see. It has never existed, not really, and now it's gone.

My head fills with static. I see my life. I see my death. I finally see my future.

Laughing. The sun shining as we run through the field, chasing each other.

Happy. He smiles. I smile and everything makes sense.

Smiling. We stand up in front of a thousand people, but the only one that matters is him. His green eyes are on me as he whispers that he loves me and I reply that I love him.

Love. I wish it were real.

The cabin begins to diminish into contorted objects as my skin glows beneath the locket. The electricity drifts from my body and one word comes to mind as I fall toward the floor.

Silence.

The last thing I see is Alex's green eyes, then my legs and arms go inert and my heart dies with them. I gasp my last breath of air as my life leaves my body, leaving behind nothing more than a spirit. I see my mom's bright blue irises, her warm smile; I see the life I'll never have. The humming in my head grows louder until I can't think anymore; can't feel. My eyelids fall shut and only one feeling remains.

Hollow.

THE BLACK WATER crashes against the sandy shore and ash rains down from the clouds and floats across the land. Alex pulls me against him, so tightly we are almost one soul. I breathe in his scent of cologne, wanting to stay in his arms forever.

"Don't worry, Gemma," he whispers against my cheek. "I'll always save you. No matter what, I'll always save you."

I nod. "I know."

He moves back and flattens our palms together forming a temple. "Ego promitto ad protegendum tibi in perpetuum."

I don't understand the language, but I know that he means what he says from the bottom of his heart and I hold onto that.

"Now close your eyes and trust me," he says softly but with strength.

As I submit and close my eyes, a bright orange flame erupts across the land and burns down on the trees. Then silence sets in with the smoke circling around us and suffocating us into the darkness. I want to run, but I cling onto him for dear life, knowing he'll save me somehow.

EPILOGUE

MY HEAD IS buzzing, like a Goddamn bug trapped in a light, over and over again. It just about drives me crazy. My skin is warm, my body relaxed and the air smells like lilacs and rain. The ground below my body is soft. I feel content.

Feel? But I'm supposed to be dead, or at least locked in a coffin in my own head.

I shoot upright, but as the blood rushes from my head, I fall back onto the mattress. I can't believe what I'm seeing. I'm lying in a bed in a room with pale purple walls and a small window that lets in the sunlight. The view outside is filled with colorful lights and flamboyant buildings that reach toward the skyline.

"I know this place . . ." I mutter. "Vegas."

"It was the safest place I could think of." His voice not only sends a chill down my spine, but it also makes my body tingle with heat and my heart wake up from its very deep sleep.

Alex walks through the doorway, taking tentative steps as he inches himself toward the bed—toward me— and every image of the last time we were in bed together flashes through my head. The way I felt, the way he made me finally breathe and then minutes later, he stole it all away from me by betraying me, ripping out my heart and shredding it to pieces; he probably still has my blood on his hands.

He's wearing a black t-shirt and a pair of jeans and his hair is damp and sticking up all over. He looks like a normal guy, completely harmless, but it's just an illusion.

I throw the blanket off me and swing my legs over the side of the bed, noting I'm no longer wearing my clothes, but a pair of boxer shorts and a t-shirt that doesn't belong to me. "Stay away from me."

"Gemma, I'm not going to hurt you." His voice is soft as he continues to step toward me; his bright green eyes are fixed on mine. "I promise I won't hurt you."

I laugh sharply as I put weight on my weak knees. "That's the biggest lie I've ever heard come out of your mouth."

Alex stops dead in his tracks, his expression filling with infuriation. "What the hell is that supposed to mean?"

My knees shake as I stand up and find my stability. "It means your promises are worthless. At least, the ones you make to me."

He raises his eyebrows. "My promises got you to Adessa's, safe and sound."

"Safe and sound doesn't exist."

"It does for the moment, Gemma, and you'll understand why, if you just let me explain."

I shake my head and take a step forward, wanting to get out of the room and away from him. "I'm leaving. I don't know why I'm walking around alive and normal, but I'm not going to waste my time listening to your bullshit."

"You're walking around normal because of me—because of how I feel about you." He moves to the side, obstructing my path. "Just let me explain."

I shake my head and dodge to the right, but I'm like a newborn deer and my knees give out on me. His arms encircle my waist and he catches me before I crash against the hardwood floor. He picks me up, carries me over to the bed, and sets me back down. I start to get back up, but he puts his hands down on the bed, one on each side of me, and lowers his face toward mine.

"I just need five minutes to explain," he almost begs. "Five minutes for me to tell you what happened and then, if you don't like it, I'll leave."

I search his eyes for the person that lay with me in the bed. "Five minutes," I say. "But that's all you have and if one single thing sounds like bullshit, then you leave, not just the house, but my life."

He nods without hesitation. As his lips part, I'm not sure if he will help me understand, or crash my world again.

ABOUT THE AUTHOR

JESSICA SORENSEN IS a *New York Times* and *USA Today* bestselling author that lives in the snowy mountains of Wyoming. When she's not writing, she spends her time reading and hanging out with her family.

OTHER BOOKS BY JESSICA SORENSEN

The Coincidence Series:

The Coincidence of Callie and Kayden
The Redemption of Callie and Kayden
The Destiny of Violet and Luke
The Probability of Violet and Luke
The Certainty of Violet and Luke
The Resolution of Callie and Kayden
Seth & Grayson

The Secret Series:

The Prelude of Ella and Micha
The Secret of Ella and Micha
The Forever of Ella and Micha
The Temptation of Lila and Ethan
The Ever After of Ella and Micha
Lila and Ethan: Forever and Always
Ella and Micha: Infinitely and Always

The Shattered Promises Series:
Shattered Promises
Fractured Souls
Unbroken
Broken Visions
Scattered Ashes

Breaking Nova Series:
Breaking Nova
Saving Quinton
Delilah: The Making of Red
Nova and Quinton: No Regrets
Tristan: Finding Hope
Wreck Me
Ruin Me

The Fallen Star Series (YA):
The Fallen Star
The Underworld
The Vision
The Promise

*The Fallen Souls Series
(spin off from The Fallen Star):*
The Lost Soul
The Evanescence

The Darkness Falls Series:
Darkness Falls
Darkness Breaks
Darkness Fades

The Death Collectors Series (NA and YA):
Ember X and Ember
Cinder X and Cinder
Spark X and Spark

The Sins Series:
Seduction & Temptation
Sins & Secrets
Lies & Betrayal (Coming Soon)

Unbeautiful Series:
Unbeautiful
Untamed

Unraveling You Series:
Unraveling You
Raveling You
Awakening You
Inspiring You (Coming Soon)

Ultraviolet Series:
Ultraviolet

Standalones
The Forgotten Girl
The Illusion of Annabella

Coming Soon

Entranced
Steel & Bones

CONNECT WITH ME ONLINE

jessicasorensen.com
and on
Facebook and Twitter

CPSIA information can be obtained at www.ICGtesting.com
Printed in the USA
BVOW08s2209121215

430104BV00002B/81/P